THE
LONE WOLF
MURDERS

THE
LONE WOLF
MURDERS

A MOTORCYCLE ADVENTURE

WAYNE LITTRELL

abbott press®

A DIVISION OF WRITER'S DIGEST

THE LONE WOLF MURDERS

Abbott Press books may be ordered through booksellers or by contacting:

Abbott Press
1663 Liberty Drive
Bloomington, IN 47403
www.abbottpress.com
Phone: 1-866-697-5310

ISBN: 978-1-4582-0828-6 (sc)
ISBN: 978-1-4582-0827-9 (hc)
ISBN: 978-1-4582-0826-2 (e)

Library of Congress Control Number: 2013902647

Printed in the United States of America

Abbott Press rev. date: 7/2/2013

To Jean, Lyn, Liz, and Ben

No man was blessed with a more understanding
family, who each in their own unique way,
provided inspiration for a leap of faith.

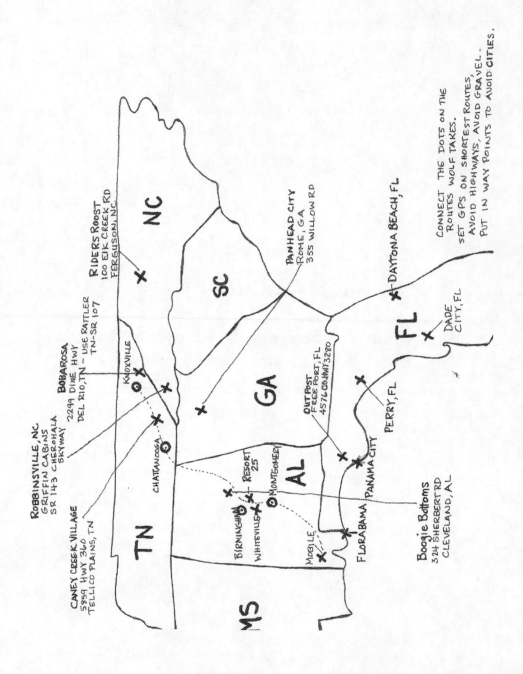

I feel the need to explain a few things before we put our kickstands up and start our ride.

I rode this ride with the exception of the murders, of course, over the past several years. The places and scenes are real or based on real places in the southeast. The routes are roads I used, often shared with me by bikers or found using GPS and other currently available maps and online applications. The scenery and perceptions described are real. This book could easily be a series of rides taken by the reader. During the summer of 2012, I did just that while finishing the story. What a fantastic ride! Some minor changes were made to the descriptions to make the places work with the storyline.

Each scene described in the story was typically begun and later finished on location. In today's current economic climate, these places may close or change names as time rides on. Readers are encouraged to visit and support these places. Too often, great biker destinations close due to even temporary declines in business.

The characters are based on actual people I met along this journey of over 100,000 miles. Much like a cherry picker selecting the best fruit, I chose the characteristics, habits, and words exhibited by the many bikers and people I met along the way to create unique and realistic characters. If we met during the rides, a character described may have something about them that reminds you of you—one never knows where a writer may get their ideas and inspirations. Maybe I was that guy at the end of the bar observing, or perhaps a rider you imparted some biker wisdom or perhaps shared a joke with. Maybe we shared a beer, a laugh, or even a ride together Who knows? In all but one case, the name was changed to protect the innocent, or perhaps, the not so innocent.

One can never say enough to describe the gratitude I feel for the bikers, coworkers, friends, and family who helped guide this story in ways they or I could never anticipate or understand at the time.

Most incidents described were inspired by actual events experienced along the way, providing the spark for what is described. While writing this work of fiction, I provided a monthly story to the local biker magazine, Thunder Roads of Alabama/Florida Panhandle about places to go, routes to take, and biker events. The owner/editors, readers, along with those with whom I shared my vision, provided support and encouragement, and indeed, the inspiration for the story. Thank you!

Throughout the book, I imbedded biker tips, humor, ride routes, and terms used by those whose paths I crossed along the way. In fact, a reader that has never ridden or perhaps just started riding a motorcycle may gain an understanding of what non-riders think of as bikers and their culture. To set the record straight, I am not an expert on being a biker, but I am one who has the passion, or perhaps a compulsion for adventure and the freedom of the ride. I feel compelled to share what I have learned and observed in an entertaining manner. Karma and totems often guided me to interesting places, amazing timing, and special people—or was it all just coincidence? I doubt it.

I tried to be a bit conservative with the language used by the characters, but let's face it . . . it is a novel about bikers, so one can only do so much.

Kickstands up . . . let's get started on the journey. Enjoy the Ride!

CHAPTER 1

I t was the kind of night predators love. The full moon overhead seemed to darken the shadows, deepening them further when luminescent clouds passed in front of it. The shadows provided abundant cover for the creatures of the night to hide and stalk their prey, who were lulled into the false sense of security provided by the bright, moonlit landscape.

The biker favored this type of night, for it soothed him to watch the nocturnal creatures graze and play in the grassy field below the picnic shelter where he sat, slowly releasing the stress from another long day at work. His bike rested nearby as he contemplated how rapidly his day had gone from a demanding, stressful one, to a peaceful, quiet scene out of a National Geographic film. The biker frequently stopped here on his thirty-mile travel path between work and home. He made this stop regularly to release his work-related anxieties before going to his home in a very typical middle-class neighborhood in a suburb of Birmingham, Alabama. His wife and kids had no idea how much they benefited from this regular stop on his ride home; they only knew him as a loving and caring biker that treasured his family above all, including his bike, "Beast." He realized he had so much to be thankful for, so he had found this place where he could be alone and at peace, while silently giving thanks to God for all the good in his life.

Just past the meadow below him, a small stone-walled church was perched on a knoll above the two-lane road even farther below, seemingly to watch over the same creatures as he. In all his years of stopping there at night, the biker had encountered only one other human, a local policeman on his rounds. Even though the law officer must have thought his night habit was odd, he bought into the explanation the biker gave him to explain his being in the lonely spot at such a late hour. Since then, he even waved when the biker rode past him while he was on patrol.

On this cool, moonlit, late February night, the biker was somewhat startled when he saw headlights coming up the hill from the road below. In rural

Alabama, everything closed up at 10 pm or earlier unless next to a major highway, which the biker seldom traveled unless in a hurry. As he watched the vehicle slowly wind its way up the hill, he was surprised to see it continue past the church and up the packed gravel road along the meadow, stopping in the small parking area below the covered picnic shelter where he sat. He knew they couldn't see him, so he decided to wait and see what happened before flashing his lights to announce his presence. *Probably just some teenagers wanting to get naked or high,* he thought to himself. As he watched, he suspected he might just be in for some x-rated entertainment, but other dangerous activity was a distinct possibility.

The vehicle below was a high-dollar black Mercedes SUV that only well-off folks could afford to drive in the current economy. With that thought in mind, he began to think of his options should he witness dangerous illegal activity. He quickly walked over to his bike waiting in the shadows and straddled it, putting his helmet and gloves on in case he had to leave in a hurry. The biker had always tried to be prepared for the unexpected, and this habit had saved his butt many times in the past. He was not prepared for what happened next. The front doors of the SUV opened, the interior lights revealing a short, older man and a large blond woman with the biggest ears he had ever seen protruding from her long, blond hair. They both got out. It was obvious from where he sat watching that the woman was much taller than the man. She was dressed in a black and revealing evening gown, and the biker could tell even from thirty yards away that this was a very hot, bodacious, Amazon woman that most men only dream of. Instead of making his presence known by flashing his lights, the biker decided to wait and see what would happen. *Might just be inspiration for a hot night with his wife later after his daughter went to bed,* he thought.

As he sat watching, the woman ran her hands down the front of the man's chest, slowly heading south to his crotch. He heard the sound of a zipper, while at the same time, he observed a considerably larger man get out of the back of the SUV and walk up silently behind the other man. Like a striking viper, the man suddenly reached out and grabbed the smaller man in a full nelson. A surprised gasp escaped from the man, who seconds earlier, must have thought he was in for a real good time. As the biker watched in shocked silence, the woman grabbed the restrained man's head in both hands, gave him a kiss full on the lips, then lifted and twisted his head in one fluid and apparently practiced motion. The biker winced and shivered slightly as he heard the victim's neck snap. He sat motionless, watching as the victim slid slowly to the ground, going limp like a deflating air mattress. The woman knelt and felt for a pulse, then grabbed his head and gave it another twist so hard the man's whole body twisted; he convulsed and was still.

"You done yet, or you want to take his head off completely?" the man asked from the rear of the Mercedes. In the glow of the open rear hatch's light, he could see the man was huge with a nose like a boxer who had run into way too many punches. He removed what looked like shovels and flicked on a flashlight.

"Shut up asshole. Let's just get him in the hole and then get the hell out of here," the Amazon lady said in a way that sounded eerily like a biker. They lifted their victim by the arms and started dragging his body toward where the biker sat frozen. "Turn that light out before someone spots it from the road," she added.

"Ain't nobody gonna see a light from there, Blondie. We've been checking this place out for a week with the game camera. Nobody but animals come here at night." He killed the light anyway and stuffed it in his pocket.

"I don't give a shit! Keep it off until we get behind the shelter," she snapped. "I enjoyed snuffing the old geezer, but I sure don't want to end up in a damn cage—bad enough riding in one."

By this time, the biker realized he had but a minute or less before the two killers would literally walk into him as they dragged the corpse up the pathway to where he sat astride his bike. Thankful for his keen night vision and the clouds passing in front of the moon, he silently cursed his trembling hands as he started his bike rolling down the path with his lights off. He turned the ignition key as he gained momentum and reached the edge of the shadows. His bike roared to life when he bumped the starter switch. He immediately let out the clutch and caught the killers in the full glare of the headlights. They froze in place, momentarily blinded by the trio of bright lights from his bike. As he roared past, kicking up gravel and spewing a cloud of exhaust in the chilly night air, he felt his bike shudder from what must have been his right highway peg hitting the Amazon's leg.

Accelerating down the gravel road along the meadow, he felt a tug at his right shoulder, causing him to skid just as he started around the curve at the church. Years of riding saved him as his instincts took over. He rolled on the throttle, straightening his bike out and preventing a high-side fall. Without looking back or checking if cars were coming, he roared onto the two-lane black top from the highway entrance to the church.

He rode for what seemed like an hour, jamming on the brakes, and then accelerating through the turns at reckless speeds before finally slowing down. He made a few more turns while checking the mirrors frequently, constantly fearing the assault of a Mercedes or the sudden impact of a bullet from behind. Realizing where he was, he turned off the highway and onto a small dirt road leading to a fishing pond he frequented. Quickly killing the lights and engine, he reached into his tank bag, pulled out his gun and shakily placed it on his thigh. After dropping his smokes twice, he was finally able to light one up and take a long, deep draw.

"Hooo-leee shit! What in the hell did I just get myself into?" he yelled after a few draws. He reached for his cell phone, hit 9, then 1, and then stopped, finger poised just above the keypad.

"The police will never believe me, a biker, wasn't part of that shit," he said to himself. "Wolf, what have you gotten yourself into this time?"

As he sat there, slowly letting the adrenaline and fear-enhanced shakes drain from his body, he began to think more clearly. He closed his flip-phone and hooked it back on his belt.

Why didn't they come after me? he thought. As he sat there, unable to get the mental picture of the killers' faces out of his head, the events slowly replayed in his mind. He figured that they didn't want the body discovered, so they most likely took it away to dispose of elsewhere. He tried to calm down and think of what to do next. As he was thinking, he walked around his bike, looking for damage from his wide open ride on this freaky, moonlit night. He felt something wet on his shoulder, along with a burning sensation. Reaching inside his jacket, his fingers came back wet. He touched his finger to his tongue and tasted blood. Peeling his jacket off, he recalled the tug and skid as he rounded the church. His small flashlight showed a laceration on top of his shoulder along with two holes in his jacket, evidence of the bullet that had passed too near to think about. "Somebody's looking after me," he muttered to himself.

After cleaning the now stinging wound with supplies in his first aid kit, he reached for his journal to write all he remembered while fresh in his mind. He could still see the man and hear the snap as his neck was broken. He remembered the killers' main features and the Amazon woman's name, *Blondie.* It struck him that they must be bikers from the terms they used. The Mercedes was black and looked new, but he had no idea about the plates . . . not much to tell the cops, even if he did call in to report the crime anonymously.

An uneasy feeling began to set in as he remembered the vanity plate on his bike. *They'll be able to find me from that, may even have seen it at a biker bar or rally,* he thought. He began to panic at the thought they might be waiting for him at home. He calmed down somewhat when he realized his plate light was out. He had been pulled over because of it by an overzealous Barney the night before as he rode through Selma, returning home from the weekend trip to Mobile. *What next?* Realizing how late it was getting, he called his wife to tell her he had stopped to have a beer at his favorite watering hole, The Hawg Corral. He started Beast and headed to do just that, and maybe something a little stronger to calm his nerves.

CHAPTER 2

A little later, after cutting through familiar neighborhoods while continuing to watch his mirrors for signs he was being followed, the biker pulled up in front of the bar. He swung his leg over his bike and stood up, relieved to see few cars or bikes outside due to the late hour.

"Wassup, Wolf?" asked Rosie, his favorite bartender as he took a seat at the end of the bar where he could see the door. He winced as she gave him the ritual biker babe hug like always. He had known her for years and fondly remembered some of the rides they had been on together after she ditched her abusive old man a few years back after ending their relationship. Funny as hell, she was the queen of one-liners and known for keeping the guys in stitches by telling off-the-wall biker jokes. Slim and well endowed, she was a pleasure to look at as she tended bar. Rosie was one smart woman who knew her customers well, remembering their names, favorite beverages, and even the bikes they rode. She could sense exactly what her regulars needed and doled out smiles and jokes accordingly.

"You must be hurtin' or something—sure are tensed up. Been working out, or is it your ole lady that's got ya that way?" She asked the question with sincere concern evident on her pretty face while closely watching Wolf for his reaction. "You sure are in mighty late. I was thinking about shutting it down, but I'm glad to see you and don't mind staying open a while. I got a lot of cleaning up to do anyway. Beer, or something stronger?"

"Both—I got some serious thinking to do."

"Now *that* sounds dangerous. You run into some trouble down in Mobile at Mardi Gras? How was your trip?"

"The riding part was great, the Biker's Ball was well, a ball, but the parade got rained on. Overall, a nice weekend seeing lots of old friends I hadn't seen in a while."

"You're so full of it, but I'm glad to hear you had a good weekend; maybe you can take me sometime if Sue's not going."

"You know, that sounds fun and dangerous at the same time." He paused and frowned. "I've just got to work out some details in my head."

"I'll be glad to listen, or if you need a place to stay, my doors always open for you," she said with an exaggerated wink to go with an obviously exaggerated, seductive smile.

"Thanks, but I don't know if I can handle what you got," he said with a grin, getting back into his normal bar routine.

He had always felt safe and welcome at the Hawg Corral, surrounded by bikers who looked out for their own. The walls and ceiling were decorated with a variety of biker paraphernalia, from wheels to helmets, to shirts and hats from all over the country. A '74 BSA bike, well past its prime, sat next to an even older piano that was rumored to have been played by Doc Holiday in Tombstone. Some nights when the place was rocking, his biker buddies provided great entertainment with tales from the road. Each story told was more outlandish than the one before, but often provided inspiration for the stories he wrote monthly for the local edition of a biker magazine. Relieved they weren't here now to distract him; he pulled out his journal and began to write.

"I'm going leave you two alone, I gotta go clean up anyway," she said in the sarcastic tone she used when referring to his pocket journal.

He wrote:

- *Who was the dead guy? He looked familiar . . .*
- *Who are the killers? They must be bikers . . .*
- *Why was he killed?*
- *What did they do with the body?*
- *What do they know about me?*
- *What could they tell about my bike?*
- *Where are they now? Where are they from?*
- *Should I call the cops? If so, will they look at me as a suspect?*

Few answers came immediately to mind. The beer and the shot of Jose, coupled with the adrenaline wearing off, began to take effect. He was overcome by exhaustion, both physically and mentally. Closing his journal, he stood up slowly. Yawning and stretching, he tried to fight off the overwhelming fatigue he felt down to his bones.

"Gotta go gal, the sack's calling me," he said, sliding a twenty over the bar.

"You be careful going home. I got a call a while ago from the Chopster, saying the men in blue were out in force tonight. Said there were a lot of unmarked cars riding around and even more in the Publix parking lot between here and where you're headed. You sure you're OK to ride? My place is just a few blocks away in case you forgot."

"Naw, I appreciate the offer, but I really need some shut eye. I couldn't keep up with you anyway," he said with a smile. "My old lady never did understand that men can have good looking women friends without benefits."

"You're a real charmer, Wolf. Honey, you ever lose her and you'll have all the benefits you can handle," she said as she came around the bar. "You call me anytime you need to talk," she said giving him a peck on the cheek and a hug.

"Offer noted," he said with a smile as he started towards the door, pulling on his worn leather jacket as he walked. "See ya next time, darling."

He paused and turned in mid-stride as he remembered her total recall of customers. "Rosie, you ever run into a biker couple that seemed like one percenters? They would both stand out in a crowd. She's about my size with long blond hair, big boobs, and ears like that guy in *Mad Magazine* . . . what's his name?"

"You mean Alfred E. Newman?" Rosie asked. "Seems pretty freaky but if that's what you prefer, ya outta check out Bourbon Street down in New Orleans," she said with a grin.

"Not my type, but the guy she was with was big, maybe six foot six or more, well built, not flabby. He had a nose and mug that looked like he had a head-on collision with a freight train."

"No, I'd remember those two for sure. They ain't been here when I was working." She dug deeper saying, "You had a run-in with them or something?"

"Just trying to remember where I saw them, could have been at a rally or maybe down in Mobile. I thought I remembered them when I was stopped at a light on the way here." Trying not to raise suspicion, he added: "If you see them, don't mention I asked about them. They can get riled real quick if they don't know you. Give me a shout if you see 'em," he said as calmly as possible, trying to prevent her from getting suspicious.

"You got it, Wolf-man, you be careful out there."

As he brought Beast to life, he thought of the cops. *Did they find the body or the killers?* He had decided at this point there was nothing to do but wait and see what was in the news in the morning. His main worry now was explaining to his wife the wound on his shoulder, stinging more now than before.

On the fifteen minute ride home, he was startled as a couple of police cars zoomed past, blue lights flashing but no sirens. Otherwise, the ride was uneventful in the unseasonably warm night air, the Eagles' song, *Take it Easy* coming from his speakers. "That's appropriate," he muttered to himself. There were indeed a half dozen police cars in the Publix parking lot, most unmarked, along with what looked like a surveillance van with a battlewagon parked beside it. None seemed interested in him as he rode by. A lieutenant on the force lived across the street from his house in the cull-d-sac. Wolf had always spoken respectfully to all on the force he encountered around town, waving when riding past them on the road.

He was aware they all knew who he was, and they seemed to forgive him when he passed by going a little too fast. He had no beef with any of the local cops, and to them, was just a good citizen that loved to ride. The town was known in the county as having little crime, or at least, very little that made the local news. Good motorcycle roads were bountiful around this section of Alabama, and there were many regular riders of the area roads.

Arriving home, all was quiet, his wife only stirring a little as he slid into bed. He had taken a long hot shower to rid himself of the chill he felt. A pain killer, chased by a generous shot of Jose helped him pass out quickly, his mind eager to put this crazy night behind him.

CHAPTER 3

The sound of the Harley ring tone startled him awake at 7 am the next morning. He didn't bother hitting the snooze button on the cell phone to catch a few more minutes of shut-eye like normal—he was wide awake and hoping last night's memories were just a bad dream. His shoulder told him otherwise when he reached up and touched the bandage.

"You're up mighty early to have been out so late," his wife said from the bathroom doorway. "You could have called," she said like always when he came in late after stopping at the bar. Sue rode a motorcycle herself, her Vulcan 750 sitting in its spot next to his bike in the garage downstairs. He had bought *Beast*, a '07 Kawasaki Vulcan Nomad 1600, 4 years ago and had ridden it daily, rain or shine unless there was a monsoon-like downpour outside when leaving for work. He had selected the bike when he purchased it new after thorough research. His internet surfing had revealed that the full bagger had a reputation for low maintenance and durability. In his mind, it was set up like a car—water-cooled, fuel-injected and with a drive shaft; oil changes, tires, and brakes were the only maintenance services regularly required.

On the rare occasions he had to leave it at a dealer for warranty work, he borrowed hers. She didn't really mind unless it was a gorgeous day with mild temps, preferring to drive a Beamer or Lexus from the new car dealership where he worked as a manager.

Today was not one of those days, a cold front had moved in overnight, and the high was forecast to be in the low 50's and predicted to get much colder when the late winter sun went down. He didn't mind, preferring the cold, crisp air to being cooped up inside a four-wheeled cage. He was reminded occasionally of the adverse effect riding in a car took on his back with its bulging discs. He was fortunate to have a friend in the physical therapy business that taught him how to do exercises while riding to strengthen his abs, preventing back pain. The regimen had kept him from giving in to the doctors that recommended surgery to solve the disc problem in his 57 year old back. The pain from old injuries from his days as a jock had come back as he had gotten older. Determined to continue riding on two wheels, he exercised his 6 foot 2 inch frame daily to keep his weight under 220. This helped his back and had kept him from lining the pockets of the surgeons. He often told others he thought the doctor should write him a prescription for a Harley to allow him a medical tax deduction from the IRS.

It was ironic that he knew so much about cars and trucks but avoided riding in them unless necessary. He made a living training his sales team to sell them. He avoided driving or riding in cages for more than a short time, due mainly to his back. He did enjoy trying them out, and could be found occasionally putting new models through their paces on curvy roads. None could really compare to the thrill of taking a bike through the twisties on a back country road. He felt uneasy being inside a cage, watching the world go by through the glass from inside, reminding him of TV—*watching* instead of experiencing nature. Some of the latest luxury models were not only climate controlled, but could park themselves and had alarms and sensors to warn the driver when too close to another cage. He wished his employer would sell bikes like they did cars; he'd be in heaven with a bike as a demo!

Wolf went through his morning routine, trying to take his mind off the events of the previous night. After starting coffee, he went out the rear of the house, down the stairs, and casually strolled down the driveway to the curb in front to retrieve the newspaper. He followed this routine daily to let gravity have its effect on his internal plumbing while stretching his muscles after a night's sleep. This morning, he was extremely alert to his surroundings, warily looking for unfamiliar cars or strangers outside. Out for their morning exercise, women in groups of two or three frequently walked or jogged outside throughout the morning. This morning was no different from many others, him noticing nothing unusual or suspicious in the quiet neighborhood he called home.

Returning to the security of his house, he poured a cup of coffee and opened the newspaper, scanning it quickly for news of the previous night's murder. In the local news section there were pictures from the new city hall dedication, held last night. He froze, staring at the picture of the mayor posing with various town officials and others involved in the construction. He suddenly realized that *this* was the man he had seen murdered last night. He had been expecting the murder to be front page news, but found no mention of it anywhere in the paper.

Having time to spare due to rising early, he turned on the TV and flipped it to the local news channel. A breaking news story was about Whiteville's mayor, who was missing and had not been seen after he departed the previous night's celebration. The reporter implied that a scandal was in the making, but foul play was also thought to be a possibility. The local city administration and police were scrambling doing damage control. The police chief stated they had leads that were being followed up on, and more details would follow in the noon briefing. In his gut, Wolf doubted they would find much until the body was discovered, and then who knew where that investigation would lead. He was worried about his part in the disappearance, and as a result, he felt a growing sense of pending doom for himself, his family, and his future freedom to ride.

The broadcaster advised viewers to stay tuned throughout the day for more information. In reality, Wolf knew that this advice was given primarily to drive up the ratings and get more almighty dollars from their advertisers. Knowing better than to waste his time on that source of information, he went to the internet seeking more recent details. Finding little additional information on the story, he checked emails and the weather, then closed his laptop and went to prepare for work.

After a quick shower, he dressed and packed the smaller Vulcan with gear he would need later when the temperature dropped. He had decided to take his wife's bike in case his bike was one of the leads the police were following, or worse, one the killers were looking for. Being much cooler, there would be few bikes out today. He had a unique flashing taillight, making his bike stand out from others, *and* his plate light was out. He'd have to take care of both the next day when he went to his buddy's repair shop for the parts. He'd need a receipt for the repair of the plate light to show the court in order to get out of the ticket Barney had written him down in Selma.

Riding the 750 was a fun change of pace, similar to riding a Harley-Davidson Sportster. Quick and maneuverable, he always had a blast riding the bike and enjoyed skidding around the curves on some of the nearby gravel roads. He took a gravel back road today, figuring he needed a little fun to get rid of the gnawing fear he had of getting blamed for the murder, or for not coming forward. *Too late now*, he thought, having little doubt that his employers would distance themselves from him, leaving him high and dry financially. He didn't need that right now with both kids in college, burning through his savings. Wolf wanted to do the right thing, but without knowing more, wasn't sure what that was. He did know one thing—he had to keep this to himself and not breathe a word of what he had seen to his family or coworkers.

As he sped to work through the wildlife area's winding gravel roads, his tension began to drain away. When on this bike, he plugged in his mp3, listening to ZZ Top as he slung the bike around corners as fast as he dared. As usual, when he arrived a few minutes late at work, he was upbeat and ready for the onslaught of the day's business. The dealership had been selling cars at a record-breaking pace lately due to the abundance of tax refund money many car buyers had at this time of year. Birmingham had begun to rebound from the recent economic slump, and his staff was ready and willing to take full advantage of the increase in traffic using the skills they practiced daily.

The sales team and managers had exceptional work ethic and it showed, resulting in a huge increase in comparable sales and making them the envy of the other new car dealerships. Surveys indicated that customers really appreciated their expertise in locating the perfect vehicle for them by providing options few other dealers had available. The support staff consistently worked together to put out great quality reconditioned used cars, and all took pride in their work. This atmosphere helped Wolf lose himself in the demands of daily sales tasks, thankfully putting the previous night's escapade out of his mind.

The problem with busy, demanding days was that they passed too quickly, and when over, left Wolf stressed out but with a natural high he got from the success his staff was having. He felt a sense of accomplishment and joy for the financial rewards his employees got for themselves and their families, coupled with the satisfaction he himself felt helping customers find the right vehicle. His main reward was in the satisfaction he felt knowing he was preventing buyers from being taken advantage of by the many unscrupulous dealers the industry was known for. Most of the staff had hung in there during the slower months of the bad economy, believing in his prediction of increases in traffic and sales in the near future. In fact, many even seemed to enjoy practicing their sales skills, working with little complaint to get ready for the expected increase in business. The team truly worked well together.

Several on staff followed his lead by acquiring and riding motorcycles to work as weather permitted. Knowing the public and upper management's misperception of bikers' reputations, Wolf had to rein in the "biker speak" that was heard occasionally at work. His co-workers were well aware of his alter ego, many looking forward to his stories of rides and rallies published monthly in the Alabama edition of the biker magazine that he regularly wrote for.

"What's happening Wolf?" was occasionally heard as a greeting when passing employees in the hallways, to which he'd typically reply, "that's John to you here," with a slight smile on his face. He secretly enjoyed the biker nickname he'd picked up during his years of riding back when he attended NC State University in Raleigh, NC, its sports teams known as *The Wolfpack*. He and his fellow riders in those times were known simply as "The Pack" in their hometown when they rode into town while on breaks from school. His riding buddies had christened him "Lone Wolf" after he was transferred by the company he worked for to Alabama, mainly due to his preference of riding alone, coupled with his inability to ride with them after the move. Shortened to "Wolf", he felt his nickname fit and made him a bit anonymous due the many "Wolfs" he encountered when riding and attending rallies across the countryside. In reality, he truly enjoyed riding alone, avoiding the annoyances of riding in a group, while allowing him to find little known roads and discover bass fishing holes along the way. When riding, he frequently had a fishing rod in his custom rod holder on the back of his bike, ready to use whenever the opportunity presented itself.

This group of now middle-aged riders didn't ride together much after each left school to start their own lives, many becoming "weekend warriors" due to their obligations to family and careers. They reconnected yearly when they gathered at a small biker resort in the mountains of North Carolina, catching up and remembering the exciting times they had in their younger days. During the day, they rode again as "The Pack" on some of the most beautiful, curvy roads in America. New riders came and went, but the core group remained the same. Not a motorcycle club, they were bound by shared past experiences from a time when riding together was for safety. Mechanical breakdowns happened frequently back when motorcycles weren't as dependable as they were now. Mostly Hondas, Kawasakis, and Yamahas with a Harley thrown in, many of the bikes were held together with duct tape, coat-hanger wire, and prayers. Unplanned stops often led to unexpected adventures and acquaintances, and their recollection of them seemed to get more interesting each year when shared with fellow bikers gathered for the weekend party at Rider's Roost. Nobody really cared, as bikers are similar to fishermen in their tendency to embellish the facts for the entertainment of the listeners.

Wolf always looked forward to those weekends, but could do without the group rides. He wasn't unsociable, he just loved to ride unencumbered by others, riding and stopping wherever and whenever he chose. He typically would ask the group leader where the next stop was, and then plug it into his GPS. He often took unexplored alternate routes, unless the group pleaded with him to take the lead. He did enjoy sharing his finds with others, but was well aware of how quickly bikers' skills become rusty when not riding daily. Often, these rural mountain roads turned into loose gravel, difficult to ride and extremely hard to turn around on. Some could be nearly impossible for a group with various skill levels to handle, so Wolf preferred to ride them by himself before taking the chance of leading others on a less than enjoyable ride. With appropriate gear along with the electronic devices now available, he was very comfortable riding alone.

Having discovered that local folk were less intimidated by a lone biker, he would often shoot the breeze with them, getting tips that led to great places, roads, and stops, along with some really interesting stories. Many were bikers—past, present, or future and seemed to enjoy talking with him in order to take a break from their same old day-to-day routine. It gave many something new to talk about at the family supper table. He'd often been invited to have a beer, share a meal, or wet a line at a favorite local fishing hole.

His boss was an outspoken, middle-aged northerner from Chicago that frequently voiced his feelings about the need to keep his two worlds separate.

Being a car buff and extremely savvy about the auto industry, his boss never really seemed to understand the passion Wolf felt for riding motorcycles. Unfortunately, he was influenced by the stereotyped image of bikers that many others have, and consequently not overly supportive. Over time, he had morphed into a bit of supporter and mostly granted his frequent requests for the time off needed to attend various biker events for the magazine. This favor was returned by the effort Wolf put into his duties on the job, along with the loyalty and support he showed for new initiatives his boss wanted to implement in the dealership. The daily stress of his job was counteracted by his 30 mile, scenic ride to and from work each day.

Today was like any other at work, a steady stream of customers coming through the doors as soon as they opened at 10 am. Many on staff lived in the same town as he, and therefore today, the main topic of discussion was the mayor. Many speculations were voiced, most revolving around the speculation of an anticipated scandal with a hot blond. The local news had added more details at noon, along with interviews with the mayor's family and staff. The description of a long haired blond, medium build, just over six feet tall was given by the police as a "person of interest" in the disappearance. As expected, this added fuel to the suspicion of improprieties, and it had been rumored in the past that the mayor was a bit of ladies' man. This was zealously countered by his wife talking about what a great "family man" he was, insisting that something terrible had happened to him. She pleaded for anyone with knowledge to come forward.

"What do you think happened to him?" asked GQ, a biker with whom he worked. "You ever run into a big bodacious blond like her in your travels?"

"Too many to remember their names," he said with a grin and raised eyebrows. "Don't reckon any that would run with the mayor's crowd," he added. "I sure would hate to get involved in that mess."

"Roger that, I heard the Feds have been called in. You know we gotta ask Bob when he gets in, bet he knows the scoop. He'll be here at six when he gets off from his job at the police dept. You know he's a school resource officer and hears about everything from the kids and teachers."

"It wouldn't surprise me if he calls in. I'll bet they're working overtime down there. By the way, do you mind working later if necessary?" Wolf asked, eager to change the topic.

"You know I got your back if you need me, buddy. Besides, might just sell another one . . . I could use some new tires before going down to Thunder Beach."

"I really appreciate it, I gotta go see Mark and get a new tag light . . . I got pulled by Barney Fife coming back from Mobile. Guess I'll need a receipt to prove

I got it fixed." He immediately regretted telling him. *One never knows what may get repeated to the wrong person at the wrong time,* he thought.

"Gotta go, my new set of tires is walking in the door right now!"

"Okay, later," he said, immersing himself in paperwork.

Bob did call in as predicted, saying the station was flooded with reporters and the FBI, and he was needed to help with crowd control. He was unable to give more information about the investigation due to his position in the department. Wolf was relieved at the development and really just wanted to ride and try to plan a way to get out of his predicament. He was now, and always had been, a law abiding citizen but was a realist in knowing how screwy things got when it came to public figures and murder. Apparently, the body had not been found, and the media was comparing the situation to the South Carolina governor that had been screwing around with a woman in South America a few years back. He too, had gone missing at first.

By four, he was caught up with all urgent tasks, and left the store to take the long route to do some serious thinking that could not be done at work or home. Thankful his boss had not added any additional burdens to his daily workload, he changed clothes, fired up 'baby' Beast and left, relieved to be away from work and all the talk about the mayor. Normally staying later than scheduled, today he didn't care if his coworkers did think it was odd he left earlier than normal. He decided to swing by his buddy's repair shop, pick up a couple of bulbs for his rear lights, and get a receipt to give the clerk of court in Selma.

He started by taking his normal route which ran by the entrance to the church, knowing many bikers used this road daily. He was thankful for his foresight to ride his wife's bike. He pulled over just short of the entrance in the pretense of making a cell phone call, all the while watching warily for any signs of activity up the hill and behind the church. As he sat there, his memories of the previous night's panicked departure came flooding back, sending an involuntary spasm down his back when he remembered how close the bullet had come to taking him out. As it was, he had nearly lost control and crashed in his haste to leave the scene. He unconsciously touched his shoulder and rubbed the tender area.

"I'll bet there are some serious skid marks up there," he whispered to himself, remembering how as a kid, skid marks were proof of your riding skill to your buddies. He wondered what the killers did with the body.

As he sat beside the road with his cell phone held to his ear, he froze when he saw movement behind the pompass grass planted at regular intervals below the church. Unable to move, he watched as a doe, followed closely by two fawns, appeared from behind the shrubs, grazing on the freshly sprouted grass that had popped up recently due to the mild weather. The protective mother suddenly froze in her tracks, ears swiveling forward and looked right at him, apparently seeing him sitting there for the first time. Seconds passed before she bolted out of sight followed closely by her fawns.

Unnerved by the deer and not having the intestinal fortitude to ride up the hill to see if there were signs of the previous night's fiasco, he started off at an apparently leisurely pace, fighting the urge to roll on the throttle and get out of there as quickly as possible.

He was immensely relieved when he was positive he was not being followed. There were no blue lights or sirens, and, after a few turns and a short ride down a lonely gravel road, he decided to continue to his buddy Mark's shop as planned. As he approached, he became uneasy when he saw the police car parked outside. As he slid to a stop in the loose gravel from the crumbling pavement out front, Mark came walking over, thrusting his hand out and shaking Wolf's in the traditional biker handshake.

"Waz up Wolf, I haven't seen that bike in a while, your ole lady still riding it?"

"Yep, but lately she's been riding a Lexus when it's cold in the morning. She's been getting up early and teaching in Pelham. 'Fraid she might be getting soft . . . not a bad thing, I do like 'em soft if ya know what I mean," he said with what he hoped was his typical smile.

"Where's Beast? You get to Mobile and back alright? I thought you might have had a problem when you pulled up on that scooter."

"Yeah, Beast came through like always . . . got a bit more spunk since you took the goat bladder off."

Mark laughed, then said, "you still need some pipes to do it right and make it sound as good as mine." Mark also rode a Kawasaki Vulcan, an older model that had been stripped down, lowered, and enhanced in ways only a master mechanic could. It would put most other V-twins in the dust with little effort.

"Probably going to be a long time 'fore I put that loud shit on Beast— I like to hear my tunes when I'm riding. When I'm behind your bike, I can't hear myself think. Besides, it scares them poor little Bambi's half to death. I think that's what gets them confused and wantin' to commit suicide by bike."

"You know, I saw the other day that loud pipes save lives," referring to the latest ad he had in the current edition of Thunder Roads of Alabama magazine.

"That BS was started by the people selling them, and I ain't ever seen it make a damn cager take notice or hang up their cell phone. Most of 'em got their music up so loud they can't hear the pipes anyway."

"Well if it's up to the mayor, I won't be selling them around here anymore with that dang new city sound ordinance he got passed," Mark said with disgust in his voice. "You heard the latest on the old fart?"

"Heard a little about it at work today, but I was too busy to find out more," he said with as much calm in his voice as he could muster.

"Come on in and grab a beer, it's close enough to quitting time for me," Mark said as he stepped inside. "Lute's been telling me all about it . . . sounds like the mayor's finally showed his stripes," he said as he headed to the fridge in the back to get a couple of Coronas.

"How's it going, Lute?" he said, taking his weathered leather jacket off and throwing it at the couch. He greeted his buddy in the typical biker way.

"It's been like a three-ring circus today, and I needed a break to get away from all the crap down at city hall," he replied as he took a big swig of the beer in his hand. "We've all been at it since we got a call from the mayor's wife about 3 am. They don't pay enough for all we do to cover his ass if you ask me," he said in his typical, matter of fact demeanor.

"What's up with all that—y'all got any leads, or is he just shacking up with some bimbo?" Wolf asked nonchalantly. "There's a bunch of rumors in the news, but you never know what's for real."

"Well, you gotta keep this to yourself, but I think he got mixed up with a hot blond he was seen with after the dedication last night. Probably still basking in the glow of some really great poon-tang she laid on him last night. Probably afraid to face that bitch of a wife he's got. She's on the council and is the one that really pulls the strings around this town. She'll probably take over as mayor if he doesn't turn up real soon." He paused and then added, "Maybe the blond screwed him to death . . . not a totally bad thing or way to go," he said with a big gut laugh. "Anyway, I gotta go see if anything new has come up."

Wolf was a bit uneasy after the comment. He suddenly felt the need to end the banter.

"OK, see you later . . . let's go riding out to Resort 25 this Sunday. Sounds like you need a break from it all."

"Ya got that right, I'll let you know. You bringing Sue?"

"Don't know yet, it depends on whether it's a purty day or not. You know how it is."

"Yes I do. What I'd like to do is hook up with that blond, and bring her . . . she could probably take care of us all if she looks like we've been told." He paused, a thoughtful look on his face. "On second thought, I ain't interested in any bitch that's been with the mayor. You never know what unwanted goodies she might be giving away," he said with a sneer.

"You're probably right; see ya later—let me know about Sunday."

"See you later, Lute," Mark yelled from the backroom.

"So what's up Wolf?" Mark asked as he handed him another cold beer.

"I need a couple of bulbs. One for the taillight and one for the plate light. I got a ticket coming through Selma, and I need a receipt to get out of it."

"You got it, man, whadda ya think about all that mayor shit?" he asked.

"Well, *I* think he's a pussy-whipped asshole, and that the new sound ordinance is a bunch of crap, but he *has* done a lot for the town with the new school system and that new fancy, overpriced City Hall complex, not to mention all the new businesses that have opened up recently. I don't like that I can't fish in the lake that is now in the middle of the complex, but overall, he'd probably be ok if he would ditch that wife of his and maybe learn to ride a bike so he can understand the biker lifestyle." He paused and added, "you know, I never did meet him in person."

"Wow, I would have never thought I'd hear ya say anything good about him, let alone that much. Last month at the sound ordinance protest outside city hall, it sounded like you and all the others there would like to string him up from the tallest tree you could find."

"You're right, but he has done a lot of good for the town," he repeated. "Hoover ain't got nothin' on us now if we could just win some football games."

"Well, he sure has put a hurting on the pipe business lately. If they start pulling bikers leaving here, I'd be glad to help make him disappear."

"Be careful what you say, if he don't turn up soon, they'll be looking for somebody to blame."

"Well, I'm not blond and I don't have big boobs, except in my dreams," Mark said with a laugh. "Did ya hear the description of that babe?"

"No, tell me about it."

"Lute said she was a tall, well-endowed blond gal, dressed to kill in a revealing black evening gown." He looked him in the eye. "*You* ever run into a woman like that?"

"Only in my dreams," he replied, remembering last night's encounter. "Anybody else involved?" Wolf asked, remembering her huge accomplice.

"That's all I know. Lute didn't seem to be real forthright with the details. Guess he was fishing around and couldn't say too much."

"Sounds right, he has been a detective for a long time. Becomes second nature after a while, I guess."

"I'd be the same way if I had Feds hanging around. I'd hate for anyone to think I was involve—you know they're always looking for somebody to blame, and us bikers are probably at the top of their list of suspects."

"You got that right, Mark. The Southern Vet Club members are still pissed about the sound ordinance the mayor got passed. Probably his wife's doings, anyway. The cops hassle them about their loud pipes, and the clubhouse is close to the police station. That's just plain messed up in my book. They're even talking about moving the clubhouse outside of town."

"You know bro, after all you and that biker's rights group said in front of city hall at the protest, y'all might just be on the list of suspects. I remember the vague threat of "*kill the bill or there will be consequences.*" There was a lot of emphasis on the word, *kill*," Mark said with a concerned look. "These days it seems like everybody's looking for someone to blame for anything that ever happens to 'em."

Wolf had a thoughtful look on his face.

"Yeah, you're right, dude. Hey, you know, I've been thinking about putting pipes on the bike like the ones you been givin' me the business about every time I come in here. How much do ya think it'll run and how soon can ya get 'em?"

"As much as I can get from you—naw, just pulling your leg. I've got a deal for real for you," he added.

"Naw, really man, I'm serious."

"Me too. You see that Vulcan with the wrecked front end over there? It was totaled, and I'm parting it out. Only got a few thousand miles on it, and it's got a power commander to go with the Vance and Hines pipes. It can be yours for two bills, installed."

"What ya been smoking, dude, it's worth several times that."

"I owe ya Wolf, and besides, I bought it for salvage and wanna pay ya back for the extra business, thanks to that plug in your story a few months back."

"Don't know 'bout that, but I'm takin' ya up on it before ya loose the buzz you must have."

"You know I don't smoke that shit—Wild Turkey and home brewed beer are my friends now," he said reaching under the counter and pulling out a bottle and a couple of shot glasses. "Let's drink on it, my friend. How soon you want 'em put on?"

"Never turned down a deal or a shot . . . here's to you, buddy." Trying not to sound suspicious, he added, "you getting real healthy in your middle-aged years with all that marathon BS. How soon can ya put 'em on?"

"If your lazy butt will help me and ya ain't working your real job, how's tomorrow morning sound to you?"

"Sounds good to me, I feel a cold coming on already. See ya at seven in the am with some biscuits. Bro, I gotta go, Sue is cooking her chili tonight. Can I get those bulbs and a receipt to go?"

"You got it, man." Mark said as he headed for the parts room.

He returned with bulbs in hand and printed out a receipt.

"I really appreciate it. Thanks for the shot, gotta roll," he said, heading out the door.

Passing the police station on the way home, he observed much more activity than normal.

Don't know what it means, but I sure want to stay as far away as possible, he thought to himself as he cranked up the music on his bike.

CHAPTER 4

The man known as "45" lay silently in the underbrush on a hill across the road from the church. He had a clear view of everything from the picnic area down to the road below the scene of his latest kill the night before. Dressed in camo, a casual observer would think he was like any other Alabamian, stalking and lying in wait for a something to shoot to wander by. In reality, he was waiting for the biker to return to the scene to see what had happened. To him, it was unbelievable that he and his accomplice had been caught totally by surprise after more than a week of reconnaissance and planning. Indeed, it was the first time in the more than ten years he had spent as a killer for hire that he had left a witness alive. That the biker had surprised them was bad enough, but what made it worse was that he had few clues to the identity of the lone biker he must now eliminate.

Typically after completing a job, he and Blondie would celebrate with a sexual abandon considered by the clueless public to be lewd, degenerate, and unlawful in many states. Not this time. Here he was, lying on the ground on a chilly, damp afternoon after killing and disposing of that wimp of a mayor in a way that would never be traced back to him or his partner. When the body *was* discovered, the crime would remain an unsolved mystery as long as they could find and silence the witness. He smiled thinking of the wasted hours the cops would spend looking for clues, perceived by the public as bumbling idiots.

Another thing that really pissed him off was that the biker had spoiled his record of clean kills, and was now a loose end he'd have to tie up before leaving this redneck town. He wasn't worried much about being identified; his appearance had already been altered since last night and there would be no picture the biker could point at to give the cops a suspect. Instead, they might just hold the biker as a suspect when the freshly dug hole behind the picnic area was found. That would make the job tougher, as it was hard, but not impossible to silence a target in jail without assistance. What puzzled him

20

the most was that the biker had not come forward or made an anonymous tip, as evidenced by the lack of cops sniffing around the area. This led him to believe that their mystery witness also wanted to avoid the law.

Since beginning the surveillance, he had seen only a few bikers go by, but none fit the profile of the bike they saw as it sped by them the previous night. He had an extensive knowledge of motorcycles, frequently acquiring new ones of various types after a good payday, riding as a lone wolf biker for most of his adult life. That had changed a few years back at a rally in Monteagle, Tennessee, when he met Blondie. What had initially drawn her to him was her curiosity about his handle, "45". It got her really hot seeing the damage a .45 caliber slug did to a body, smashing through bone and flesh.

He didn't kill that way as often as in the past unless necessary, mainly due to the mess it left coupled with the improvements in modern forensics used to solve crimes. He had an extensive film collection from his days as a Ranger and the jobs he had done later as a mercenary. He was thankful for the training he had received courtesy of Uncle Sam, and now earned a good living doing what he enjoyed most—killing. He had been drummed out of the service for his love of doing what they trained him to do best—what hypocrites!

Living on an isolated property in the mountains, he enjoyed raising hogs and slaughtering them with his Colt 45. This really got Blondie turned on, especially when they were dressed to look like human pigs . . . come to think of it, he enjoyed it, too. He used them occasionally to process and eliminate evidence of human victims brought back to the secluded farm when torture was required to obtain information for various employers. He immensely enjoyed the benefits of his personal recycling program.

He became instantly alert when a biker pulled over just short of the church's entrance from the road. Training the sniper rifle's scope on the leather clad rider, he knew at once it was not the bike that had almost run them down as it sped by last night. He knew by the sound that the bike had been a Jap-made, Harley wannabe, and was certain it was a Kawasaki Vulcan with a big V-twin engine. The Japs now made those big cruisers with light bars, full fairings, and hard bags. The bike had been dark with lots of chrome, reflecting the moonlight as the lone biker rode away. He recalled the brake light that came on like a strobe briefly when the rider took the turn around the church.

The biker below stopped and pulled out a cell phone as he watched. 45 knew it was a much smaller Vulcan 750 cruiser by its size and profile. He confirmed this by reading the badges on the tank and side cover.

Probably some nerd riding back and forth to work to save gas to put his snotty nosed kids through one of those local church schools, he thought to himself.

21

There was only a small percentage of riders he thought of as real bikers. He often made sarcastic remarks to weekend warriors and trailer kings he saw at rallies, them putting only a few hundred miles on their high dollar, chromed out Harleys and custom choppers. They bought the latest in shiny new leathers in order to impress their women and buy their way into being part of the biker culture. *Impersonators!* What a shameful waste of a scooter.

He tended to avoid members of hardcore motorcycle clubs, knowing that by insulting, threatening, or harming a member, he would incur retribution from the entire club with disastrous results for all involved. He believed his only weakness was his unwillingness on occasion to back down from a conflict even when outnumbered.

He knew the biker from last night was the real thing by the way he handled his big cruiser in the gravel, throwing it around the turn at the church. He could have sworn he hit the guy with a round when he seemed to lose control, but knew if he *had* hit him, it would have knocked him off the bike, and he wouldn't be looking for him today. *Must have been distracted by the bitch,* he thought.

His easiest kills were those that rode motorcycles. He would often strike up a conversation and tell of a great road in the area. He then found it easy to set up the kill, waiting for his victim on a blind curve where he would cause an "accident" and finish them off by breaking their neck or impaling them with anything handy. After all, *everybody knows riding motorcycles is dangerous*, especially after a few drinks. Many times, he and Blondie would practice just for fun to figure out new ways to initiate crashes. It was no surprise that many curvy roads not far from their isolated place in the mountains were thought to be death traps due to the fatal single bike crashes that occurred frequently on them.

He waited another hour until dusk before breaking cover and going to his bike, parked out of sight in the clearing below. The low pitched rumbling of his CVO Street Glide was soothing to him after lying on the ground for most of the day. He had arranged to meet up with Blondie at the local biker bar to ask a few discreet questions that needed answers after their waste of a day lying around. He sure could use a shot and a beer after today. However, he had to ride over to the scene of last night's near disaster to fill in the hole before heading out. He also wanted to look for tire tracks, while resetting the game camera to get a close-up picture in case the biker returned. He hoped the mystery biker showed up while he was there . . . he had both a bullet and a grave ready.

Shame to kill a real biker, he thought, but shit happens. Seeing no one, he finished his tasks quickly, and then got back on his Harley to ride to the bar. Having decided to take the long way to remove the kinks from his powerful, muscular body while having a little fun enjoying the power of his scooter, he smoked the rear tire a bit as he started off, quickly accelerating away from the church. About to shift into third gear, he immediately let off the throttle when he spotted a cop car headed towards him. After he went by, 45 watched his mirrors and saw the brake lights come on. He quickly realized when he didn't turn around that the sheriff was just on patrol and making his rounds, obviously not interested in busting a biker for going a little too fast.

CHAPTER 5

Just after six pm, Wolf pulled into his driveway, pushing the button on the garage door opener and pulling in next to his bike with the practiced ease that comes from riding every day. As he dismounted, he gave Beast a pat on the tank and rubbed the fur covered seat. "Missed you boy, but there's trouble in Gotham City," he whispered to his everyday companion. Beast had been purchased new four years back, and been his constant companion wherever he went ever since, carrying and protecting him for over a hundred thousand rewarding miles, through all kinds of weather conditions, never complaining or letting him down. He had feelings for his bike similar to what the Lone Ranger demonstrated with his horse, Silver in that TV show he watched as a kid. He truly understood the bond that develops between a man and his ride, be it a horse, bike, plane, or indeed, even a cage.

Beast, a big V-twin cruiser with a silver and black paint scheme, was the center of his life when not at home or his day job. With a few additions that included a fairing, Wolf's iron horse fit him like a good old pair of jeans. With so many hours in the saddle, the Vulcan was an extension of himself when riding.

After removing his leathers, he went to the tool bench, got a screwdriver and replaced the taillight bulb with the conventional, non-strobing one, then replaced the license plate bulb. He was reasonably sure his vanity plate wasn't readable last night, as it had a layer of road grime on it that he seldom removed. He was very lucky. He realized with all the resources of the internet, the plate would have led those obviously experienced killers to his doorstep. He hadn't thought he was lucky when he was hassled by the cop in Selma, but he had recently changed his mind.

Still got good Karma working for me, he thought to himself. At that moment, his wife of twenty plus years appeared in the doorway.

"You think more of that bike than you do of me," she said, giving him a hug and squeezing his butt cheek. "You know I can do a few things for you that Beast can't," she added. "Supper's ready and your biker show is about to come on."

"Beast don't never complain 'bout 'nuthin, and is always ready to be ridden," he said in his best southern drawl with an exaggerated leer on his face.

"You might better teach him a new trick if you keep talking like that . . . besides, that sounds pretty gay to me."

"Yeah, I'll show you what gay don't sound like later. Smells like chili and cornbread, right?" he asked.

"You got it, kimosabe, and it's getting cold. I got something special for you later."

Sue was the kind of woman most bikers dream of. She understood his biker ways, never complaining when it took hours for him to get home after work on a nice day. She never bitched even during the long riding season, when he left for days to attend a rally or to go on a charity ride. She enjoyed his tales from the road, often sparking ideas for his stories saying, "you should write about that," after he told her about a particularly interesting place, person, or an exciting, unusual event upon returning from a ride. Since their boy had followed his sister and gone off to college, she had, after a few weeks of moping around, returned to the playful ways and quick wit that had led to him falling head over heels for her so many years ago.

She didn't seem to still have the same passion for riding that she had in those days, and had added a few pounds, but the same playful, mischievousness was still there. He felt it was his mission with the kids grown up to bring the zest back fully. She would surprise him at times by getting leathered up, then waking him after a late passion filled night saying, "you gonna stay in bed all day, or you wanna ride? Daylight's burning . . . you getting old or something?" She knew that always got him going, and would frequently cause an even further delay due to how those leathers clung to her ample womanly curves. She didn't seem to mind too much.

As usual, the chili and cornbread supper was great, the beer was ice cold, and later, after he watched the news for more developments, they headed to bed.

The motorcycle ring tone announced a call from one of his biker friends. When he looked at the name, he became instantly alert when he saw the call was from Rosie, the bartender at *The Hawg Corral*.

"You ought to get yer ass down here, Wolf, I think that babe you were talking about is here, although she don't look exactly like you described her . . . she ain't no blond tonight, and her ears look normal. She's asked me and a few others if we know a big guy that rides a dark Jap cruiser bike with a fairing. What's really scary is the guy that just came in and hooked up with her. He was checking out the bikes in the parking lot before he came in, according to the Chopster. You got some bad blood with those two?" she asked with concern evident in her voice.

"Don't think so, everybody loves me; I may have pissed off a few cagers for good reason, but I've made no real enemies that I know of," he said, trying to sound unconcerned.

"Not like me," she snorted. "What's weird is she's not blond anymore, ain't got big ears, but she looks like she could be a linebacker at Alabama except for those big boobs of hers. Everybody was checking her out until this guy came in and hooked up with her. That guy's a real dangerous bad ass if you know what I mean, but his nose looks pretty normal to me."

"What'd ya tell them?" he asked, trying to breathe normally.

"Nothing, ain't nobody gonna say anything. Besides, since that story you wrote about your bike came out, a lot of guys have gone out and bought Vulcans similar to yours. Toad's here tonight on his and it looks a lot like yours. Maybe Harley Davidson sent 'em."

"Y'all real busy tonight?"

"Yeah, we got that dang karaoke goin' on, can't really stand it, but there's a big crowd and everybody's drinking and cutting up. Some of 'em even sound pretty good," she said. "Some of the guys from the Vet's club got up to do that Motown style shoo-op backup for a singer doing an old Temptation's song. They must have been practicing—it was funny as hell to watch. Maybe you can get 'em to do another one and get a picture."

"Sounds like a good idea. Anybody from the magazine there? If not, maybe I *should* cover it."

"Nobody from there is here. That sounds like a great idea, I'll buy; we can always use the plug in the magazine."

"You got it, I'll see you soon. Bye."

Sue rolled over in the bed and made eye contact. "Really—you going down there now? You know, I think Rosie's got the hots for you, but I'm not worried after what we just did. You want me to come?"

"Naw, you already did at least twice. You get some rest, you might need it for when I get back," he said with a faked leer on his face. "Duty calls."

"What I really think is you can't go a day without riding Beast—not complaining, it does seem to get you in the mood."

"Gonna take yours again if you don't mind, the light's still out on the plate."

"You better not put a scratch on my bike, and you better still be in the mood when you get back."

"You know I'm always in the mood around you," he said drawing her close and giving her a big kiss. "See ya later."

CHAPTER 6

Arriving at the bar, he was extremely relieved to see twenty plus bikes outside as he rolled up. One was leaving that had been parked just outside the door, next to a new Vaquero. As he pulled into the vacant spot and cut his engine, he heard a deep baritone voice from behind him say, "nice bike, dude," in what he thought was a somewhat sarcastic tone of voice. He got an immediate uneasy feeling that he tried to put aside.

Dismounting, he turned to face the biker and said, "Thanks, which one's yours?" He noted that the speaker was a huge, old school looking biker.

"It's the Street Glide over there. I just got it a few weeks ago. The name's 45," he said, shoving his hand out.

"Mine's Wolf. That's a fine scooter ya got there. Wanta trade?" he said with a smile while pumping his extended hand. Old habits are hard to break, and meeting bikers frequently, he often got kidded for riding a metric bike, too often by Harley riders who really just wanted to brag about theirs. This time, he felt uneasy as he watched the seasoned biker closely. He had been ribbed recently while stopped for gas by a Harley rider that made the comment, "*if it don't use oil, it ain't a real bike.*" That statement had played a part in a subsequent run-in with a deer a few miles further down the road on that recent trip. He had been somewhat distracted thinking about the comment and was riding with the music turned off. That deer hit him in the same hard bag as the one before. Odd, two deer hits on the same route; maybe somebody was trying to get his attention.

"You ride much at night? Heard there are a lot of deer around these parts," he said in an accent Wolf couldn't quite place, but had an ominous feeling he had heard it before and recently.

"I try to avoid the back roads at night when I can; had a couple of run-ins with deer not too long ago."

"You're that writer guy from the rag I was reading." he said without emotion. "That shit really happen? This is the replacement?" he asked with a sneer, referring to his wife's 750.

Instantly pissed off, but with a growing sense of unease, Wolf replied. "Yeah it did, scared the shit out of me. I see deer everywhere now when riding at night, real or imagined. I despise those deer statues in the yards and especially those reflectors that look like deer eyes from a distance. Now I try to stay on well-lit roads at night as much as possible." He intentionally let the insult slide, allowing him to think Beast was out of commission to allay any suspicion.

"Get you a real bike like my Glide over there and they'll hear you coming. Say, you know anybody that rides a Vulcan like that one of yours in the magazine that has those flashing rear lights and a batwing? Met him last year in Daytona and forgot his name. Said he was from Birmingham, but we were pretty wasted at the time," he asked in a somewhat less confrontational manner.

Thinking quickly while appearing to consider the question, Wolf answered, "I used to have that type of light last year, but I took it out when a trooper picked me out of a bunch of riders in Panama City. Seems like I've seen a few bikes with them, but most were crotch rockets." He added, "I'm sure it wasn't me you ran into, I'd remember you no matter how wasted I was." His uneasy feeling was getting worse.

"Maybe I'll run into him around town. Any other decent biker bars around here? The entertainment and scenery's kind of lame in there."

"You might try the one in in Bessemer, they advertise in the magazine. Nice jawin' with ya, 45, but I've got a cold one calling me, and I need to take some pics for the magazine. By the way, where are you here from?"

"Tennessee," he replied and then headed toward his bike. "Be seeing ya."

Wolf, not usually unnerved by any biker encounter, knew in his gut that this guy was more dangerous, had absolutely no conscience, and would in fact, be glad to stick a knife in anyone that pissed him off. Most bikers he knew had big hearts under their leathers, and would stop to help others in need. *Not 45*, he thought, *this guy would rob you, then kick you and your broke down bike into the ditch as he rode off laughing*. Most of his type were one percenters or ex-cons, gone renegade after riding in gangs and clubs. Seasoned bikers could usually pick them out and avoided them. He was relieved when 45 walked away.

Most bikers he knew were good, charitable, and friendly, even though they cloaked themselves in a tough-looking shroud. After all, that "bad ass" reputation was the only shield they had from being messed with by local rednecks and thugs on lonely backroads, as well as in the small towns and bars they stopped at while out enjoying the freedom of the road on their bikes. Wolf's biggest fear was being caged in a jail cell, and therefore avoided trouble like the plague. He remembered being told by his dad to "know your enemy," and headed for the door with this in mind.

Going inside, he found a party going on complete with a couple he knew singing a sappy duet on stage. All the tables near the stage were full, with many in the crowd cheering the singers on with alcohol-enhanced enthusiasm. One of the loudest was his buddy, Chopster, who yelled at him to make his way over and join the party. Waving him off, Wolf held up his index finger and then pointed at the bar and made a circular motion, indicating he'd be back after getting a beer and making the rounds. With a thumbs up back from his buddy, he continued making his way to the bar in the back, stopping occasionally to return the ritual greeting to bikers he knew, many from fans that read the magazine.

Wolf had a case of CRS, or in layman terms, a terrible memory for names, finding it easier to put faces with the bikes they rode. He had a good idea of who was inside the bar from the bikes he saw outside, but had never before seen the one he had parked beside. It was a new solid black Vaquero like the one he had tested out the previous year during the Daytona Beach bike week. He had been really impressed by the bike, and was hoping to run into the owner and find out what they thought of the obviously newly acquired ride.

As he approached the bar at the rear of the Hawg Corral, he got a big hug from Rosie, followed immediately by more of the same from Comma, a young vivacious blond, who stuck an ice cold Corona complete with a lime, into his hand.

Rosie looked over at Comma and said loudly, "he's mine bitch, and I got something to bend his ear about." She grabbed his hand and led him away.

"Watch the bar for me, I'll be back in a few minutes," she said as she walked toward the back door. Wolf went along, giving an innocent shrug as he was dragged outside.

The Hawg Corral had an area out back with a few old, well-used and weathered, solid wood tables, complete with a fire pit and a rusty, but well maintained old grill frequently used for biker gatherings. The area was used frequently by many as an escape from the more than occasional off key singing on karaoke nights, quick romantic meetings, and phone calls. No one thought there was anything strange about them to heading out back. In actuality, a frequent topic among the staff was about the relationships of patrons that at times, was used to rib the regulars. The good-natured joking around was never taken seriously by the biker crowd. Some of the local non-riding cougars that were frequently looking for a new ride added to the gossip, especially on the weekends. In fact, to most of the regular bikers, this was a great source of entertainment, watching as others become more aggressive as the nights grew late and more alcoholic beverages were consumed.

"Did you see the big-boobed chick at the end of the bar when you walked by?" Rosie asked after they moved away from the bikers gathered around the fire.

"Kinda hard to see anything after you dragged my ass out here so fast," he said.

"Shit, I saw your eyes on the way out. You've never missed checking out a nice pair of boobs since I've known you."

"Well, I did kinda notice her a little as I went by," he admitted.

"She's a brunette tonight, guess your eyes got stuck below the neck," she said in her normal sarcastic tone.

"Yeah, like most the women I know, you're always right," he admitted.

"Well, she really is a blond; that hair's out of a bottle."

"How in the hell you know that, you changed your preferences and been muff diving lately?"

Rosie gave him a smack up-side the head then said, "look asshole, I'm trying to tell you, she sure looks like the woman you described. Ain't no friend of yours, she's real big trouble." She smiled and quickly added, "You know, us gals are pretty good at assessing the competition."

"So why do you think she's trouble, she piss ya off or somethin'?"

"No, did you see that big guy in the parking lot with the Harley 'glide when you rode up? He was in here and had a beer with her. They acted like they just met, but I could tell it was just a ruse. She's been asking about a bike that sure sounds like yours. One thing's funny though, she didn't say nuthin' bout that tag of yours."

"What makes you think she's trouble? There are lots of chicks that come in here trying to pick up bikers."

"The guy that was talking with her is a real bad ass. Chop believes he's ex-Army, Ranger or something. One thing he's sure of; he's a real bad dude. The woman has been looking through the magazine and seems real interested in you and Beast. You got some bad blood with them, like did you screw her at a rally or something?"

"No way, I'm getting old, but I would have remembered those boobs. You of all women ought to know better . . . me and Sue are real tight. I don't need no complications in my life with all I got going on. Besides, you never know what unpleasant goodies might come home with you."

"All I'm saying is that there's a reason she's sitting alone at the end of the bar. You know your buddies; they'd normally be all over that like flies buzzin' around a pile of crap."

"Well, if she's looking for me, I need to find out why. Maybe she just likes my stories."

"You be careful with that one. Her man's real dangerous and she looks like she could be treacherous, too."

"You're beginning to sound a bit paranoid, *mom*, but your concern is acknowledged and noted. Let's head back inside before she gets antsy and comes after you. If I'm going to find out more about this babe, you need to play the part of a jilted woman."

"You're a real asshole sometimes Wolf, but you know I love ya and will always be there for ya. I hope you know what you're doing."

"Not completely sure, but you know, a guy can't never have enough friends, and I'd rather find out if she's a friend or foe." She grabbed his head and gave him a big kiss full on the lips, then grabbed his hand and pulled him towards the door. He stopped and pulled away.

"I need to say hello to a few of my adoring fans, see you in a few minutes," he said with a smile meant to put her at ease.

"OK, but you remember what I said." She turned and went through the door. He walked away from the bikers at the firepit, pulled out his cell phone, and pretended to make a call to buy time to plan his next move while waiting for the intense, uneasy feeling to pass.

After a while, he opened the door and went directly to the empty chair next to the big blond sitting at the end of the bar. Rosie walked over, slammed a beer in front of him and stormed off.

"Looks like you got one pissed off bartender there, Wolf. My name's Cheetah," she said, extending her hand towards him. Her grip was surprisingly strong for a woman.

"A real pleasure to meet you, but have we met before? Can't believe I'd ever forget you," he said glancing directly at her boobs.

"We've never met, but I read your story in the rag there," gesturing to the magazine lying on the bar. "I enjoyed it, especially the part about the bike. Matter of fact, I liked it so much I went out and bought a Vaquero. It's parked out front."

"I wondered whose bike I was admiring out there. That's an outstanding ride, and it looks like you added most of the options I mentioned. How do you like the way it handles?"

"I can't get enough of it; lots of power and it hugs the corners well. I appreciate the advice on the add ons you had in your story."

"Yeah, I was really impressed with it down in Daytona."

"You riding your Vulcan tonight?" she asked. "I'd love to see it in person."

"Afraid not, mine's in the shop, so I'm on the old lady's bike. Kinda fun for a change of pace, it's real light and pretty quick for a 750."

"What's wrong with your bike?" she asked quickly with a little too much interest.

"Just having the hard bag on the back fixed where the deer hit me a while back. Bad thing is, I see deer everywhere now at night since it happened. I've gotten so I hate all those damn reflectors people put on mailboxes, they make me jumpy thinking they are deer eyes. I've even started avoiding the two lane backroads at night. A real shame; I used to really enjoy the solitude of riding after dark."

"That's too bad. You and that bartender serious?"

"Not at all, she's a good friend though, we go back a ways," he said and then quickly added, "I'm a lucky guy, I got a killer wife at home, kinda reminds me of you." He instantly regretted revealing more information than he wanted to.

"Y'all real tight?" she asked in a low, sultry tone of voice, looking directly into his eyes. He felt her leg rub up against his in a way he knew was less than innocent.

"Yep, we're real tight, and she'd kill me if she thought I was screwing around." He pushed his leg against hers as he turned to slide out of his stool. "Gotta take a leak, be right back." He noticed a slight wince of pain quickly cross her face as he stood up.

"You all right? Didn't mean to hit your leg."

He could tell when she seemed slow to answer that what was coming next was bullshit. "Yeah, I hit a damn cart in the parking lot that some lady with a snotty-nosed kid let go of. I let her know what I thought of her and the brat. You should have seen her face, thought she was going to wreck her car getting out of there. I hate cagers," she said with way too much emphasis.

I got your number now, he thought, remembering the tug at his bike as he sped down the hill and away the previous night in his panicked hurry to flee the murder scene. He could not be positive it was her, but he did vividly remember the feeling he had when the Amazon woman had gotten such pleasure snapping the mayor's neck. It was hard to believe that this could be the same cold-hearted killer, but he suddenly felt the need to get away from the bar and her. He resisted the urge, knowing it was safer to learn more. He retreated to the bathroom before the person he thought could be the merciless killer noticed his discomfort.

While away, Cheetah signaled for her bill, paid in cash, and told Comma, "tell Wolf I had to go, but I'm sure I'll see him again real soon." It was obvious when she said it a little too loud, it was meant for Rosie to hear. There was little doubt in those nearby that she was serious trouble for anyone that messed with her.

Wolf returned just in time to see her back as she walked toward the front door, the crowd parting as she went through like it does when a big cop comes through a crowded room. She stood out in the crowd, seeming to dwarf most she passed. He still wasn't one hundred percent sure but—

He quickly crossed the room to the door and watched as she straddled her bike, put on gloves and helmet, then started the Vaquero and rode off with the practiced ease of a seasoned biker.

"She's a looker alright, bet she could put a hurting on ya without even trying," said Chop, suddenly appearing from behind him. He shook his hand enthusiastically.

"Just admiring her bike," he replied with an innocent look.

A microphone was thrust into his hand as the DJ said, "*Love This Bar's* on next, and Wolf, you're up. Let's hear you belt it out for everybody."

"This is your doing but I really don't feel much like singing tonight," he said, looking at his friend.

"I figured you'd might say that, so here's a shot of Jose to git ya in the mood," he said, holding an oversized shot glass up in front of his face.

"Guess I don't have much choice in the matter, do I?"

"Not unless you want to answer to big old Term over there," he said pointing to the group that had been singing when he walked in. "His babe really gets turned on when you sing like 'ole Toby, and I believe he's looking to get lucky later."

"Oh shit, crank it up then," he said, taking a big gulp and stepping up on stage.

While singing, he walked over to the bar owner, an old school biker, and stuck the wireless mike in his face to get him to sing the main chorus line, "I love this bar". His antics were followed by familiar cat call whistles, applause, and backslapping, all knowing this old school biker did not do karaoke. After he finished, he joined Big Dog, Term, and the group at their table. The group of bikers were all members of the local Southern Vets Motorcycle Club, most of which he knew. After greetings all around, he leaned over and spoke in Big Dog's ear.

"Got a minute to talk out back?"

"Sure, Wolf, I need a fresh beer anyway," he said and stood up.

They headed to the bar in the rear, grabbed beers, and went outside.

"Wassup?"

"You or anybody else ever seen that big-boobed Amazon that was up at the bar before?" He added, "And maybe the big guy that was with her earlier?"

"Never seen her before—Bunny whacked me side the head when she caught me checking her out a little too long. She was talking with that big ass ex-Ranger at the bar earlier, and they looked real chummy. No one knew either one of them."

"Those are the ones. Anybody talk to her while she was here?"

"Several guys were hitting on her until the big dude showed up and scared 'em off. You know, she was looking at your story and asking if we knew you. You thinkin' about tapping that one, you better reconsider. That guy is a real mean bad ass. He's killed before, I've seen that look. He'd rip your head off and spit down your throat without thinking twice, especially if you were hittin' on his babe. He ain't exactly the friendly type, for sure." He looked Wolf in the eye and slowly said, "You got some bad blood with him?"

"No, I just met him in the parking lot, and he'd have no reason to have it in for me. He just seemed way too interested in Beast. You got any idea why?"

"Don't know bro, but the babe's got a Vaquero like you wrote about in the story. Maybe's he's ticked that his babe liked your story and bought a rice-burner," he said, slapping him on the arm.

"Never would have thought writing a story could be dangerous."

"You know that's the price you pay for being famous, just stay clear of the babe and don't pursue it."

"She's not my type . . . you know about me and Sue."

"Yeah, you're a real lucky guy with that one."

"Yep, and she knows how to shoot a gun real good. Kinda keeps me in line."

"I hear ya, let's get back unless you got something else bothering ya."

"Nope, I'm good. Thanks for the info, I gotta head out anyway. Tell everybody I said bye."

"You got it. Be seeing you," he said as they headed back inside.

Wolf moved quickly through the bar, saying goodbye to those in his path, and waving to friends he saw across the room. As he went out the front door, he stopped to light a smoke, allowing him to scan the parking lot for potential danger. After hitting the start button on his bike, he allowed the engine to warm up while looking across the street for any unusual activity. This was a typical action most cautious bikers did after having a few beers, trying to spot the local cops, eager to bust bikers that had consumed one too many. He stubbed out the smoke, put his gloves and lid on, and rode slowly out of the parking lot, relieved to see nothing suspicious.

Frequently checking his mirrors all the way home, while taking the long way by cutting through quiet neighborhoods, he was more tense than he ever remembered being when riding. His apprehension slowly passed as he noted no unusual activity or out of place cars before turning into his own neighborhood. He pulled into the parking lot in front of the neighborhood clubhouse and lit a smoke while contemplating the evening's events. He knew the two bikers at the Hawg could easily be the ones he had seen commit the brutal murder, but he just couldn't be sure. *How could their appearance be so different in such a short time?* There were a lot of bad-ass bikers around he had met before, but that didn't make them killers. Many came in the Hawg when just passing through, drawn by the popularity of the place, along with the abundance of good looking babes seeking to hook up with a biker. He had no idea how to put the police on their trail without implicating himself. It would be some seriously bad karma if he was wrong about them. He decided to start by covering his own butt in case the killers were out there looking for him. He would see what the police investigation turned up before making any rash moves.

After a while, he started his bike and rode the few blocks home, again noting nothing unusual. It had been a long day and he was beyond tired.

CHAPTER 7

Wolf was sitting on his bike in front of Mark's shop before opening time when he heard the rumble of a motorcycle still more than a block away. A bit of a showoff, Mark pulled up in front, sliding to a halt in the loose gravel a foot from where Wolf sat. Mark's bike was an old style Vulcan 1500 that had been customized for speed by removing anything unnecessary in order to lighten it, while doing things few knew how to in order to maximize the big V-twin motor's output. The 24" ape hangers along with the flat black paint completed the bad boy look, and the straight pipes could be heard from a long way off, getting the attention of the locals. Wolf suspected that Mark's bike had something to do with the new sound ordinance. He did seem to enjoy revving it as he often rode out of his way to pass by the mayor's home, just outside the city limits while on his way to work early in the morning.

"Ready to make the Beast roar?" he asked as he dismounted.

"Hope you don't plan to make it as loud as your monster," he replied. I got a cop across the street, and Sue will probably cut me off if I wake her up when I get home late."

"I'll tone the noise down if you insist, but it'll make you hold on real tight when you open 'er up. Glad ya got that backrest."

Wolf reached in the saddlebag and tossed him a sausage biscuit. Mark opened the door and headed straight to the coffeemaker, taking a bite as he went.

"Man, there was some serious traffic near the mayor's house this morning. Don't know if there are new developments, but the cops and the news folks were thicker than flies around there. You see the news this morning?"

"Nope, I had a late night and didn't want to be late and give you a chance to come to your senses about that price you gave me."

"Screw you, a deal's a deal."

"Just kiddin' bro. I can't wait to see what ole Beast can do."

36

"Never be as fast as mine, but it'll be close. Turn on the idiot box while I get some coffee and open up shop. Bet that mayor's down in New Orleans, laughing his ass off about the whole thing. His ole lady's gotta be really pissed. I heard she wears the pants and pulls the strings. Probably runs the city but nobody knows it. You know I heard her family's connected to big money from up north. Mayor probably got fed up and left with that hot babe Lute mentioned."

"Sounds like you got it all figured out. I sure hope those news reporters don't interview you for the six o'clock news, probably get ya sued or something," Wolf said.

"Nobody ever listens to my opinions except when it comes to bikes."

"Not a bad thing, you *are* kinda radical with the opinions lately, especially about the mayor—you be careful about that shit. They'll be looking at both of us if anything bad happened to the old fart. I don't much like the idea of some big ugly dude feeling romantic when it comes to my backside," Wolf said, grinning. "Besides, I couldn't stand to be in a cage, even for a few days—you know I got a bad case of claustrophobia."

"You've got that right, dude. Let me know what they're saying in the news . . . be back in a few and we'll get started after it cools down a bit."

"You got it bro. Take your time, I've got to get Beast ready for the new pipes."

There were no new developments, but the mayor's wife was putting on quite a show for the media. She seemed to use the media coverage to spotlight all the progress that she and her missing husband had made on behalf of the city. It was apparent to him that her tearful pleas for help during the interview were rehearsed. The good things she said about his merits as a devoted family man and dedicated public servant were expected, an obvious attempt to make him seem honorable to the viewers. Wolf knew better, and could tell in subtle ways that her comments did not come from her heart. *She would have made an excellent actress,* he thought. It occurred to him that the most successful politicians were also very believable thespians.

Relieved there was no mention of bikers having anything to do with the mayor's disappearance, he went outside to get his bike ready by removing the hard bags and leaving them outside on the bench. When he was done, he began to roll it inside. Mark appeared and helped him push it up the ramp on the lift.

"How long you reckon it'll take to do the job," he asked.

"Not long at all, I took the parts we need off the other bike last night after you left. You'll be left with the whole afternoon to see what it'll do . . . just don't get yourself pulled for excessive noise or anything crazy, most of the cops around here aren't very friendly right now."

"Darned, thought I'd do a burnout in front of that new city hall—guess I'll have to settle for just riding out to the lake instead," he replied, chuckling.

"Grab a wrench and help me take your pipes off. On second thought, you just hold 'em while I loosen the bolts. When was the last time you cleaned under here?"

"Haven't had the time since I got back. Thought I'd wipe it down as we go today."

"You get the prize for having the dirtiest, well maintained bike in town. Hard to believe it runs like it does with all the miles you've racked up."

"Don't let it go to your head, but you have a lot to do with that. You reckon I ought to start looking for a new one and retire ole Beast? Been hearing a metallic ticking at first when I start it up on cold mornings, but it goes away."

"No, it's probably just a hydraulic lifter. The worst thing you can do is just let it sit up for a while. I ever told ya how many times that those parts go . . ." Wolf cut him off before he went into more detail in his familiar discourse on V-twin engines.

"Maybe once or twice. Not riding's bad for me too . . . gotta be free," he said, flapping his arms like a bird. "My back always reminds me when I go more than a day without riding."

They were done by eleven, interrupted only a few times by customers stopping by. Starting the bike, they both admired the throaty roar of the 1600cc V-twin's new pipes. They rolled it off the lift and outside. Wolf grabbed the hard bags, and with practiced ease, quickly put the bolts in place, then stood up to admire his new slant cut pipes.

Mark came up behind him. "Take it out for a long ride and then come back and bow down to the Vulcan mechanical guru, namely me. You can pay me when you get back."

"You got it bro, see you in a while. Can I bring ya some lunch?"

"No, I'm good. Be careful . . . I'm not sure you can handle all that extra power."

"Kiss my leaving, going down the road while you gotta work, ass, my friend. Handle this—"

"Back at ya, have fun." He started Beast, revved it a few times while Wolf put on his helmet.

"See you later, bro," Wolf said, mounting his two-wheeled companion.

He shifted into first, gave a twist of the throttle and quickly let out the clutch. Beast kicked up gravel, while sliding a little until the rear tire gained traction and surged forward. Turning out onto the road, he accelerated with power he had never experienced from his bike before. A big smile crossed his lips as he forgot the reason his bike had been upgraded with the new pipes. He was impressed by the increase in torque. The deep throaty roar when he rolled on the throttle, coupled with the extra low-end power made him forget his recent worries. He headed out of town, determined to see what this power would do on the highway.

He headed out towards one of his favorite curvy stretches of road on Highway 25. Heading towards Chelsea on Hwy 11, he quickly gained confidence in the responsiveness of the motor, passing cars and trucks every chance he got. He wanted to twist the throttle wide open and see what Beast could really do, but didn't. He knew the local cops regularly set up speed traps to contribute to the county coffers, so he waited for the straightaways in the route ahead. After crossing 280 and onto Bear Creek Road, he pulled over, got off his bike, and gave Beast a quick walk-around, checking the tires and looking at the pipes for signs of bluing, a sign of running too rich due to the new power commander and exhaust. Seeing nothing out of ordinary, he looked for any traffic in the area, and slowly pulled onto the highway, coming to a complete stop.

"Let's just see what you can do boy," he said, giving the side of the tank a pat.

He revved the throttle a couple of times, then let the clutch out swiftly and smoothly to get maximum traction, utilizing the extra power from the new mods. He had already discovered that Beast could now smoke the wide sports car tire he had on the rear, a feat it couldn't do before unless on loose surfaces. Beast responded by pushing him against the backrest, then chirping the tire when he shifted into second gear. He pushed the bike close to redline before shifting into the next gear, finally letting off the throttle as he approached 120 mph.

"Whoa boy, you really got some spunk now, but you're going to scare those deer shitless if I do that when we're out riding," he said, caressing the side emblem on the tank with his hand.

He let the bike's engine slow him down until the speedometer needle was just past 65 mph and continued down the road towards Resort 25 and the curves just down the road.

Resort 25 was south of Leeds on Hwy 25, a twisty, curvy, two-lane state highway known as Copperhead Road by the locals. Bikers loved this stretch of road where the thunder of their bikes was heard often as the riders put their bikes through the curves, the more daring riders dragging pegs on some of them. Near Leeds and Pell City, with Barber's Motorsports just down the road, this biker resort was a favorite stop of his and popular with the locals. The bar and restaurant drew bikers from around the country, to whom the area was a destination, especially during race weekends at Barber's.

The resort formerly was known as 29 Dreams, a name that confused many, possibly contributing to its ultimate closing. The new owners had renamed and reopened the resort, investing much time and money renovating the bar and grill, and then paving the parking lot for the bikers. The gamble had paid off—large crowds of bikers now flocked there on the frequent mild weather days Alabama was known for. The resort had been opened up for cages, bringing in a more consistent base of regular patrons. All mingled and partied with little trouble between the groups, due in part to the attentive and attractive bar maids. For partiers with too much to drink and no designated driver, there were clean, comfortable cabins out back to stay in overnight. The setting was rustic and scenic, nestled between the hilly ridges in the area.

Wolf came out occasionally with his wife and spent the night after having a few too many for him to feel safe to drive home, 40 miles away. Indeed, he and his wife would go there after infrequent arguments to "make up". He had been inspired at times to initiate a totally ridiculous disagreement in anticipation of later rewards.

As he turned into the resort, Wolf noted a dozen cars and a few bikes. Being a weekday, this was not unusual, but was in fact, more traffic than the biker bar had in the period before it had closed when known by its former name. Having plenty of open space right in front of the main building housing the bar and grill, he pulled up next to the door. He stood up, removing his helmet and gloves while scanning the other bikes nearby, looking for familiar ones to indicate who was inside. He saw the Vaquero from the previous night and inwardly jumped when a low, raspy voice came from behind him.

"Admiring my new scooter are you? I'd have thought after writing the review you'd be riding one by now."

"When I get ready to put Beast out to pasture, I probably will be," he said, turning to face the woman. He stuck out his hand, but was pulled into a biker babe style hug instead.

"I've been reading your stories all day. They had several old issues at the bar, and I found a few more here. You really get around. Would you show me some curvy roads around here?" she asked.

"Nothing personal, but I mostly ride alone, as you must know after reading the stories."

"You wouldn't need to worry about me; I can keep up with anybody I ever met."

"No doubt, I watched you take off when you left the Hawg. How's the Vaquero treating you?"

"Awesome bike. It sure blows most others away, just like you said in your story. Sure is quiet though."

"You know, I kinda like 'em that way—it don't spook the wildlife as much, not to mention the local law."

"Loud pipes save lives," she said, "but it is kinda nice for a change to be able to clearly hear my tunes. My other bike was loud as hell."

"I don't want to argue the point, but have you ever seen a deer run across a field, then turn around to run back the other way, and usually in front of you?"

"More than a couple of times, made me think they were trying to commit suicide. Stupid deer."

"My theory is that it's the loud rumbling of the exhaust pipes that spooks them when the sound bounces off the trees. Loud music gets their attention, but it don't make 'em panic. I've seen many just stand there and watch me go by . . . kinda like they enjoy rock-n-roll music," he said with a straight face while raising his eyebrows.

"Maybe you got something there Wolf, but I think you could just be full of shit. Your pipes aren't exactly quiet," she said, laughing.

"Been told that before but not quite as nicely. What did ya used to ride, sorry, but I forgot your name."

"It's Cheetah to my friends. Used to have a '04 Road King with lots of chrome and some bad ass pipes. Great bike, but this one's faster and really hugs the curves."

She went around his bike, pausing at the rear, then bent over and appeared to look closely at his rear tire.

"That a car tire you got on the back? I like the tread pattern, but don't it handle crappy when you got it leaned way over in the curves?"

"Naw, a lotta bikers have asked me the same question. To me, it handles better by hugging the curves, especially the banked ones, then wants to straighten back up coming out of them. Puts a bigger patch of rubber on the road. It does takes a little getting used to is all. It's saved my butt several times like when I got hit by deer twice in the side . . . didn't break the rear end loose. Also makes it more stable in the loose stuff and the rain."

"You're screwin' with me again, aren't you?" she said.

"Not at all—did I mention they last three times as long? I get about 25 to 30 thousand miles on each one. I'll never go back to a bike tire on ole Beast here." he said, patting Beast on the tank.

"Tell you what, let me buy you a beer and you can tell me about some good places to ride and bars to go to. Looks like I may be here for a while," she said, taking his arm and heading for the door.

"Never turned down a free beer," he said as they headed inside.

After a couple of beers and too many questions about places to go and others that rode Vulcans, Wolf stood up and left to take a leak. Standing at the urinal, the door opened and he heard the snick of the latch being turned. He glanced around, and was surprised to see the bartender, Millie, standing just inside the door. He finished his business and slowly turned around.

"Please tell me you're not looking for a way to earn extra money," he said with raised eyebrows and an exaggerated shake of his head as he looked her straight in the eyes. "I thought business was good lately."

"Shut up with the jokes Wolf, I have to tell you something really important," she said in a tense whisper.

"Must be pretty good to follow me in here—what's up?"

"That bitch you been shootin' the shit with is bad news *and* she's got a real dangerous old man that's about a hundred yards from here in one of the cabins. He's real big and looks dangerous, and I mean scary bad. There are other strange things about those two. They're staying in separate, side by side cabins and they rode in separately. Even stranger, they never come in the bar together."

"Maybe they're cousins or well—this is Alabama. Maybe they're just having an affair and don't want anybody to know about it."

"That's not all. I've heard them both ask about bikers that rode Vulcans. It's like they're looking for somebody."

"Maybe they're just looking for people to ride with that have Vulcans. She's got that real nice Vaquero parked outside," he said, trying to put her at ease.

"We both know better—" she said, looking him in the eye with a worried expression on her face. "You need to be real careful in case he's the jealous type of mean."

"Well, I was getting ready to head out after I got back inside. Two beers are my limit when riding. I want to get in some curves before heading home."

"You be very careful. Tell Sue I said hi."

"I will, but I'm not gonna tell her where we were when you said it."

"Screw you Wolf," she said as she opened the door and stormed out.

Going back inside the bar, he noticed Cheetah standing by the door watching. "You really got a way with the bar maids, Wolf," she said sarcastically.

"Yeah, they just don't like it when I say no."

"How about that wife of yours, aren't y'all real tight?"

"Tight as can be, but she gives me a lot of space knowing how I like to mostly ride alone. Hard to find a good woman like her."

"Does she ride with you very much?"

"Every now and then she'll go along to take pictures for the magazine on my follow up rides. We ride together to Thunder Beach down in Panama City each year."

"Shame to waste a good bike like that," she said.

"Well, I can hardly blame her after the spill she took last year. I don't want to push her, and like I said, I don't like having to be worried about anybody else when I ride. You know, I've found folks are more likely to talk to a lone biker when stopped. Leads to some great stories and invitations."

"Well I'd love to ride along with you to check out that tire . . . here's my number," she said handing him a card, brushing his hand with her nails.

"I'll keep that in mind. Gotta go ride some before I go home. Be seeing you."

Blondie gave him a biker shake and hug in a way typical for guys or butch women. He turned and strode out the door. As he mounted the bike, he lit a smoke, noting her watching through the window. He could tell from his years of dealing with car buyers that the camaraderie was not genuine. He didn't dare turn to look in the direction of the cabins. He knew there would be a black Street Glide parked nearby. A quick glance in his rear view mirror confirmed it, and he could just make out the outline of a very large man standing in the shadow of the porch. He waited for the engine to warm up and started off. He revved his engine more than needed, then gave it full throttle and rode towards Leeds and the curves ahead.

Pleased with his timing in adding the new pipes, he was somewhat relieved, thinking he had headed off the biker couple's suspicions. Even if these two weren't the ones that had dispatched the mayor so coldly just a few nights ago, he knew that the sound of the pipes would keep him from being easily discovered by the actual killers if they were looking for him. Although the overall descriptions fit, the faces were drastically different. He just couldn't be sure, and knew he couldn't pick them out from mug shots. Cheetah was OK in the way he wanted his woman to be. She reminded him of Sue when she was with him during biker events. He had to be sure before he cried wolf.

"That's funny, Wolf crying wolf," he said to himself.

He relaxed and enjoyed the rest of the ride, getting used to the extra acceleration when he twisted the throttle starting out, enjoying it even more going through the curves. He was pleased with the power, but hated the noise. He knew the new pipes would be annoying on his next long trip, but realized it would be hazardous to his health to go back to the old ones. *Have to get some ear buds.*

Returning to Mark's shop, he pasted an exaggerated smile on his face and slapped Mark on the back.

"I gotta admit Beast runs like a scalded dog now!" he said.

"Never a doubt, man, but what's with the bullshit grin? What's bothering you?"

"Nothing really important. Let's settle up, I gotta get home."

"You owe me nothing; those pipes are pretty scratched up on the bottom side. Didn't think you'd care, seeing how often you clean the bottom of your bike." He paused, looked thoughtful, and looked him in the eyes.

"Really Wolf, no bullshit, whatever it is that's got you worried, I'm there whenever you need me. Don't know if you can count on how good the advice will be, unless it's about bikes."

"I appreciate it Mark, I might just take you up on your offer before you know it. You serious about the pipes?" he asked. "It just don't seem right to me."

"I'm not taking any money from you for 'em, bro—I'll get more than my investment back from the other parts. I tell you what; you get the tab next time at the Hawg."

"Now that's a deal, I think . . . gotta go," he said, shaking hands.

Wolf got on his bike, bumped the starter button, then revved it to signal his approval of the pipes. With a wave, he turned out and accelerated quickly down the road.

On the way home, he took the route that passed in front of City Hall, where he again noted the excessive activity. There were even more cars than the previous day, many with federal government tags. Clustered in a group that reminded him of a venue at Thunder Beach, were TV news vans with their antennas extended high in the air. There were several small groups consisting of a reporter with a cameraman and anyone willing to give an opinion and be on the news. There was even a food vender truck, completing the similarity to a rally, minus the bikes. Uniformed policemen were outside directing traffic, and as he passed, he saw one throw up an arm and wave. Probably Bob, his buddy from work getting overtime, he thought.

He continued past, careful to avoid excessive noise from his now much louder pipes. An idea began to form in his mind about what he should do next, and soon. He warily watched his mirrors as he wound through the extra turns taking the long way home. Seeing nothing to be alarmed at, he turned into his driveway, pushed the garage remote button, then rolled to a halt inside. He killed the engine. As he closed the garage door, the rain came pouring down in huge drops, soaking everything it hit.

"Good Karma's still with me, must be doing *something* right," he muttered to himself.

He was happy to see supper on the stove and grabbed a plate of Sue's hearty pot roast and a beer. He paused at the bar, got out a bottle of Jose and took a long pull of the golden liquid. Flicking on the TV while sitting at the bar to eat and check his emails, he watched in fascination as the police chief pleaded with the viewers for anyone with information to come forward. A police artist's sketch, along with a physical description of a woman wanted for questioning followed his plea. The sketch looked vaguely like the actual killer's appearance, but could easily be mistaken for several other women he knew.

No new developments were announced, and the reporter that followed hinted at the incompetence of law enforcement officials. The mayor's wife came on next, begging again for anyone that knew anything to come forward. Wolf looked closely at the high definition screen making note of what he thought was deceit in the woman's message. To him it seemed she knew more than she was saying, similar to a card player that had drawn a winning hand. A $50,000 reward was mentioned.

He got ready for bed, his earlier idea now a decision for the next day's action.

CHAPTER 8

After Wolf left, Cheetah headed to where 45 stood watching from between their cabins. She went directly inside, followed closely by her huge partner. Quietly closing the door, she turned the chair around, wrapping her long, shapely legs around its back. He sprawled on the queen sized bed, then propped up against the wall to face her.

"Well, is it him?" he asked.

"Don't think so, he didn't act like someone that had recently witnessed a murder. His bike did fit the profile, but the pipes and rear light weren't the same. I checked those pipes to be sure; they've been on the bike for a while."

"You sure took your time talking with him. What did you talk about for so long?"

"All kinds of typical biker bullshit. He does have a way of pissing off the women."

"What did he do to piss you off? Y'all seemed real friendly right before he rode off."

"Not me, you prick . . . he pissed off the bar wench while they were both in the same bathroom. I asked about it, and he explained that he had turned her down."

"He must be gay . . . she's a looker, but way too sweet for my tastes."

"No he's straight . . . got a wife that rides, remember?"

"Ain't much of a biker, turning women down like that. Gonna give us all a bad reputation," he said with disgust.

"He's harmless, just a family man that writes and rides. He is a real rider, got over a hundred thousand miles on that bike, even has a car tire on the back. Probably thinks he's a bad ass in his own mind."

"Got no use for his type. Maybe we ought to help him have an accident just to be sure."

"No, I've got something else in mind. I was talking to a guy at the bar last night that told me about a sound ordinance the mayor got passed. It really pissed off the local bikers and a group of 'em staged a protest about a month ago. He told me Wolf was there being very verbal on what he thought about the ordinance and the mayor—sounds like motive to me. Cops just want to pin it on somebody, it doesn't matter who."

"Maybe you got a point. Not a bad idea, but aren't you forgetting about the guy on the Vulcan that saw the whole thing? We need to find him soon. Got any brilliant ideas about that?"

"We need to find you a better place to stay while I find the guy. There can't be that many big Vulcans with fairings and those rear lights around here. We can arrange an accident when we find him. We do need to split up in case that witness comes forward or sends in a tip."

"Do it fast, we don't want the guy coming forward, even if he can't pick us out from a mug shot. I miss the nose, it was funny seeing citizens' reactions when I pulled up beside them. A few even ran off the road," he said with a nasty grin.

"You just be careful and don't go getting yourself picked up for being stupid—just be cool until we find the guy."

"I can handle myself. Now, how about a little lovin' to help me sleep?"

"Screw yourself, 45. You'll get your reward when we get this finished. Try hitting on that bar whore instead. She seems to like bikers. Now get out of here while I do some research on the internet."

"Not my kind of bitch, besides, she'd probably scream so loud they'd call the cops. See you in the morning," he said, getting off the bed and heading toward the door.

She opened her laptop and started surfing the web, looking for new developments in the news about the missing mayor. Not finding anything to cause concern, she began a search for local groups of Vulcan bike owners. She checked on Craig's list and Ebay for ones for sale, figuring the mystery witness might just be trying to get rid of his bike. She wondered why the lone biker hadn't come forward, again concluding that he must want to avoid the law himself.

Too bad, he might just be my type of guy, she thought, thinking of the mysterious biker and imagining what tortures she could utilize before killing him. That would be fun if she had the opportunity.

Blondie, aka Cheeta, Butch, Ronnie, and other names she had used in the past, was unique. She had played football in high school as a linebacker, and was a vital part of the state championship winning team. After graduating, she was offered a full ride at a major university due to her quickness and instinct at anticipating what offenses would do. She was kicked off the squad after it was discovered that he (at the time) was more sexually stimulated by some of his teammates than the slutty cheerleaders that often hit on him. Blondie found New Orleans to be to her liking, and with the help of cosmetic surgeons, had become a popular stripper on Bourbon Street. She had on occasion gotten revenge in various sadistic ways on former acquaintances that showed up from time to time at bars where she was performing.

She had been forced to leave New Orleans in the aftermath of hurricane Katrina that devastated the area and flooded her home. For days she was trapped with little freedom, but had used the time to devise a plan for a future full of unbridled freedom as a biker. She had flown to Europe where she completed her sex change, becoming the woman she believed she was intended to be. Afterward, she took on a new identity and earned her income in ways the government couldn't track and wouldn't approve of. She was still very competitive, but rarely thought of women as worthy competitors. In her mind, men were simply used to earn a living, but she was always in control and found the current arrangement to be of her liking. She was a planner, seldom leaving details to chance that would put her freedom to do as she wished at risk. Her companion, 45, was a strong and talented partner, but she would not hesitate to sacrifice him if her freedom was in jeopardy.

After planning her next day's activities, she shut her computer down and got ready to sleep. As she closed her eyes, the rain came pouring down.

CHAPTER 9

The rain was still coming down when Wolf was startled awake by the sound of the Harley ring tone. He had been dreaming of being in a jail cell, a thought that troubled him greatly. Not one to hold much stock in dreams being predictors of things to come, he believed them to be the mind processing fears and events of the previous day. The dream quickly faded away.

As was his daily routine, he went outside to retrieve the paper. The lightning thundered overhead as a warm front passed through the area, chased by a much colder one swooping down from the north. Returning inside, he poured a large cup of coffee, opened his laptop computer, and brought up weather.com. He looked at the hourly predictions and then the weather map in motion which showed that the storm front would last until 11 am, then be followed by another about the time he got off work. He resolved to take his truck to work, a decision he frequently regretted as the weather predictions tended to change rapidly in Alabama.

He normally rode daily, rain or shine, realizing a long time ago that the ride affected his mood at work, where his demeanor could impact the morale of the sales staff. He did his best to hide this from the staff, but coworkers that had known him for a long time, knew and understood his feelings. His biker buddies on staff tended to do things and tell jokes to lighten the mood, causing him distress at his weakness. He would sometimes go overboard to prove he could handle the extra stress by taking on additional tasks. On the positive side, he did get ahead on his planning, and used his time to help the new or struggling sales associates hone their skills thru practice and self-discovery. Still, the day would pass slowly, especially when the sun came out between the weather fronts.

Miles away in the small cabin at Resort 25, Blondie was chafing at the delay the weather caused, and she too, was using the time to plan. She had discovered the Vulcan Owners Riders Club's web site, and was browsing local member's pictures, looking for bikes like the one that had almost run her down. She rubbed her shin where the bruise was a reminder of their discovery, even after all her careful planning. She found several VROC members in the area with bikes that loosely fit the description, and sent them messages to learn more. Earlier, she had dispatched 45 to retrieve the game camera, left at the church's picnic area. 45 wasn't happy about riding in the cold rain, but went without argument, knowing she was the reason for his increase in jobs, money, and the resulting freedom to ride.

She had kept him from getting caught more than once with her careful planning. She was indeed the brains of the pair, keeping him in check from his love of the kill. If left to him, he'd kill with that damn 45 caliber Colt model 1911, typically shooting them in the face. Inevitability, this would result in their loss of freedom and a life behind bars, followed years later by meeting a quack with a needle, the victim's relatives watching through the window.

She too, clicked to the weather channel and planned her day to revolve around the forecast. She planned to visit local dealers and bike shops in the area, inquiring about fairings and that flashing rear light.

There were no new developments in the news regarding the missing mayor, but she knew that sooner or later, the body would be discovered. She had hoped to be long gone by then, but the lone biker had thrown a monkey wrench in that plan with his unexpected arrival on the scene. She too believed in Karma, but knew from experience that it could be trumped by carefully planning the details, something she excelled at.

They had gone to "plan B" after the kill, driving the Mercedes to a secluded rock quarry filled with water several miles away, past Pea Ridge and out in the sticks. The area nearby had some future development activity planned, but the quarry was very deep, and she was sure it would be a long time before the SUV was discovered with the mayor's body inside. When discovered, the only sign of violence was a broken neck, easily occurring in that kind of crash. She had planted half a bottle of his favorite booze in the vehicle and, after pulling the old geezer's pants down to his knees, figured the investigators would come to the logical conclusion that he had been tending to his own needs, fueled by the encounter with the blond outside City Hall. The Mercedes with the body had sunk quickly after going over the steep quarry wall.

A new message appeared on the screen from a VROC member in reply to her inquiry about the bike he owned. The member did have the rear lights that she had asked about, and said he knew several others that did, too. Thinking it through, she believed he would be a good source of information. She sent a reply asking to meet, and attached a picture of a thirtyish blond biker babe from the web to get his interest. He replied immediately, agreeing to meet that evening at a local night club. Her plan was working, as usual.

She turned her attention to searching for a secluded place to stay in the area. As she read the postings in the local classifieds and on Craig's list, she realized that many of the locals were ignorant rednecks. A joke she'd seen while browsing the VROC website came to mind, causing her to laugh aloud. Two things make it hard to solve a redneck murder; first, the DNA all matches, and second, there are no dental records. She agreed with that assessment of the locals.

She struck pay dirt when she came across an ad to rent out a "mostly nu" mobile home in a "rurul settin not fer frum Shelby" with a "large garage wurkshop cross the yard". Two somewhat blurry pictures showed enough to peak her interest. She called the number and made arrangements to meet the literary genius that had such an entertaining way with words.

Blondie dressed quickly in jeans, boots, and an undercoat topped with her leather jacket and chaps. Her hair was pulled back in the fashion that biker guys do, and a thick, biker mustache had been added to complete the transition. She often disguised herself as a man, and used the name Butch, finding this to be an advantage when dealing with redneck men.

She headed out after the rain stopped before noon. After riding for an hour and passing through Columbiana, the Shelby county seat, she passed a political sign showing Senator Shelby was up for re-election. She took this as a good sign—leasing a safe house in Shelby, in Shelby county, with a sign saying "Vote for Shelby" nearby—hilarious. She thought about assuming the name of Butch Shelby for the lease if needed, thinking it must be a very common name in the area, and all the Shelbys were related in some way.

The meeting with the owner went without a hitch, and few questions after she paid six months' rent in advance in cash. Her only request was that the old man keep the transaction to himself, saying she wanted to avoid any attention from the ex-wife, and would pay a bonus later. The old man readily agreed, counting the hundred dollar bills with an agreeable smile. He figured this was just more biker trash that wanted to hang out; getting drunk and stoned until the money ran out. He couldn't care less—cash was cash, and the place was over insured.

The property was well maintained and hidden from view from the road by thick brush and trees. The entrance had a gate and the workshop had room for both bikes with plenty of space to spare. The internet was easily accessed via cell phone service. She called her partner, gave him the coordinates along with a short list of items needed to make the place secure. She knew he'd be at home here, as he was accustomed to living in seclusion on a farm in the sticks. She returned to Resort 25, leaving 45 to make the needed changes.

CHAPTER 10

Stag was looking forward to meeting Cheetah, hoping her name was indicative of her sexual preferences in men. He had heard of, but never been to the bar she named, but was always willing to try out new places, and fantasized about the upcoming meeting with the blond biker babe. He had been a VROC member for almost five years, joining within a month of purchasing his black 2005 Vulcan Nomad. He frequently purchased accessories to give his bike more bling, and was extremely pleased with the addition of a fairing, purchased from an ebay seller in Maryville, TN. He rode mainly on weekends, frequently meeting others for group rides around the area. His wife seldom accompanied him unless the weather was perfect—70 degrees, sunny, and no chance of rain. She talked constantly when they were riding and didn't seem to fit in with the others in the group. He secretly envied the guys with the younger, well-endowed biker babe companions that dressed in sexy, skimpy leather outfits. *That* was his vision of the ideal biker companion.

Stag had agreed to meet Cheetah at the Chrome Rider Saloon at seven. He arrived ten minutes early, planning to wait outside to check her and her bike out as she rode up. He was surprised to see only two bikes in the bike parking area in front, both decked out with lights. A toy hauler was parked nearby. *Not much of a biker bar.*

Stag's real name was Eric Wilson. He was a branch manager at a local bank where he had worked for over 15 years. His kids had gone off to start their own lives a few years ago, leaving him and his wife of 25 years alone. She was very active with her friends and relatives, but he yearned for the excitement and freedom that bikers enjoy. He made the plunge one day after meeting a seasoned biker that came in to do some banking. The biker had given him a copy of the motorcycle magazine he wrote for when he left. After reading it cover to cover, he was hooked. He took the MSF beginner course, bought the Nomad, and rode as often as possible. He had even added a fairing and some lights that he had seen on the writer's bike. Being just over six feet and somewhat heavy set, the bike fit him well and was an easy and low maintenance motorcycle to ride.

He sat in front of the bar, noting the much younger crowd of biker wannabes arriving in fancy cars, dressed in biker leathers. Most of the women showed an abundance of cleavage, and many were blessed with shapely young rear ends framed by tight leather chaps. As he admired the view, he heard the rumble of a motorcycle downshifting as it turned into the parking lot. Dressed in leather for the cool 50 degree night, it was hard to tell if the rider was a guy or gal. The biker gunned it around the corner, braking hard and pulling between the neon bikes.

The lights reflected off the gleaming black paint of the Vaquero. The rider had a long blond ponytail hanging out the back of a black skid lid. He knew it must be Cheetah from the curves he could see in the tight leather pants and her well-tanned, attractive face. He had planned well, telling his wife he was staying at a buddies' house due to an early morning departure for a group ride. He had done this before, and as a result, it was not thought of as unusual by her.

He admired her curves even more as he watched her dismount, remove her helmet and gloves, and then partially unzip her jacket to reveal ample cleavage. Dressed from head to toe in snug, black, weathered leather, he knew instantly that she was the biker babe of his dreams—an experienced rider, and real easy to look at. He could easily imagine grabbing a handful.

"Wassup—you must be Stag," she said boldly as she strode over and extended a hand. When they greeted each other, he could feel the strength and abundance of upper torso development when their chests touched.

"That's what my friends call me. You must be Cheetah."

"Yep, that's me. This doesn't look like the type of biker bar I'm used to. Are there any real bikers inside?"

"Looked like many are dressed the part, but my guess is they're mainly weekend warriors and wannabes in there. Sure is a nice night to ride, shame to leave a bike at home." It was obvious he was trying to impress what he hoped would be a "riding" partner in the near future.

"Let's go check it out and get a beer . . . I'm buying," she said with a smile.

Pulling the door open, they were greeted by a huge bouncer and asked if they were riding. When they acknowledged that they were, he passed them on inside, advising them that bikers didn't have to pay a cover charge.

The crowd seemed to part for them to pass as they made their way to the bar. The band had just started, and was doing a decent job playing their rendition of a ZZ Top tune. Arriving at the horseshoe shaped bar, Blondie leaned over and got the bartender's attention immediately, who openly admired her cleavage.

"What are you having?" she said, looking at Stag.

"Corona."

"Two Coronas with limes," she yelled at the bartender and flipped out a twenty.

They grabbed their beers and headed toward a small area behind the pool tables. The noise level was lower, making it possible to talk without yelling.

"Here's to the great ride ahead of us," she said, holding her beer towards him.

"You got that right," he said, lifting his eyes to meet hers from where they had been gazing at her boobs. They clinked their bottles together.

"You like what you see?" she asked, leaning forward and touching his knee.

It was obvious she had taken him off guard by the way he responded with obvious excitement, much like a teenaged boy excited about the prospect of his first sexual experience.

"Damn right, there's a lot there to like!"

"Just wanted to make sure—let's slow down and get to know each other better. Where are you from, Stag?"

"Right down the road a ways. Been living here all my life."

"Sounds pretty boring. What do you do for fun around here?"

"Mainly ride my bike and go to rallies and on rides with the club."

"You got a main bitch or wife?" she said as she stroked his hand across the table.

He lowered his head and said in a less bold tone of voice, "Yeah, I got a wife and she's a real bitch—we don't get along too well. Going to kick her ass out soon as I get a chance."

"She ride?"

"Not often, thank God."

"I understand. Most men need a little more excitement than their women provide." She was very direct and understanding.

"You got that right," he said, noticeably encouraged while looking into her eyes.

"I like excitement. You been riding long?" she asked taking his hand and stroking his palm with her nails.

"Most of my life, but I took a few years off while the kids were young."

She could tell this was not the whole truth by the way he looked away. She let it pass.

"Well, I really like your bike . . . Vulcan Nomad, right?"

"Yep, sounds like you know your bikes. That's a fine ride you got. How do you like the way it rides?"

"It does pretty good for a metric. I need to do a few more things to make it right."

"What are you looking to do to it?" he asked.

"Pegs, rack, and I really hate that fairing. I want to change it out for a batwing like yours. Where did you get that cool blinking tail light?"

"It's really just a replacement bulb, found it on Ebay. I'd be glad to swap fairings, or I can tell you about a place in Maryville to get one."

"You ever had any problems with the bulb or the fairing?"

"Nope, best deal on a fairing around."

"How'd you find out about them? Anybody else tried them out?"

"I know a guy named Wolf that writes for that biker magazine. He told me about them, has them on his bike. Several guys I ride with have them now."

"You know, I met him at a bar in Pelham a few days ago. Nice bike, nice guy," she said.

"Yeah, he's real cool, I read his story every month. Several of the guys in VROC have made similar changes to their bikes."

"Any got stock pipes, a fairing, and a blinking brake light? I saw one the other night like that near Helena."

"Maybe—that sounds like Bones or it could have been Toad; they both live out that way. We ride together from time to time."

"When's your next ride? I'd love to ride with the VROC gang if they're all as cool as you," she said giving his hand a gentle squeeze.

"I'm sure they wouldn't mind. We're supposed to meet on Sunday at Resort 25 for biker church and then a ride to Mt. Cheaha."

"That's really wild, Stag, it must be a sign. I'm staying out there while I'm in town."

Cheetah leaned back and looked thoughtful while seeming to check him out from head to toe.

She leaned forward and squeezed his knee.

"You know, this place is pretty lame for a biker bar. Nothing but preps and wannabes. What do you say we ride out to the resort and have a few. Might be other benefits if you catch my drift."

"You got it babe. Sounds good to me," he said with enthusiasm.

Cheetah stood up and led the way through the growing crowd. Stag was elated as he observed the envious stares of the guys they passed. In fact, he felt much like he did back in his college days when he had picked up that hot chick at a party in front of his fraternity brothers.

"You lead and I'll be right behind you. Don't take it easy, I promise you I can keep up. If you go too slow when we get to the twisties, I'll take the lead. You can meet me there."

"If I do go too slow, it'll be 'cause I want to check you out from behind."

"I'll bet you do," she said, giving him a full kiss on the lips while grabbing his butt. He stammered a bit when he replied. "I actually meant the bike, the other view is one I've already been admiring."

They put on helmets and gloves, then started their bikes. She pulled out her phone, punched a button, then stood her bike up, revving the big 1700 cc V-twin motor. Stag started off, followed closely by the Vaquero. He increased speed quickly, shifting smoothly through the gears. Cheetah stayed with him, her bike's front fender twelve feet behind and just off his left hardbag. He took the entrance loop to the interstate with her maintaining that position throughout the entire curve. It was as though there was an invisible line between the bikes, keeping them perfectly spaced.

Fourteen miles away, a lone biker was parked in the shadows next to an abandoned grocery store on a stretch of Hwy 25 known as Copperhead Road. He sat there watching the blip on his smart phone steadily closing on his position.

Stag took the Grants Mill Road exit, avoiding the lights on Highway 280. As he wound his way through the curves, Cheetah stayed right with him, and at times, it seemed she was attached to his rear fender. He had traveled this road several times in the past, but quickened his pace this night trying not to be outdone by this obviously skilled rider. He became tense at the thought of an unseen road hazard, and hesitantly told her so at the four way stop. She laughed then said she'd take the lead, and would take it easy the rest of the way. After another set of curves and a left turn onto 119, she took a fork to the right, bypassing the lights in town and cutting off the first stretch of Hwy 25. Coming to the stop sign on 25, Cheetah stopped and waited for him to pull up alongside.

"I'll race you to Resort 25 . . . whoever loses buys the first round," she yelled.

"Sounds fun, but I've never done this road at night. I'll just try to keep up."

"Alright then, but I'm going to see what this thing will do. Meet me at cabin one . . . I'll be waiting, so don't take too long. Riding makes me frisky."

Without waiting for a reply, she took off, spinning the rear tire before it caught and took off. He took off quickly behind her, not noticing the lone bike and rider in the shadows of the old store they passed. As he watched her taillight get smaller on the road ahead, he didn't notice the headlights in his mirrors. His focus was completely on the road ahead, determined to try to keep up in order to take advantage of the implied prize at the road's end.

Riding Hwy 25 was exciting to Stag in the daytime, but tonight, he was so excited about the reward, that he went into the curve after the railroad track too fast, almost losing control. He came to his senses, and slowed down before going into the next few curves. He regained his composure, and was excited to see the Vaquero's taillights not far ahead, going through the last hairpin curve before their destination. Coming out of the same curve, he twisted the throttle and quickly shifted to third gear as he approached the final set of s curves.

Unnoticed by Stag, the bike that had been following him through the curves was barely 10 yards behind with the headlights off as he came out of the hairpin. 45 twisted the throttle on his Street Glide and quickly caught up, staying a few yards directly behind. As they went into the final curve, he came alongside the Vulcan. A steel toed boot reached out and gave Stag's handlebar end a shove, causing his bike to veer to the right, the rear tire losing its grip on the asphalt and sending the bike and Stag careening off the road and into the woods on the slope below.

The Harley's lights came on immediately as 45 downshifted and braked hard. He turned onto an overgrown gravel driveway just past the spot where the Stag had left the road. Killing his lights, he jumped off and ran through the woods to where the Vulcan Nomad had come to rest nearly thirty yards off the road. It had clipped a small tree, resulting in the bike spinning around, the lights shining back up in the direction where it had left the road. 45 reached down, turned off the key, and stood there listening. The creak of cooling metal sporadically broke the total silence, accompanied by a low moan and the rustle of leaves off to his left.

In a low voice he said, "you OK down there?"

There was no response except a faint moan. The sound of a vehicle coming down the road from above grew louder as it neared where the bike left the asphalt. 45 froze and watched for signs of brake lights or slowing as the car neared his position in the dark woods below. Instead, the car sped up as it came out of the curve and passed where his bike was parked, hidden by darkness. He flicked on a small, powerful flashlight and headed in the direction of the sound of rustling in the undergrowth. The bluish glow of the light made it easy for him to see the trail of broken branches that started just past where the bike had come to a sudden halt, stopped by the trunk of a medium sized pine tree. The Vulcan had hit the tree on its right side, partially wrapping around the base.

As he parted a low brush, the small beam of light reflected off what he thought was the rider's helmet, helping him easily pick out the dark lump moving around. As he looked down upon the injured rider, he was amused by the unnatural bend of a leg and an arm, reminding him of the Gumby figurine he had played with and tortured as a child. He shone the light full into the biker's face and noted the blood infused white froth bubbling between his victim's lips.

"Help me," he gasped in a whisper.

"No problem," he replied with a sinister snicker, his thin lips curled upward to form a facial expression that could make many lose bladder control.

He knelt down beside the shattered rider, grasped his helmet in both hands, then slowly pulled and twisted until he heard an audible snap. The helmet encased head lolled in his huge hands like a tootsie roll pop with a broken stick. He shone the beam full into the man's eyes and watched with pleasure as the eyes fully dilated and the loosely attached body convulsed and went limp. He waited for a minute, then checked for a pulse. Finding none, he stood up.

"Serves you right, trying to get more woman than you could ever handle."

He moved quickly and silently as he made his way back through the woods to where his Harley was hidden just off the road. Before starting the powerful motor, he turned it around and pointed it back at the road while listening for passing vehicles. Two high performance cars went by with their engines screaming, apparently racing. As the sound of the cages faded down the straight stretch of road leading to his destination, he started his bike and turned back in the direction from where he came. He did a tight U-turn in the hairpin curve and accelerated through the s-curves. As he approached the final curve, he locked his rear brake, quickly releasing and straightening his bike back up. Coming out of the curve, he again locked both brakes and came to a halt just as he came to the edge of the road where the Vulcan had gone airborne into the woods below. He shone his light at the skid marks, and satisfied with the results, started off down the straightaway. He enjoyed the feel of acceleration and passed the entrance to Resort 25 at over 85 mph. He slowed as he approached the next curve and then, a short distance past, did another quick U-turn and headed back, this time roaring into the entrance and skidding to a halt just outside the side door.

Dismounting, he noted several dozen cars and trucks parked outside and a couple looking in his direction from near the fire pit. The couple had been romantically engaged, but were startled by his sudden arrival. He was not surprised there were no bikes present. He was aware that the locals were mostly fair weather riders, the chilly night air providing the only excuse most needed to drive their cars. The two piece band was playing rock and roll as he entered the door. A crowd of thirty or forty were eating, drinking, and singing along to the music. Several looked his way as he took a seat at a stool at the end of the bar.

"What can I get you," asked a perky, brunette bartender.

"Double Jack on the rocks."

As he waited for his drink, he cased the room, observing that this young crowd consisted primarily of redneck guys and plump redneck women with a few lookers mixed in. Several middle-aged cougars tried to make eye contact with him as he scanned the room, smiling as he glanced in their direction. His drink arrived, and he drained it in one swallow. He set it down and ordered a Corona.

As he sat nursing his beer, a curvaceous leather clad woman entered the room from the back. All eyes in the room turned and looked as she walked past, her bubblegum colored hair bouncing in pace with her ample breasts, highlighted by the plunging neckline of her revealing black leather vest. As she stood at the other end of the bar waiting for the bartender to approach, an obviously intoxicated, well-muscled redneck grabbed her arm and pulled her over next to him.

"What're ya having, babe," he said with an alcohol enhanced leer on his face and slurred speech.

"Nothing from the likes of your scrawny ass," she replied twisting her arm away in an upward motion that caused him to hit himself in the face with his own arm. The lightning quick move caught him totally by surprise, and his slow reaction and flash of pain gave his buddies time to intervene before he did anything stupid.

Blondie spotted 45 at the end of the bar, turned, and said loudly, "What I need is a real man." With that, she turned and strutted to the other end of the bar, sitting on the stool next to 45. She ran her hand inside his black leather jacket and snuggled up to him.

"Let's blow this joint, stud, I've got something for you in my cabin. By the way, what's your name?"

"45 is what my friends call me, and I'm guessing we're going to be real good friends soon."

"You got that right."

45 threw a twenty on the bar, got up, took her arm, and headed out the door.

The band had stopped playing when the incident started, and all eyes in the room were on the couple as they left. Outside, they got on his bike. The Street Glide started with a roar. Rubber squealed as 45 engaged the clutch and crossed the parking lot, headed for the cabins beyond. There was silence in the bar, and more than a minute passed before anyone resumed talking.

Pulling up beside Blondie's Vaquero, they dismounted and went inside. Blondie hit a button on her laptop on the bunk bed by the door, starting a porn DVD with the noise of loud and raunchy sex. She removed her wig and sat on the bedside table facing her partner on the bed.

"Everything go as planned?" she asked.

"Smooth as silk, no witnesses. The guy never knew what was happening. You sure he's the one?"

"No way, he was one of the biggest dorks I've ever met. I did get some useful information from him."

"I thought it was way too easy. That guy couldn't ride worth a shit. He almost lost it without my help in one curve. It felt good watching him wreck and then putting him out of his misery."

"I thought you'd like it. We can't leave any loose ends. I've been thinking about our next move. They'll probably have a funeral that should bring out most of the local VROC members to ride escort. It'll give us a chance to scope out the bikes and find our mysterious witness. I still think it is damned strange he hasn't said anything about what he saw."

"He probably has his own reasons for not wanting to get involved with the law. Maybe he's afraid he'll get blamed for it," he said.

"That's a reasonable theory. Might just come in handy to pin it on somebody else. Sooner or later, the body will be discovered in that quarry."

"He's bound to live in the area. We'll find him soon enough. If he hasn't come forward or called in a tip by now, he probably won't come forward at all."

Cheetah looked him dead in the eye and said, "we aren't leaving until we're sure we got the right guy. I'm not going to spend a day in a jail cell. I'd sooner be dead."

"You got that right—ain't nobody going to take me in, and I'm taking a bunch of them to hell with me."

With that, she handed him the bottle of Jack and watched as he took a long swig. He handed the bottle back, took out a joint and lit it. After taking a long pull on the medicinal grade marijuana, he passed her the burning joint. She took a quick hit and passed it back.

"That's enough of that shit, I've got to be clear headed in the morning."

"Blondie, you're turning into a real puss," he said.

"Wait until dawn to leave. Until then, I'll show you what a real puss is."

"Now you're talking," he said, taking off his shirt.

CHAPTER 11

D awn came too soon and as a result, 45 left with little sleep, feeling drained and buzzed from the night's activities. The temp was in the high 30's, and a cloud of exhaust surrounded his bike as he sat letting it warm up. He watched the rosy glow brighten the edge of the sky as the sun slowly came up, accompanied by the chirp of birds and the rustle of squirrels in the trees overhead. He took it easy as he rode out, comforted by the total lack of activity in the resort. He passed a car straddling the edge of the rock-lined ditch as he left the cabin area, evidence of the alcohol consumption in the bar last night. Traffic was light on this ride, his Harley passing less than a dozen vehicles on his way to the rented trailer. Arriving less than an hour later, he left his bike in the shed and went inside. He drained the last of a bottle of Jack and killed the rest of the joint. Stumbling off to bed, he fell asleep quickly.

Back at the cabin, Blondie was startled awake by the sound of sirens. Instantly alert, she listened as they went by, stopping a few minutes later. She dressed quickly and left the cabin, starting her bike and riding up to the bar, stopping outside the side door. Several people were outside, talking while looking at the road as a sheriff's car with lights flashing sped by the entrance. Cheetah got off her bike and approached the group.

"What's going on?"

A cute, slim, brunette girl spoke first. "One of our cooks spotted a bike that went off the road about a mile from here just before the first curve. He says the rider is dead. We're all hopeful it wasn't a customer on their way home."

Blondie recognized the speaker as one of the bartenders from the previous night who seemed to be in charge. She was ready for the next question.

"You look like you had a good time last night. Your man still in the cabin?"

"No, I kicked his butt out at dawn. Don't worry sugar, it's not him. He called me when he got home a few minutes ago."

An old Nissan pickup truck turned in, pulling up next to the building. A thin, Hispanic young guy got out and approached the group.

"Sorry I'm late boss . . . they got the road blocked and just let me leave," he said in near perfect English.

"Did it look like a customer from last night?" the bartender asked.

"No, the skid marks were from the other direction. The police said it looked like he was going way too fast for the curve and skidded off the road and into the woods. His bike was wrapped around a tree and he broke his neck. His head was almost turned backwards—nearly freaked me out," he said in a shaky voice, pausing for breath after every sentence.

"Somebody you've seen before?"

"I think I've seen the bike before, but they were both messed up real bad. Can't be sure . . . oh yeah, it was a Kawasaki Vulcan . . . dark blue and gray I think. Had a fairing."

He paused and took several deep breaths before continuing.

"Oh yeah, boss, the cop said he'd be down to ask some questions in a while," he said then suddenly grabbed the truck and gagged.

"Jose, let's get you inside and give you a drink or something—looks like you need something to calm your nerves," the cute bartender said, a look of concern evident on her face.

"I'll be OK, Miss Millie—it'll get busy soon, and I've got to get everything ready."

"We got you covered, Jose. You take it easy for a while. We'll let you know when we need you. Sure am glad he wasn't leaving the bar. You sure he was headed toward the bar and not away?"

"Sure as can be," he said, then turned as another employee supported him, holding his arm and leading him inside.

Millie turned to Blondie and said, "I sure hope that doesn't mess up your weekend . . . bad to hear about a biker accident right down the road."

"Shit happens. Bikers get killed all the time, usually by being stupid or drunk," Blondie said without emotion. It was obvious to the listeners by the cold, dead look in her green eyes, that she was not upset at all.

"Still, always bad to happen to a biker, and even worse when it's someone you know. There are enough hazards out there with the cages, deer, and those damn cell phones," Millie replied, tears welling up in her eyes.

"Don't get all mushy about it honey, he was probably cheating on his ole lady or something like that—bad karma don't ya know."

"I just pray he didn't suffer. His family will sure be tore up."

"Honey, after it's all said and done, they'll probably be better off with the insurance money they'll get."

Hearing that, Millie turned and stormed inside, her distress from the conversation obvious to all.

"Sure is sensitive to be running a biker bar. Probably just needs to get laid."

With that, Blondie laughed loudly, then turned and straddled her bike. She started the Vaquero up, putting on gloves, glasses, and a skid lid while the motor warmed. She stuck a cigarette between her luscious lips, lit it, and started off with a chirp of rubber as she let out the clutch and headed for the road entrance. Turning left, she slowed as she approached the accident scene and was stopped while traffic was directed around the numerous emergency vehicles. She watched in satisfaction as several emergency workers struggled to bring the body, encased in a body bag strapped to a bright yellow scoop stretcher up the slope. She snickered as one lost his footing, resulting in the entire group, body included, sliding halfway down the slope in the loose fallen leaves, reminding her of the Keystone cops.

The cop directing traffic winced, but continued to move traffic along. When her turn to move came along, she twisted her throttle and swerved to pass the two cars ahead of her. She let the engine wind out, shifting just before it red-lined. She enjoyed the responsiveness of the Vaquero, grinning with pleasure as she aggressively dragged pegs in the hairpin curves on Highway 25. Turning southwest, she headed towards a local greasy spoon in Whiteville for breakfast and to hear firsthand, the gossip from the locals in the small southern town. Stopping outside, she bought a paper, and then went inside to catch up on the local news and developments surrounding the mayor's disappearance.

As she had expected, the waitresses and diners were talking and joking about the mayor, offering up all types of speculation as to his whereabouts. A middle-aged, chunky waitress finished her conversation and walked over to where she sat at the counter.

"Git ya some coffee, ma'am?"

"Yeah, make it black. What's everybody talking about?"

"It's that mayor, ain't ya heard 'bout that sleazebag? Ya must not be frum roun here. Most folks hereabouts think he's shacked up with some blond he was seen with, and now he's too scared of his wife to come home. Always was a chicken, anyway. Right there on the front page of yer paper."

"Seems like I heard a little about it on the news last night. I'm just here for a few days. Don't the police think foul play is involved?"

The waitress guffawed loudly, "now that's a real funny play on words, him bein' chicken an such. You see that skinny young blond over there? That old mayor was hittin on her the last time he wuz in here, even asked her out to that fancy Mercedes of his. Why, he's got younguns older than she is—now that's really fowl if you ask me."

"Well, that's the way those old guys with money are, thinking that money and fancy cars will get the young babes in the sack."

"If my ole man tried somethin like that, I'd cut off his bidness in his sleep an he knows it. That thought keeps him from screwing around. That mayor's wife is mean enough to do that, too."

Blondie chuckled at the thought, remembering her experiences from a few years back.

"What can I get ya shug? The boss is givin' me the evil eye, says I gossip too much."

"Give me the big breakfast with eggs over easy, grits, toast, and sausage."

"Coming right up, more coffee?"

"Yeah, keep it coming."

Blondie browsed the paper while waiting for her food to arrive. As the food was placed in front of her, three plainclothes cops came in and sat down in the booth behind her. She pretended not to notice, but was attentive to the conversation. She watched as her waitress walked over and greeted them.

"How's the hunt for his highness going guys? Y'all figured out where he's shacked up yet?" It was obvious that she knew the cops well.

"Mabel, you know we can't discuss police business with you. Besides, we might as well be talking to those reporters," he said with a laugh.

"Now that's a plain mean thing to say, Joe! Didn't your mama teach ya to be nice to your elders?"

"Yes, and she also taught me that a good job is hard to find. How about taking our order, we gotta be getting back to that zoo all too soon."

"Sorry boys—didn't mean to piss ya off, just askin'. What can I get y'all?" she said smiling with obvious sarcasm.

She took their orders and returned with coffee. They waited until she went back behind the counter to talk.

The cop named Joe spoke first. "You know it's the locals like Mabel that get all those rumors started. Sure does make our job tough, interviewing people with tips that started as speculations dreamed up and repeated by the locals."

The tall cop named Lute said, "keep your voices low guys—lots of ears in this place. I'm sure one of those rumors or tips we get will lead to what really happened. We all know something bad happened to him, even if he was seen with that blond. Besides, why were the feds here before he was even reported missing? Something's going on we don't know about."

Joe nodded his head in agreement and said, "let's talk about this shit someplace else, we don't need any loose talk getting back to those reporters or our boss, not to mention the freaking feds. Besides, we came here to take a break from work for a while. Hey Bill, I heard that boy of yours might be getting an offer from Auburn. That right?"

Their conversation turned to sports, hunting, and other stupid bullshit that Blondie had no interest in.

Typical small town rednecks, she thought. Probably not a good idea to be hanging around here, anyway.

She signaled for the check, handed Mabel a ten, then walked outside to her bike. She could feel the eyes on her as she started it up and rode off, headed to the trailer in Shelby.

CHAPTER 12

The sound of a Harley exhaust came from the cell phone next to the bed. Wolf stirred, hit the snooze button, then rolled over, still dreaming. In his dream, he was being chased by the two killers riding black Vaqueros. He rounded a curve and could see blue lights flashing ahead with police cars and bikes forming a roadblock across the road. In his dream, he came to a stop in the road. All weapons were pointed at him with Lute standing in front, bullhorn in one hand, handgun in the other. At that moment in the dream, his cellphone rang with a screech designed to be heard over a rumbling V-twin motor. Wolf was instantly awake and relieved when he realized it had been just a dream.

He got out of bed and went through his morning routine. After starting coffee, he looked out the window for anything unusual. He had recently changed his routine in small ways, and now took the rear steps from the rear deck instead of going out the front door. Vigilant to new sounds, people, or cars in the cull-de-sac where he lived, he went down the driveway to retrieve the morning newspaper. Even though he'd seen nothing unusual, he was still startled when a car pulled up next door to pick up his neighbor's kid, probably to go play a round of golf with the local high school team. Like most bikers he knew, he had little use for the sport, and openly made fun of the clothes they wore and the money and real estate that was wasted just to hit a little ball around. To him, watching a golf tournament on TV was more boring than listening to congressional debates.

Back in the kitchen, he poured a cup of coffee then scanned the paper, stopping to read stories of interest. Finding little of interest and no new developments on the missing mayor, he flipped open his laptop to check his emails. He froze when he read the most recent message's subject line.

Member Eric 'Stag' Wilson Killed in Bike Accident on Hwy 25

He looked at the time and realized the message had been sent to all on the email list of Resort 25, a favorite biker resort of his, just minutes ago. He immediately recalled his visit to the bank where he gave the guy a copy of the magazine. He could picture his bike and its' similarities to his own. He remembered that Stag admired his own bike, Beast, asking for info on the fairing and rear taillight. They were both members of VROC, and Wolf had seen Stag's Vulcan Nomad with its new fairing in a picture posted on the site. A sense of unease washed over him as he turned on the TV. As expected, there was no news about the accident. He decided to ride out and talk with Millie at the bar to get more details.

After a quick shower, he called his work buddy, GQ at home and asked him to swap shifts, saying a personal issue had come up. GQ readily agreed to the swap and asked no questions, preferring to get off early instead of closing. Wolf got on his bike and drove as fast he could, while still being able to avoid a traffic stop for reckless driving.

Arriving a half hour later, he found dozens of bikes and their riders outside. He recognized several from VROC, and pulled up near where they stood talking next to a dark blue and gray Nomad that looked remarkably similar to his own. He had met its owner before, but couldn't remember his name. The owner walked over and greeted Wolf in the traditional biker way and spoke first.

"Good to see you Wolf, you hear the bad news?" Wolf looked at his name patch.

"Yeah I did Lucky, I got the email this morning. It's always bad to hear about a biker going down and worse when they don't make it, especially someone you know. Heard what happened?"

"Millie said it looked like he was on his way here last night, but lost it going around the last curve. Real strange for old Stag to be riding 25 at night, and especially going too fast for that curve. We've ridden with him and he's a careful rider. Something must have spooked him—maybe a deer. Strange."

Wolf thought of another possibility, but didn't voice it.

"I gotta go talk with Millie. How's she taking it?"

"She's real upset, Stag used to flirt with her all the time. I can't imagine how much worse she'd be if he had been *leaving* here when it happened."

Wolf looked surprised and said, "you sure he was on his way here?"

"No doubt, I talked with the investigating officer myself. You know old Grey—rides a black Goldwing, been out here several times. He said when he saw the bike, he thought at first it was your ugly mug he was going to be looking at. Something about the way you ride sometimes. Anyway, he said there were skid marks coming from the other direction right where he went off the road. Damn shame."

"His wife know yet?"

"Grey said an officer was headed over to notify her. You know, she never did seem to like him riding that much. I thought we'd wait until later to check on her, maybe get one of the women to stop by. I don't think it would be such a good idea for us to show up on our bikes right now."

"You're probably right about that. Call me and let me know about the arrangements. I'll be there for escort at the service. I gotta go check on Millie and go in to work afterward. You guys be real careful out there, especially you, Lucky."

Millie was indeed upset, a fact recognized by all the regulars who knew her for her playful antics while tending bar and directing the others that worked there. She was very somber today, and seemed to just be going through the motions. Wolf got her attention and motioned her outside. He greeted her with the usual hug, but Millie was slow to let go. He saw a tear run down her cheek as she finally released her hold and seemed to sag in his arms. He sat her in a nearby chair, then knelt down in front of her while taking her hands and looking directly into her eyes.

"Listen to me girl, ain't nothing you could have done about it, he was on his way here when it happened; you know that. Ole Stag would not want you to remember anything but the great times we all had out here. Besides, they'll be a lot of sadness here today from those that knew him. You need to be strong and try to act your normal self when we leave this table."

She seemed to be thinking about it, and squeezed his hand.

"You're right, thanks for the reality check. I'll be OK," she said pasting a fake smile on her face while wiping her tears away.

"I gotta ask you a question that I need you to think about, but I need you to forget I asked it, no matter what, afterward. Can you do it?"

"That sounds pretty deep, Wolf. What are you talking about? You know you can trust me about anything. Ask your question . . . it better not be some bullshit."

"I'm very serious, don't ever repeat anything about what I ask, and you gotta forget about it later."

"Alright, ask your damn question already."

"Promise?" he said, looking directly into her watery eyes to let her know he was serious.

"You got it. What the hell is the big question?"

"Anything strange happen last night? Maybe a new customer asking about bikes like mine, or just hanging out?"

The color slowly drained out of Millie's face as she listened. As he watched, her face suddenly flushed red and she started to shake. She grabbed his arm and squeezed hard.

"This got anything to do with the accident?" she asked suddenly.

"No, just asking . . . don't jump to any conclusions," he said in a way he hoped was convincing. "*And*—don't forget your promise."

"I'm not, but if she had something to do with Stag's accident—"

Wolf cut her off before she finished, "who is she?"

"*She* is the big biker bitch that was in here last night at the bar. She's in cabin number one—been there all week. Same one I warned you about last time you were here. She asked about you and your bike. Last night she came in with a pink wig on, and all the regulars were practically drooling when she came strutting in the bar. Stoney grabbed her arm and she practically knocked his head off. Afterward, she picked up this big biker stud at the bar and took him back to her cabin. What a slut!"

"You catch her name?"

"The name she goes by is Cheetah. She ain't real friendly except to the big biker she picked up."

"She seem to know him?"

"Yes, but she put on quite a show while she was in here. He stayed here earlier this week. You know her?" she asked in a concerned tone of voice.

"Not really, but if she's who I think she is, I've run into both of them before at the Hawg, and her, here too."

"You be careful with either of them. They both look like they would enjoy putting a hurt on anybody that pissed them off without thinking twice about it. She's got real cold eyes and some very quick moves. You should have seen what she did to Stoney's face . . . made him hit himself so fast I didn't even see it."

Wolf took this in then said thoughtfully, "any cameras in the bar?"

"Yes, but some asshole turned them around in the last few days and all they show is the ceiling. I went to watch how she made the move on Stoney, and that's when I discovered they were messed up."

"Too bad, I'd like to get a picture of them both. Any ideas?"

"I do have an idea—my boyfriend's got one of those game cameras he uses during deer season. We could set it in a tree outside her cabin."

"That's a great idea, just don't take any chances with anybody seeing you do it, could be dangerous based on what you said. Did she fill out any paperwork when she got the room?"

"This ain't no motel operation here; she paid cash."

"Let me know if you get anything. Don't forget what I said about repeating any of this, or even looking funny at them if they come in. Not a word to anybody, even those you trust, like your boyfriend. Tell him you're looking for varmits. I mean it."

"Thanks for your concern, dad, but me and Mr. Glock can take care of ourselves. Don't worry," she said with a weak smile, pausing. "You know you're a real softy Wolf, but thanks."

"Well, I gotta go to work. Call me if anything comes up, or if you hear about the arrangements for Stag. More importantly, be careful," he said, getting up to leave.

She stood and hugged him a little longer than normal once again.

"You be safe . . . I'll keep my promise, you can count on it."

With that, she smiled and went back in the bar. Wolf walked over to the VROC members, said his goodbyes, and left.

The ride gave him time to think back over the conversation. He hoped it was just a coincidence, but in the back of his mind, he suspected it wasn't. Somehow he knew the accident and the mysterious biker couple were connected, and most likely, to the murder he had witnessed at what seemed like just yesterday. He turned up the music and tried to focus on the ride. He knew that distracted driving had put way too many bikers in the ground and didn't want to be added to that long list. As he rounded the curve before his turnoff from Hwy 25 that would take him back to 280 and its distracted cagers, he spotted five turkeys in the road ahead. Two went left, two went right, and one came running down the road towards him, trying to take off in a way similar to a duck on the water, finally getting off the ground. He ducked and swerved, narrowly missing the huge bird as it flew over his head. He could feel the air disturbance as it passed, so he slowed down and focused on the road. It never seemed to fail that when he got distracted, some dang animal brought him back to the present reality of the ride. He was thankful for the close call.

Turning onto Hwy 280 and its eight lanes of traffic, he passed a woman in a black Mercedes SUV, similar to the one he had seen at the isolated, country church a week earlier. As he passed, he glanced at the driver, fearful of seeing one of the killers. Instead, he saw a typical, middle-aged woman driver with her ear glued to a cell phone. He moved over to a center lane, and watched as she did likewise. Glancing again at his mirror, he noted that she had sped up and was less than two car lengths back. He slowed down when the speed limit changed and she got even closer, seemingly not to notice him while she continued to talk, at times using both hands. He sped up and moved to the inside lane to put more distance between them and allow him an escape route. When the light ahead changed to red, he came to a stop behind an old Ford pickup truck. As was his habit, he watched his rear view mirror and was not surprised to see the Mercedes in the same lane as he, and not appearing to be slowing for the light. He quickly moved over into the turn lane just as he heard the sound of squealing rubber, chirping as the ABS system took over. The Mercedes came to a complete stop mere inches from the truck's rear bumper, passing through the space where he had been sitting a few seconds earlier.

Wolf turned and gave the woman the most scornful expression he could muster, and pointed to his ear. She visually answered back with upturned palms, shrugging her shoulders, while pasting a stupid apologetic smile on her face in the way women drivers do when trying to say "oops, my bad." It was a wonder he had ridden as many miles as he had without getting killed by some distracted cage driver. He noticed that she had put the cell phone down. Somebody has got to be looking over me, he thought to himself.

Arriving at work a few minutes early, a young sales associate, texting on his cell phone almost walked into him as he backed his bike into his customary spot on the concrete pad outside the rear door. Wolf gave the young man a short, emphatic piece of advice about cell phones and moving vehicles. He went inside and quickly changed clothes while trying to put the morning's events out of his mind. He focused instead on what the company referred to as "Game Day" due to the abundance of Saturday customer traffic and the resulting sales activities. The hours went by quickly, assisting sales consultants and customers in their quest for their "perfect car". As usual, the staff was enthusiastic and pumped up for the day, going about their jobs with well-trained ease. He had found that a key to their success was heaping praise for their actions, and happily sharing in their joy with each successful customer interaction. Mistakes and missed opportunities were thought of as "teachable moments", and he greeted each one as an opportunity to help the staff grow and become more self-reliant. Most understood this and took his advice seriously, often seeking his advice when needed. Laughter was heard often as he was in and out of offices, helping him to put the morning behind him.

Around five, he went to the break room to eat a late lunch. He was joined at the table by the young sales associate that had almost run into him earlier.

"Sorry about earlier, it won't happen again. You know, I thought I saw your bike outside the Chrome Rider last night. I started to go inside to find you, but before I could, this guy came out with a really hot, tall blond chick and got on the bike. She had her own bike, too, kinda like yours but really slick looking. She was all over the guy and he looked old enough to be her dad. Wolf, I gotta get me a bike . . . you guys get all the hot babes!"

Wolf didn't bother to chastise him as he would typically do when someone used his nickname at work. Instead, he put his sandwich down, saying he'd just remembered an urgent call he had to make. The young associate watched with surprise as his normally fun-loving manager walked quickly out the door without saying anything else, opening his cell phone as he went.

"Millie, thank God I got you! Forget about putting that camera up, and if you see either of them, call me immediately," he said as calmly as he could. He had really been shaken by what the associate had told him, and panicky at the thought of what he feared could happen if she was seen by either of the two bikers when placing the camera.

"Too late, it's already in place. I hate to tell you this, but Mary Jo just came back from taking fresh towels to the cabin and told me all her stuff is gone. I don't think she's coming back. You alright?"

"I'm fine. You call me if you see them, but stay clear of them—got it?"

"Yes sir, *dad*. You can count on me," she said with a little too much sarcasm.

"Okay then, I'll see you later, bye."

He hung up and dialed his buddy Mark's number.

"What's up Wolf? You do know its Saturday. Beast break down or something?" Mark asked.

"No, but I really need to talk to you about an urgent matter. I don't know of anyone else I can talk to about it."

"You got it dude, I'm here for you. What time and where?"

"Probably be late after we close . . . that OK with you?"

"You know it is as long as you bring the beer. Come on over to the house. Sounds like this could be a long conversation. Everybody will be in bed by the time you get here, so we can talk in my newly refurbished garage man-cave undisturbed."

"Sounds great dude, and thanks. I'll text you when I'm on the way."

"See you then. Wolf, whatever it is, it'll be OK."

"I hope so; see you about ten or so."

Wolf returned to the break room. He wasn't hungry anymore, but finished his sandwich anyway.

CHAPTER 13

After locking up the store, he headed toward his buddy's house in the country, a few miles outside of town and not far from where he lived. He took the back way, again frequently checking the mirrors for any sign of being followed. Mark's house was on a lightly traveled county road. He had recently built his new home behind the old farmhouse he had lived in for many years. It was huge compared to the old one, and stylish with country charm. The house was situated with a view of the surrounding horse farm. A deck that wrapped the rear and side of the house overlooked the surrounding fields. Mark had put his heart and soul, as well as most of his income from his repair shop into this home, and it showed. The upstairs was stylish, comfortable, and functional for his wife and daughter who were the center of his life.

The downstairs was finished well after they had completed the upstairs and moved in. It was completely devoted to manly tastes. Half of the space was taken up by a fully functional repair shop with lifts and tools that could accommodate almost any type of vehicle. Another room was an exercise area that Mark used to train for his newest passion as a cross-country runner. The last part was the lounge area that would be the envy of any guy. It was complete with a full bar, beer distillery, big screen TV, rustic furniture, and sports team memorabilia. Two friendly, well-trained Labrador retrievers were always in attendance, completing the manly environment.

Wolf pulled up outside the garage door. The door came up immediately, seeming to invite him to pull inside. Mark was nowhere in sight, so he got off his bike and went into the bar area. Behind him, he was startled as the garage door came down and Mark was still nowhere to be seen.

Mark's voice came from upstairs, "Grab a drink, Wolf, and pour me a beer. I'll be right down."

He did as instructed, grabbing two frosted mugs from the large freezer, then pouring two drafts from the tap. Mark came down a few minutes later and joined him at the bar.

"How 'bout that high tech garage door sensor? I just set it on auto, and it opens when you pull up outside. I had a hard time programing it to pick up an old road dog on a bike, but it worked," he said with a grin, greeting Wolf enthusiastically.

"Real cool, and funny at the same time. What did you have to enter to program it to pick you up? Comedian mechanic or something? There a setting for that, too?"

"Naw, I just put in the term "smart ass" and it just automatically figured it was me. What's up buddy, you sounded real serious and mysterious on the phone—you OK?"

"No, I got a real big problem, and I don't know what to do. If I don't do something, I'm afraid more people will die in the near future." The concern was evident by his tone of voice and the look on his face.

"That's some really deep shit there, bro—you're not bull shittin' me or something, are you?" Observing the look on his friend's face, he could read the answer. "You really are sure about it, aren't you?"

"I wish I wasn't, but after today's events, I know."

"Let's get a bottle of Wild Turkey. I think we could both use a shot or three before you get started." He grabbed a bottle from behind the bar and a couple of shot glasses. He turned and looked at his friend.

"This got anything to do with the missing mayor?"

"Worse, it's about him and a friend of mine that got killed last night on 25."

"Wolf, before you go any farther, I think we need to get Lute over here to hear it, too. He'd know what to do more than me, and he owes you his life . . . you know he's got your back, no matter what," Mark said in a somber tone.

Wolf was worried where the full disclosure might lead, but shook his head in agreement. "You're probably right."

"Darn tootin I'm right! He'll be here in ten minutes if I call him. He just left here an hour ago . . . we were talking about the mayor and all the stuff going on at City Hall at supper."

"Alright, make the call, I'm going to check the internet for news about Stag and have a shot while we wait."

Wolf pulled up Facebook, then the VROC site, followed by the Alabama news site. He noted there was to be a memorial service at biker church the next day for friends of Stag. No details were posted about the upcoming funeral. There was nothing new about the missing mayor, but mention was made that his wife had been made acting mayor in his absence. He was startled by the garage door opening and the sound of Lute's bike pulling inside. The engine went silent as the garage door came down.

"Glad you didn't program that computer of yours for "no cops". It's starting to rain outside. Good to see you Wolf! Mark says you need to talk about something important. Y'all gonna hog that bottle all to yourselves?" Lute said, entering the bar area and greeting them the way biker buddies always do. A round of shots was poured and Lute made a toast to another "Wolf tale".

Wolf looked his friend in the eye, tossed the shot back, then chased it with a swig of beer.

"I'm not so sure you're going to like this story when you hear it, bro. This is the first time I've told it. Wait until I finish to ask any questions. Lute, you may want to grab a pad and pen and take a few notes. This is some real serious shit I'm getting ready to lay on y'all. I'm not so sure you'll want to get involved—there won't be any going back after I start."

Lute had years of experience interrogating criminals, and could read body language extremely well. This talent had served him well in the past, helping him to put more than a few criminals behind bars. He could tell that Wolf was not lying, and was in fact, extremely concerned about what he was about to tell them. He was reminded of confessions he had prompted after hours of grilling the suspect relentlessly. His friend's demeanor worried him greatly, as it was similar to the way criminals sometimes would finally just give up trying to hide their guilt and then confess. Being able to understand and reflect a perp's cultural background was a natural talent he used as needed. Having grown up in a rough, culturally diverse neighborhood in Birmingham, he had learned to fit in. He could have easily have had a career as an actor.

"Well I don't know about Lute, but you certainly got my attention. This had better not be the start of some book or story you've been thinking about writing, or I may have to cut you off," Mark said.

"Go ahead man, lay it on us, you know you can tell us anything. Think of me as your Catholic priest taking confession. We'll decide what to do together afterward—you good with that?" Lute smiled slightly, trying to put him at ease.

"Yeah bro, you're right, but I'm Presbyterian. You ready?"

"Yes, my son, what sins have you come to confess . . . come on already, the suspense is killing us."

"Alright then, here we go. I saw the mayor get murdered Monday night when I was stopped at a church on the way home from work. I saw the two that did it up close and personal in my headlights as I busted ass to get away from there, but I think they were wearing some kind of facial disguises. They didn't see me good enough to know who I am, but they got a good idea of what my bike looks like. They are still in the area, and I'm pretty damned sure they killed

Stag because he rides a bike like mine. If I hadn't been such a chicken shit and had come forward when it happened, Stag would still be alive today. I'm pretty sure I ran into them a couple of times this week, once at the Hawg, and then again at Resort 25. I think the woman was staying out there all week, but now they've both disappeared. The problem is, I'm not completely sure they're the ones I saw do the killing, their faces are different. However, they do seem to match the ones I saw, except for their faces and hair. Both are bikers, and the man is huge, about 6 foot 6 or maybe seven". The woman is over 6 feet tall, well-built and strong, with big boobs and real sexy. I know they are looking for me, but I changed the way my bike looks and sounds, so I'm pretty sure they don't suspect it was me that saw them. Stag's accident wasn't really an accident, I'm sure of that. He was a conservative rider, and I can't imagine him riding 25 fast at night. I do think anybody that crosses their path is in danger, and they're looking for anybody with a bike like mine that lives around here." He paused and took a deep breath of relief. "That pretty much sums it up."

No one spoke for a few minutes while they digested the story.

"That really is some deep shit Wolf," Lute said with a thoughtful look on his face. "You really believe it was the same two you saw later at the bar, don't you?"

"Yes I do. Why else would they be asking questions about bikes like mine?"

"Alright, then, let's assume what you said is right. Why are they still hanging around?" A transformation came over him, reflected in his face. "Mark, how about putting some coffee on, we're going to be pulling an all-nighter. Bro, don't worry, you know I believe that you believe everything you just said. I got your back, no matter what. What we have to do now is go over details and time lines, then come up with a game plan to find those two. I can't give you any details, but there's a lot more to this than the mayor's disappearance. Have you said anything about this to anyone else?"

"No, but I do have a couple of close friends keeping an eye out for them. They don't know why." He paused, then asked, "Does this have anything to do with the feds having a mini convention in the Publix parking lot the night of the murder?"

"Damn, Wolf, you better be glad I'm your buddy, you know enough to get you killed or charged with the murder. The scuttlebutt is that they were setting up a sting when the mayor went missing. Not sure of the details, but I am sure there are more people involved than just the mayor. All this is unofficial, and you didn't hear it from me."

The silence was thick as they thought about the last bit of information, trying to imagine what crime had brought the FBI to their little city. Mark got up, then returned with freshly brewed coffee and a bottle of Bailey's.

Lute spoke first. "Alright then, let's get started. Wolf, get out that journal of yours, I know you've been making notes about all of this, right?"

Wolf nodded and reached inside his jacket pocket, pulling out his well-worn, leather enclosed book. He opened it and waited.

"Mark, take notes. Wolf, start at the beginning and don't leave anything out. I want to know anything you saw, heard, smelled, tasted, or even dreamed about since Monday. Take it slow, we can take a break whenever you need to—just don't leave anything out. Close your eyes and visualize it. Before we get started, who are the friends keeping an eye out for them?"

"Rosie at the Hawg, and Millie at Resort 25. I told them to stay clear and give me a call if they see them. What do you think we should do about them?"

"Nothing right now. Let's get started."

Mark and Lute both had pads and were ready as Wolf started at the beginning by telling about being stopped for his tag light being out. Mark looked at Lute with raised eyebrows, wondering about the relevance of the stop, but said nothing after Lute made a subtle nod of his head to prevent him from interrupting. He continued on for more than an hour, pausing to go back and fill in details of his thoughts and observations. At times, Wolf would refer to his journal, painstakingly trying to leave no detail out. They knew he was through when he slumped in his chair and let out a long breath. Lute had seen this reaction in the past when suspects confessed to crimes or when the burden of a secret kept was lifted.

Lute broke the silence first. "Let's take a break and grab a beer before we start the interrogation—just kidding, no water-boarding involved here, just follow-up questions. Dude, I can tell you're a writer by the details you gave. You should have been a detective."

"You been drug tested lately Lute? Imagine me, a cop. You must be smoking some serious shit," he began to relax and regain his sense of humor. He was relieved now that he had confessed what to him, had been a deep, dark secret. He knew now he had brothers that shared the biker code of trust, sharing in the secret and watching his back. He knew in his gut that together, they would come up with a solution.

"I'm going outside for a smoke guys, be right back."

"That's cool, take your time, me and Mark need to compare notes. Take the dogs out with you, too. That's kinda funny, a wolf taking out the dogs."

"Pretty lame if you ask me, but it *is* getting late and we *are* still sober," Mark pitched in, laughing.

Wolf went out the door and lit up. The two labs went about their business, then one walked over and sniffed a bike he had not noticed when he rode up.

He walked over and took note that it was a Nomad, probably an 08 model due to the color combo, red and black. Other than the color, it was a twin of the Beast, even had a black fairing instead of the stock windshield.

Walking back inside he said, "when did you get the Nomad, Mark? Nice looking bike."

"A customer brought it by today to get Progressive shocks put on and some other stuff done to it. Wants me to get rid of the loud pipes but keep the commander and intake on it. I installed slip ons to make it quieter without restricting the air flow. That bike's got as much get up and go as yours does now. Thought I'd ride it home and check it out for him. Gonna take a few days to get all the parts. I'm having a hard time finding a few he wants."

"Good, but don't be in a hurry to get it done. If I'm right, it might be bad for a biker's health to ride a quiet Nomad with a batwing on it around here right now."

"Guys, let's get back to work. Wolf, tell me again, why you thought those two were bikers."

Lute started asking questions, a task he was extremely talented at. He used a gentle, non-accusing demeanor, and threw in bits of humor to make the interview seem more like a normal biker conversation than an interrogation. Another hour flew by.

Mark handed everybody a beer and said, "Lute, your turn now. We need to know what's going on from your end; only fair you fill us in on what you know. Between the three of us, we might just be able to think unconventionally and figure out a way to catch these killers before somebody else gets killed. Does that make sense to you?"

"Makes a lot of sense, but you may be disappointed; I don't know much that you haven't heard about in the news. Those FBI guys aren't being real forthright about anything. Those assholes, especially the agent in charge, treat us like we're all a bunch of country bumpkins. Pisses everybody at the station off real bad. They know things about this, but they won't say anything about why they were already here when the mayor went missing."

He continued. "The blond was seen sitting inside a grey Crown Vic, right behind his black Mercedes SUV before the mayor came out. She is wanted for questioning but the descriptions vary. Several witnesses got a pretty good look at her. All of them agree that she was a real looker. She does fit the general description of the woman you saw. When the mayor left the dedication, most folks had already gone, including his wife. The mayor was seen getting into his SUV. Nobody else was seen inside her car. The guys in the police department think those feds had a tail on the Mercedes when it left the parking lot, but lost it. One of the guys overheard a conversation about an unmarked Crown Vic involved in causing them to lose the Mercedes in a development off 17. Turns out the car was owned by some old guy that lives in Helena. Had to keep that one quiet. The feds went in with six men and scared the crap out of this old retired couple. The guy had a bad ticker and had to go to the hospital, but he's OK now."

"So why were the feds here in the first place?" Wolf asked. "There were several of them and a big van in the grocery store parking lot the night it all happened."

"Nobody seems to know or they're not saying. I think the mayor was dirty and the feds were either going to bust him, or he was an informer on some sting they had cooked up. Everybody thinks he's dead, but nobody knows for sure. He is officially, just missing, and there are few clues. I liked the mayor, he was always nice to me. His wife is on the council, and now has almost taken over down at city hall. She's a real cold bitch, but she did have a lot to do with getting the new city hall and the new school built, spent a lot of the city's money to do it. Maybe the feds are after her. Don't know, just mainly wild speculation going around in the ranks. I sense that she doesn't seem to be too tore up about her husband. Spends a lot of time with the chief and my boss about it, and seems to try to avoid the feds."

"Sounds to me like she might be the one that hired those two and had him killed," Mark piped up.

"That's some pretty wild speculation, but you got a point, with this new info. Definitely sounds like a professional hit to me. The problem is, how do we keep you out of it and still get the new information to the right people so we can get everybody looking in the right direction. Tell you what, I need to get on the internet and look up a few things, maybe come up with something about those two bikes—might get lucky with some names. You guys take a break for a few. One thing, Wolf. How do you feel about coming forward?"

"Lute, you've known me for a long time, so you know how I feel about the loss of my freedom. I want to do the right thing, but a day behind bars, or even being cut off from riding ain't worth it. I'd rather be a dead biker than spend any time without the freedom to ride. Not to mention what it would do to Sue and the kids along with my job security. You gotta keep me out of this."

Lute got real serious, looked him in the eye and said, "Wolf, I'll always have your back no matter what, but I had to ask. I didn't want to mention this, but maybe now's the time. When we were talking about who might have it in for the mayor, your name came up in regards to what you said about that new sound ordinance. Hell, for that matter Mark, your name came up too, along with many others that were at the protest. The Southern Vets are being looked at, too. When the mayor's body turns up, things are going to heat up for anybody that ever said anything bad about the man and that list includes a whole lot of bikers. Wolf, you were even quoted in the paper, for Christ sakes."

"Damn, this could bring back the 60's and those Easy Rider days around here—not really such a bad thing when I think about it," Mark threw in with the goofiest grin he could muster.

"Don't think it would get that bad, many guys on the force ride, and most folks know about all the charity rides that bikers do to raise money and how they provide escorts for funerals. Tell you what, you guys go take a break for a while and do some brainstorming. I'll let you know if I find out something."

"You got it bro," Wolf held out his hand, and shook with Lute in the way bikers do when sharing a confidence. "Luv ya man."

"Stop the mushy shit and get out of here," he said with a smile and a look of understanding. "It's all going to work out in the end."

Going out the back door, they sat on the bikes parked outside. Mark reached in the side bag of the Vulcan and came out with a fatty.

"A guy gave me this after fixing his bike. Told him I don't smoke the shit no more, but he insisted. Figured I'd save it for a special occasion. You remember how creative we used to get when we smoked this shit—got a light?"

"Well, Lute did say we need to do some brainstorming. I seem to remember coming up with some real outside the box thinking a few times. Too bad he can't partake anymore. Fire that sucker up, I could use a little mellow right now."

They passed the aromatic weed back and forth a couple of times, until Mark was overcome with a coughing fit. Wolf took another short pull, then stubbed it out.

"A couple of tokes is all I need, don't want to get wasted. He leaned back in the seat, put his feet on the highway pegs, and looked up at the sky. "Man, what a beautiful night. You sure can see a lot of stars out here. Man, you got a real nice place out here away from the city lights."

"Yep, it's what I always wanted for my family. I would like to grow old and see the grandkids playing in the yard there. Teach 'em all the biker ways. Gonna start building a pool over there as soon as I have enough money saved," he said pointing to an area off the rear of the house.

"You know, I could see myself settling down in a place like this, but it's gotta be on a lake. But before that, I wanna just take a year or so and travel all over the country, staying in places I like for as long as I want to. Maybe talk the old lady into driving a toy hauler and meeting me at different spots. Sooner or later, I'll find the right place to settle. Maybe an A-frame with a metal roof and a big garage for the bikes overlooking a lake . . . don't have to be big or fancy."

"You'll get there before you know it bro. Shhh, be quiet for a minute and look over there."

He looked where Mark was pointing and could just barely make out the outline of three deer about a hundred yards away. At that moment, they heard the barking of a dog coming from the same direction and watched as the deer, spooked by the dog, started running in their direction. They could clearly hear the pounding of their hoofs, and, as they got close to where they sat rock still, the snorting of their breath. The deer suddenly stopped twenty yards from where they sat on the bikes. The largest one looked directly at them for what seemed like several minutes, ears twitching and rotating like radar masts. At that moment Lute came out the door, startling them, causing them to take off down the gravel road in front of the house. In one fluid motion, Lute drew his Glock from his holster, crouched, and pointed it at the fleeing deer. Mark laughed so hard, he fell off his bike, hitting the ground with a thud. Wolf started laughing uncontrollably, and was quickly joined by the others as the laughter became contagious. One would start laughing again, and the others couldn't help but follow. This went on until they were all holding their sides in pain while wiping tears from their eyes.

Wolf thought the deer was a sign indicating he had chosen the right path in getting his buddies' help. He relaxed, but chose not to share this latest tidbit with his friends.

"What have you two been doing out here while I was inside, working my ass off on the computer? Never mind, I can tell by the smell and the shit eating grins—y'all could have at least asked if I wanted to partake of that devil weed, too," he said with an obviously fake hurt look on his face.

Mark said from the ground, "we knew you couldn't, your being one of the city's finest . . . besides, you did send us out here to brainstorm."

"I'm just envious—maybe, when all this is behind us, we can all head to the hills and have us a real par-tay for a week or so and do some riding on the Blue Ridge Parkway. So what did you geniuses come up with?" He tried to look serious.

"Nothing yet, but I for one, am glad you weren't out here with that gun of yours. Thought you were going to shoot ole Bambi there—you're pretty damn quick on the draw, McGraw, I'd hate to get on your bad side."

"Don't worry, I was just a little spooked by the fact that those two bikers are ghosts—the name and address on that new Vaquero's buyer was fake, and there is nothing in any report that mentions any out of state bikers."

"No surprise, let's get back inside, you got *me* spooked now," Mark said as he got up, wiping himself off.

"Mark, how about taking notes again. Got any more coffee?"

"Yassah, Mr. Lute, I be makin' sum mo fo ya right now, suh." He went to the bar.

"First thing we have to do is get this information to the department in a way that will keep us all out of the middle of it. I'll come up with an anonymous letter that will get everybody's attention and looking in the right direction. Have to be real careful with the wording. We don't want everybody running around hassling every biker they see—somebody would get hurt or even killed for sure. I'll work on that."

"Sounds good Lute. I think we got to figure out a way to bring the killers out in the open . . . shit! They're looking for bikes like mine, right? They're bound to be checking out the VROC bikes at Stag's service tomorrow at biker church, or, I guess today right? There were a lot of responses to that invite on Facebook." Wolf looked at his cell phone and noted the time. "Guys, it's almost 5 am. The service for Stag starts at 10."

"All right, let's get started. Here's what I got so far; you guys chime in anytime you want." Lute looked at his notes. "Send in the tip mentioning the place, time, and general description of the two killers. Next, I'll check out Stag's laptop, then go see if they got a picture or film at the dealer that sold that chick the Vaquero. Check out that cabin out at the resort for clues and evidence. Check the video at that bar."

Mark spoke first. "You know guys, all of this could still be just a coincidence. When the cops start sniffing around, the killers are going to just disappear. I don't even want to think about all the stuff that's going to get stirred up when it hits the fan. And life for you," he said pointing at Wolf, "ain't never gonna be the same if any of this gets out . . . not to mention where the cops are concerned."

Lute spoke up. "You guys have got to trust the way I'm going handle the tip. No one will have any idea you are involved at all—trust me on that. You guys go get a few hours of shut-eye, you'll need to be alert out there. We'll ride out to the service together. I'll have a rough plan and a note put together by then. It isn't the first rally I've ever been to, you know."

"All right then, the couch does look pretty good. Wake me up when you got the coffee ready to go."

Mark headed upstairs while Wolf grabbed a blanket, stretched out on the couch, and shut his eyes. His conscience clear, exhaustion took over quickly and he began to snore almost immediately.

Lute began typing on the laptop, composing a note that would give enough clues to put his coworkers on the right track. He was cautious to avoid anything that would point back to Wolf. He knew as soon as it was discovered, every arm of law enforcement that could even remotely claim an interest would converge on the little town, searching any place a body could be dumped and canvasing for more clues. His biggest fear was that by including the biker connection, he would create a hassle for anyone on two wheels, bringing distrust and even violence between the authorities and the biker community. He decided to leave that part out at this point in the anonymous note.

CHAPTER 14

4 5 was up at daybreak that chilly Saturday morning. After putting some coffee on, he went for a run around the field and through the woods, following a deer trail he had come across down by the nearby creek. As he ran, he imagined ways to silence the unknown biker that was the reason he was still staying in the crappy little trailer, in this backwards, redneck county. He remembered the shock he felt when they were blinded by those headlights suddenly coming on, not so much at the sudden appearance of the lone biker, but more at himself for allowing it to happen at all. Even more astonishing was the fact that he had missed the s.o.b. with his pistol. He resolved to get some practice in after stopping by the old church to check the camera still hidden there.

Walking in the door, he was surprised to see Blondie waiting, dressed in her familiar disguise as a man. All signs of femininity were now absent. Her total transformation was somewhat disturbing to him. It almost made him feel gay until he thought of the tricks she knew in the sack. They had spent several hours in the barn transforming the Vaquero's appearance. It now sported more chrome and bright red flames around the fairing, tank, and hard-bags. A removable sissy bar and luggage rack had completed the transformation.

As he poured a cup of freshly brewed coffee, she spoke first. "Been thinking it over. You need to stay scarce and away from Resort 25, just in case. The service may bring our mystery biker out, and he'd probably get spooked if he saw you, might even put things together. He definitely won't know me or my bike. I'll look over the bikes there and get plate numbers of any possible matches. What are you planning for today?"

"Thought I'd retrieve the camera and get in some target practice. Maybe work on the scooter. Why?"

"I've got a feeling the shit's about to hit the fan somehow. Strange nothing has come out yet, and the cops believe something happened to him. Maybe that biker has called in a tip. Don't stop at the church, just ride by and see if there's any unusual activity. Somebody could be watching. Call it female intuition, but just play it safe anyway."

"Your female intuition must not work too good dressed like that . . . today's Sunday, it'd be unusual if there wasn't any activity there," he said with an exaggerated laugh.

"Just seeing if you're paying attention. You can get the camera tonight."

"You know, I ran this op just fine before you came along. Been doing this shit for a long time, and will be long after you cash in your chips. I can't think of too many better ways to make a living. You know the old saying—*do what you love and the money will come.*"

"Yeah, and there's a song out there that says, "doing what you like and liking what you do". Some kinda acid-head hippie song."

"You know, I remember an Army sarge that used to make his platoon sing that shit when on the run in formation . . . he ain't around no more."

Cheetah looked him in the eyes and said, "maybe you ought to keep that in mind . . . it's a lot easier to get caught nowadays with all those cell phone cameras everybody carries. Be careful, lover, and don't call me Blondie—it's Ronnie."

"You got me there. It would be messy to kill some muther fucker cause he thought I was a gay anyway."

"I'm outta here. I'm going to get there early, get some breakfast, and try not to draw any attention. I'll stay in touch."

Blondie, aka Cheetah, and now Ronnie, started to tell him about her plan she was working on to frame that writer, but thought better of it.

Let's see what opportunities come up today, she thought to herself. She headed out the door, helmet and gloves in hand.

Minutes later, he heard the sound of her 1700cc V-twin motor starting. Minutes later, he heard the crunch of gravel, followed by the chirp of rubber meeting asphalt. He went in the bathroom to take a shower and get ready for a day of riding before the flowers and greenery came out and nature made the roadside scenery all pretty again. He had always preferred the bleakness of a winter landscape.

At ten am, 45 started his Harley Davidson 110 cubic inch CVO V-twin Street Glide and started out, headed for Helena. He enjoyed the crisp bite of the chilly morning air on his cheeks, and the dry, clean air that cleared his lungs. He felt alert and alive, his senses in tune to the throb of his engine and the countryside activity passing by at 70 mph. When he snapped on the radio his ears were greeted by Thurgood's tune, *Bad to the Bone.* He continued flying down the road on his two wheeled jet, connected to the ground by only two small patches of rubber.

"Ronnie" chose a spot outside to eat where she could check out new arrivals at the resort. Her meal was simple—eggs over easy with grits, gravy, and sausage all mixed together. She sat alone and waited as the new arrivals went directly inside and stayed there, unwilling to enjoy the fresh air due to the morning chill still in the air. *Guys don't get much attention—not a bad thing,* she thought. She ate in silence and observed the newcomers. As the time for biker church neared, the rumble of many bikes grew from the hill above. The sound seemed to pause, apparently caused by a dozen or more bikes coming to a halt, their engines idling. She could tell they weren't Harleys from the lack of the signature exhaust and figured they must be members of VROC, all riding Vulcans. They most likely had stopped at the place where their recently departed fellow rider's bike left the road, and he left the world of the living.

Minutes later, as the start time for church grew closer, eleven Vulcan motorcycles pulled into the parking area, came to a stop, and then parked in a line outside the meeting room where services were held. One bike was flying the Stars and Stripes, along with a confederate flag. As the bikes came to a stop, there was an obvious gap in the line of parked bikes near the middle. One biker came over and placed a wreath on the concrete surface where the missing bike would be. They were all somber as they filed inside.

She waited for fifteen minutes in case there was a latecomer. As the sound of music came from the room, Ronnie casually strolled down the line, stopping to look more closely at several bikes including a solid black Nomad with a full fairing. She took a picture of the rear including the plate, careful to make it look like she was checking text messages on her cell phone. She moved on, stopping to look closely at Wolf's Vulcan Nomad, noting the gloves draped over the tank bag. She realized that *this* was a link she could use to make Wolf the patsy if needed, tucking the thought away for later. She continued, looking at the red and black Nomad next to Wolf's bike. It too, had a black fairing, and she pondered what red would look like in the moonlight. She got a shot of the bike, then continued looking at others, marveling to herself at the money spent on all the extra chrome. After checking out the Vulcans, she continued down the entire row of gleaming scooters next to the shelter, stopping and looking at unique ones. She nonchalantly walked back to the bar and ordered a beer. Returning outside, she took a seat where she could watch the bikes, their owners, and the taillights when the bikes were started.

Ronnie's activities did not go unnoticed. Lute sat inside the bar, also observing bikers as they arrived. The weather lately had been unseasonably mild, and bikers were taking full advantage of the early spring. Usually, there would be few bikes out this early on a chilly Sunday morning, but the high for the day was predicted to be in the mid 60's. The restaurant was packed, as evidenced by the dozens of bikes outside. Bikers stood around new arrivals, taking advantage of the rapid increase in the outside temperature, enhanced by the bright sun and clear blue skies. He noticed a lone male biker; big, but not as big as the killer Wolf had described.

As he watched, he saw the man walk behind the bikes, and became instantly alert when the biker paused at Mark and Wolf's bikes. The biker took his cell phone out, apparently responding to a text. He continued down the line, pausing to look at several others, many that had no fairing or hard bags. He appeared to be just another admirer of custom bikes, a trait shared with countless other bikers. Lute relaxed a bit, but continued to observe the man as he walked around the parked bikes, then entered the door on the far side of the room from where he sat passively observing. He looked for distinguishing features and noted that he was about 6 foot two, maybe 180 pounds with no facial hair. Probably an accountant or a lawyer, out riding to get away from his dull life, he thought. The lone biker ordered a beer, then returned outside and perched on a picnic table in the rear corner of the pavilion nearest the meeting room and the bikes parked outside.

Lute saw no other significant activity around the bikes of the VROC members during the service. Being suspicious by nature, he continued to watch the biker's actions when those attending the service came outside. Most walked solemnly to their bikes, started them, and moved into a double file formation. It was hard to be sure, but it seemed the lone biker he was observing was more attentive to the procession than he'd expect, but he then realized that most of the other bikers were also watching the activity with interest. Realizing how tired he was, he wrote it off to an overactive imagination. As he sat gazing at the activities, the man made a call just as the bikes started off, then straddled a new Kawasaki Vaquero, black with flames, and, apparently in no hurry, started it and departed in the opposite direction from the group of bikers.

CHAPTER 15

Biker church was held each Sunday by members of a local Christian Motorcycle Club in a small meeting room across the parking lot from the bar at Resort 25. There was seating for forty with little room left over. At the front, a podium was set up with space to the side for a lone acoustical guitarist that would sing a few inspiring, spiritual songs. The service usually consisted of a couple of songs, announcements, then a spiritual lesson that put the biblical scripture into layman terms, targeted at bikers. Brotherhood was emphasized, and the belief in the Holy Spirit and choices had been the subject of recent services. Services usually lasted thirty to forty minutes. This service lasted considerably longer. Many that knew Stag stood up and spoke, recalling experiences and speaking kind words about him. All present pledged to join the funeral procession, even though little information was known about the upcoming arrangements. He was a veteran, and as such, most thought he would be buried at the military veteran's cemetery. It was too early to know for certain. At the conclusion of the service, several decided to pay a visit to Stag's widow to offer condolences. Others would collect donations for his widow and help in the days to come. Details of the funeral would be posted on the VROC and Facebook websites as soon as known.

The group of Vulcan riders filed out of the meeting room with the intention of riding as a group back to the crash site before going their separate ways. They planned to place the wreath where Stag's bike had left the road. Most parked beside the road opposite from where the skid marks leading off the road were still plainly visible. Mark and Wolf pulled into an old gravel driveway just below, where unknown to them, 45 had stopped two nights previously. The undergrowth was trampled as evidence of the recent activity at the scene. As they caught up with the group of bikers staking out the wreath, Mark pointed out the skid marks to Wolf, shaking his head and grimacing. Others took note, many silently thinking that the same could have happened to them, remembering times in the past when they too, had gone into similar curves a little too fast or after having a few beers. The somberness of the group was obvious. All but Mark and Wolf returned to their bikes and started off.

"Damned shame, but what was he doing going so fast on this road at night? Stag wasn't an everyday rider, but he was pretty experienced. Wonder what got into him . . . too much to drink, you think?" Mark said, with a frown and raised eyebrows.

"Most bikers I know tend to ride slower and more cautiously when they've had a beer or two. Besides, he was on his way to the bar, not from there. There was that woman he met at the other bar. I'm pretty sure she was involved, especially with him being out here at night. You know, Stag's neck was broken—very strange coincidence. Maybe his bike had a little help leaving the road."

"Lute will know soon, they always do a toxicology on drivers, especially in single vehicle fatalities so we'll know soon enough. I gotta get back to the hacienda, I promised I'd do a cookout with the family. You wanta come on out? You could bring Sue; we haven't seen her lately."

"Sounds great, but I have to work today. I don't get every weekend off like you. Maybe another time real soon. Thanks for offering."

"Tell Sue she's welcome to come out if she's not doing anything."

"You know bro, I'm going to try to keep her as far away from this as I can. She doesn't need the extra worry right now, and I want her to stay safe. Daytona Beach is coming up next week and I'm supposed to be gone for about nine days."

"We'll have her over, and if anything comes up, she can stay with us."

"I appreciate it—you be safe riding home, I still believe riding a Vulcan can be hazardous to your health right now."

"Yeah, especially if it looks like yours . . . *you* be safe. Keep the chrome side up and the rubber down."

They shook in the traditional biker way, holding the chest hug a bit longer than normal. Both mounted their bikes and allowed them to idle before starting off in different directions. Mark headed toward the curvy section of 25, intending to test the bike out before completing the work on it in the week ahead at his shop. Wolf headed back to Resort 25 to speak with Lute before heading to work.

Mark was having a ball putting the Vulcan through its paces, opening the throttle wide open coming out of the curves and into the straight stretches. He was satisfied with the now muted sound of the exhaust, allowing him to hear the music without cranking the volume wide open. The temperature was in the high sixties and the early spring had caused the Jasmine to blossom early, creating purple splashes of color that greeted his eyes. The sweet smell of the blooms met his nose, reminding him of a ride last year to the mountains. It would have been the perfect day to ride if it wasn't for the recent events that had impacted his friend's life, creating a feeling of uneasiness in his mind. He hated that feeling, as it usually preceded bad things to come.

As he turned off Hwy 25 onto County road 41, he thought he saw a headlight in his peripheral vision from the old abandoned store he had just passed.

I'm beginning to imagine things already, he thought to himself.

He continued on, again opening the throttle and accelerating away from the turn. As he went into a wide sweeping s-curve before a small lake, he saw a bike rapidly closing on him from behind. The bike's headlight was not on, making him feel uneasy and suspicious that he was being followed. He was even more worried because on this day, he was unarmed and riding a bike he was not accustomed to. He decided to play it safe by reaching the small community ahead where there would be many locals eating Sunday brunch at the restaurant there. In seconds, his speedometer read 80 mph, but his mirror showed the unknown biker still gaining ground in the straightaway. Unwilling to push his luck too hard, he let the bike catch up. He slowed to 60 mph to allow it to pass, but the biker stayed about ten yards back. From the mirrors he saw it was a late model HD Street Glide. From the rumble of the exhaust he could hear over his own, he deduced it was a CVO Screaming Eagle package. The bike was black with ghost flames. The rider was dressed in black leather with a dark shield covering the part of his face visible over the windshield. They traveled this way for several miles until Mark, tired of the game, twisted the throttle wide open. The Harley lost ground, but quickly narrowed the gap and moved even closer, staying directly behind him, not even bothering to run the typical staggered position favored by experienced bikers riding together.

"What an asshole!" Mark said to himself. As he went into the next curve, he cut into the center, straightened up, and braked hard while silently praying that the Harley wouldn't crash into his rear. As he had hoped, the bike shot past, the mystery biker momentarily caught off guard by the unexpected maneuver. Mark whipped the Vulcan onto the gravel road to his left, fishtailing as he entered the loose gravel surface. Opening the throttle to pull the rear end of his bike straight, he accelerated as fast as he dared, relying on the car tire mounted on the rear's traction and stability to maintain control. He glanced in the mirror and saw the biker come to a stop, then whip his bike around, tires smoking. He knew he would win the race on the gravel due to the extra rubber the wide rear tire provided unless the road was a dead end. He said a silent curse for not bringing a weapon, fearing what would happen if the road did end. He watched as the biker started down the road after him, but was relieved that he was widening the distance between himself and the other biker. After a mile or so riding the gravel road while gaining confidence in the bike's handling of the curves, he saw the end of the road across the lake the road was winding around. He realized the road was a loop around the lake that would end back on the paved road he had just left. Putting on the brakes, he put the Vulcan into a sideways skid like he had done so many times on the dirt bike he rode regularly at home. Coming to a stop at the blacktop, he looked both ways, and, seeing no sign of the other bike, turned onto the blacktop and accelerated as fast as the bike would go. Realizing where he was, he turned off into a small parking area in front of the town square containing the Stone's Throw Restaurant, skidding to a halt in front and drawing the attention of the diners inside, many with shocked looks on their faces.

He dismounted quickly and ran towards the door, his heart beating rapidly. He could hear the wide open scream of the Street Glide as it approached from the direction he had just come. Opening the door, he heard the bike slowing down as it downshifted. He looked back in time to see the Harley and its rider go past at what must have been close to 70 mph. As he watched, the rider gave him a one finger salute that changed to the sign of a pistol aimed at him. He stood there trying to force his racing heart to slow, while he regained his composure before facing the many diners he could feel staring at him. He turned and walked quickly to the bar, sat on a stool, and ordered a beer with a shot. The silence in the restaurant was deafening.

After gulping down the shot of Wild Turkey and half the beer, he turned in his stool to look out the window. The diners looked down at their plates, seemingly afraid to meet his glance. He was thankful for this typical reaction from ordinary citizens, preferring to avoid conversation while he regained his composure and allowed his heart rate to slow.

Mark pulled out his cell phone and dialed Lute's number, praying he would answer. He was rewarded with the sound of his voice, answering on the third ring.

"What's up dude?" Lute said.

"I need an escort, and while you're at it, probably some fresh drawers."

"Dude, I think you called the wrong number, this ain't no pimp service you dialed. Besides, what's your old lady going to think about you hooking up with an escort?"

"Lute, just get your ass over to the restaurant in Mt. Laurel and I'll tell you all about it. I'm not leaving here until I see you. By the way, you carrying?"

"Always . . . you safe?"

"Right now I am, but hurry up and get here. You and I gotta talk. This shit with Wolf is for real. I'm purty damn sure I just had a close encounter with one of the killers he was talking about."

"Mark, just stay calm and be cool, I'll be there in fifteen minutes. You sure you're safe? I can call in the troops if we need to."

"Yep, don't worry, that guy wouldn't come in to get me in front of this many witnesses. It's the ride home I'm worried about. I couldn't outrun his bike with the one I'm on. Besides, we gotta come up with a plan to get those assholes before they kill again."

"See you soon." He hung up.

Mark walked over to the window, avoiding the furtive looks from the diners. Several tables emptied as customers got up to leave, many with plates still loaded with food. He knew they left due to his presence and the unaccustomed disturbance caused by his entrance to the establishment.

Don't often see overweight citizens leave that much food on their plates, he thought. He felt guilty for the impact he had on the server's income, and laid a hundred dollar bill on the bar, telling the bartender to keep the change. More customers came in staring openly at him with looks of disapproval. They were not used to seeing bikers in what to him appeared to be an upscale restaurant in the small community. The quaint, private little town was itself a refuge from the common folk. He knew the area was loaded with million dollar homes surrounding the golf course and lake.

A middle-aged man in a suit, obviously the manager, was accompanied by a private security guard and was hesitantly making his way towards him from the lobby area. Looking out the window to the parking area where his bike sat waiting, he saw a small truck and a golf cart, both labeled with the word, "Security" on them. As he watched, a private security guard got out of the truck, then ran towards the restaurant entrance, his hand holding his holster as he ran. He was reminded of Barney Fife, but knew this cop's pistol would be loaded. More of an immediate concern was the taser in the hand of the young, pimply faced guard with the manager. From the look of nervous excitement on his face, Mark knew he was in danger of a shocking experience.

He decided the best action was to remain calm, go along with whatever was requested, and wait for Lute to get there. He was no longer thinking of the recent bike encounter, instead fearing the immediate one before him.

The manager spoke first. "Sir, several customers have complained about you. I'm afraid we must ask you to leave."

Mark's face flushed with sudden anger, but he remained outwardly calm, seeing the taser held tensely by the guard. He was more afraid of the guard unintentionally pulling the trigger of the taser, knowing he would surely be blamed.

"No problem, but I must ask, kind sir, what it was I did and to whom I need to apologize," he said in the most sarcastic, but sophisticated manner he could.

"No need to get nasty, we don't want any trouble here," the guard said in an authoritative and loud, overly excited tone of voice. The taser was now pointed directly at him and the manager had stepped back out of the way.

Mark put his hands out, palms forward, in a gesture of surrender and said softly, "I don't want any trouble either, and I'll be glad to leave. Please point that thing somewhere else, or I'll be forced to shove it where the sun don't shine. Back off Barney!"

He regretted it immediately, as the young guard stepped back and prepared to taze him. He was saved as the other guard came up from behind and pushed the younger guard's hand down. Unfortunately, the young guard pulled the trigger and the darts flew and struck the nearest window a few feet away, shattering it into thousands of tiny pieces of safety glass that slowly crumbled and fell to the floor. The unmistakable sound of 10,000 volts of electricity being discharged along with the window breaking, created a panic amongst the diners who, up to that point, were enjoying the sight of the heathen biker trash being hassled as they believed all of his kind should be. Screams were heard, and dishes crashed to the floor as many scrambled to get outside as fast as they could. Mark stepped back against the wall, trying to stay out of the way of the chaos, or from any more actions of the guards. The now broken window pieces created even more problems as they bounced and slid across the polished wooden floor, causing the manager and several diners to slip and fall in their hurry to leave.

Mark stepped in to help an older lady up from the floor, reassuring her that there was nothing to fear but the young guard standing like a statue with his mouth open. The tazer was held loosely in his hand, wires dangling and leading to the window. As quiet returned to the room, all eyes were upon him watching for what would happen next. At that moment, the rumble of numerous V-twin engines was heard, quickly becoming louder. All eyes turned to the window as a dozen or more bikers turned into the parking lot from the road, coming to a halt double file outside the front door. The room was again quiet as the engines were turned off.

All Mark could do was laugh and point as he watched a wet spot slowly spread downward from the crotch of the young guard's pants, a pool of golden liquid spreading at his feet. He turned and started towards the door. After a few steps, he paused, then turned and looked directly at the guards.

"Clean up on isle three," he yelled. "Y'all have a nice day!" He turned and headed to where Lute and several others were waiting in the lobby, a big grin pasted on his face.

Lute was shaking his head when he said, "I thought I asked you to be cool, dude. Everything under control in there?"

"It is now, but the young hero over there sure will have some explaining to do—he started to shoot me with his tazer, but missed and killed the window instead. You might want to speak to the manager on my behalf."

"You sure are a lot of trouble sometimes; this might just make the evening news. By the look of those teenyboppers over there with the smart phones, the whole scene is liable to be on youtube by now. Hope you didn't do anything I'll have to arrest you for later."

"No, but I'll bet these folks will be more respectful of bikers in the future."

As they stood talking, a distinguished looking man came over. "Sorry about the trouble, young man. I'm the mayor of this town and saw what happened. I'll take care of everything. Unfortunately, the folks around here are real quick to judge a book by its cover. Many moved here to get away from the violence and crime in Birmingham. You know, I used to ride a bike in my younger days, and the police were always hassling us back then. Y'all come back and visit sometime. Here's my card."

"Thanks, mayor—I really am sorry about the mess. My name's Mark and this here is Lute. Most of all those other guys are public servants, too; police, fire, and such. Me, I run a motorcycle shop. You ever think about getting a bike again, give me a call and I'll hook you up. Good luck with your townsfolk. You might just need it if you get back into riding a motorcycle." Mark waved at the customers that had stayed, still watching as he turned and walked out the door.

"Y'all enjoy the rest of your day," he said loudly to those left inside.

The ride home was uneventful. Lute stayed with him after the rest of the riders went their separate ways, splitting off one or two at a time as they got closer to his house. Before making the last turn onto the road that led to Mark's, Lute pulled into an abandoned development's entrance and made a call. He said a few words, listened to the reply, then started back out onto the road. Arriving at Mark's, he waited as his friend pulled inside the garage. Taking a last look back at the highway and satisfied that no one had followed them, he followed Mark inside.

"I didn't want to ask with all the others around, but what the hell happened before you called me? I don't think I really want to know what happened in the restaurant, I've got a pretty good idea that you and those private cops didn't get along too good. Just tell me what happened before you called."

"You got it. I had just turned onto that road off of 25, and was just tooling along going the speed limit, when I noticed a bike coming up fast from behind me. The guy got right on my ass—I mean a few feet right behind me and stayed there. I slowed down to let him pass, but he just stayed there, so I sped up to almost 100, but he was still right on my butt, maybe inches back. I got to worrying, so in the next curve, I went inside and braked hard, and he shot by. Saw him hit the brakes as I turned onto that old dirt road that goes around the lake. He came after me, but thanks to the tire on that Vulcan, I put some distance between us. Got back to the blacktop and beat it to that restaurant, figuring I'd be safe with all the people there. I was safe, right up until those two private cops showed up; end of story. Oh yes, the guy was riding a black '11 or '12 Street Glide with that CVO Screaming Eagle package like the one Wolf described. That bike had some serious giddy-up. Not much info that will help you out, I'm afraid.

Didn't get the plates—the guy did look pretty big and was dressed in black with a dark shield on his skid-lid. *And,* he flipped me the bird when he went past."

"Did you see the guy parked anywhere before you turned off?"

Mark thought back for a moment, then answered. "You know, I thought I saw some headlights come on from beside the old store when I turned—not sure though."

Lute asked a few more questions, then made a couple of calls.

"What now?" Mark asked, obviously relieved to let Lute take charge.

"There's some stuff I have to check into before we do anything else, but it'll be a while before I hear anything. Don't tell anyone what happened today on the road. Right now, I need some shuteye, mind if I crash here for a while?"

"No man, you have a nice nap, I gotta go do the family thing for a while. Let me know if you need anything, bro."

Lute stretched out on the couch and fell asleep immediately. Mark went upstairs. The sound of a small child's laughter was soon heard throughout the house.

About eight pm, Wolf returned to Mark's house. As he entered the man cave, he was immediately concerned by the looks on his friend's faces. Typical greetings were exchanged, but the mood was somber.

"What's goin on . . . something happen after I left today?"

Mark looked at Lute. "You wanna tell him or should I?"

Lute said, "your story, you tell it."

"You have got to see this dude." He picked up his laptop and pushed a few buttons. On the wide screen, a video started, starring Mark. As he watched, the scene in the restaurant played out, the video shot by a nervous teenager that was shaking with predictable results. Mark paused the video as the window broke and then pointed at the biker in the background on the road. He zoomed in closer to reveal a big man, dressed in black leather, helmet, and riding a shiny black Harley Street Glide. The picture was grainy and unclear, but Wolf was reasonably sure that it was the biker he had spoken with at the Hawg Corral. Additionally, the bike was the same color and type. A knot of fear for his friend grew in his stomach.

"This thing's gone viral on the internet. I just hope the news channel doesn't pick it up. That guy look familiar?" He went on to tell Wolf about the encounter before the video was taken.

"So what do we do now?" Wolf looked at Lute. "What should our next move be? We gotta stop this guy before he kills somebody else."

"The bad thing is we can't prove anything, not to mention we don't know who or where he is. Oh yeah, did I mention that there's still no body?" Lute said.

"What about that anonymous tip? That should get them on the trail of the mayor's body and the killer."

"I thought you should read the note before I leave it." He handed the one page typed note to Wolf.

The note read:

> I want to be anonymous cause I'm scared for for my life. On Monday night of last week, I saw the murder of a man I believe is that missing mayor of Whiteville. This happened about 10:30 that nite in the field behind the church on Highway 52 near Helena. The mayor rode up in a shiny black Mercedes suv, and had a tall and well built, (not a fat one) woman that was wearing a black evening gown, and had straight blond hair, just past her shoulders. She was very good looking, like a prostitute with large boobs, long legs, and ears that were big and stuck out from her hair. She was much taller than the man maybe about 6 foot 1 or 2 and was very strong. A man that was much larger, maybe 6'6" or even taller, maybe 6'8", well built and very strong got out of the rear of the suv and put the mayor in a headlock. The woman grabbed the mayors head and broke his neck. I heard it snap from where I was hidden. After he fell to the ground, the woman checked his pulse, then twisted his head again. I am sure he is dead, his body jumped like in the movies. They started to drag the body up to the woods behind the picnic area. He may be buried there. I don't know for sure. The man also had a big and crooked nose that looked like it had been broken. He was bald or had very short hair like in the army.
>
> I think the killers planned to kill the mayor by things they said. They said they had a hole dug for his body and said something about a camera. They also said words that I heard on that biker show, like cagers. I saw them in my headlights as I drove off before they came after me.
>
> I think they may have worn disguises. I dont want to come forward cause I'm scared they will find me or my family and kill us. They are very mean spirited, cuss a lot, and dangerous. They reminded me of bikers. He called her Blondie.
>
> Please do not try to find me. That is all I know. I am sorry to have waited so long to come forward, but I thought you would have found them by now. Please be careful because those two are very dangerous and have guns. One of them shot at me as I drove off but missed.
>
> A good citizen

After reading the note, Wolf relaxed, then sat back in his chair and read it again. He appeared to be thinking, really concentrating as evidenced by the squinting of his eyes. Several minutes went by before he spoke.

"You know Lute, that's a real fine piece of literary work you got here. My first instinct was to correct all the grammatical errors, but then I realized the experts in the FBI will analyze it and profile the writer. It doesn't sound like me or you, but yet it doesn't sound like a hoax or some redneck that it won't get taken seriously. Nicely done, bro. You should write for a living."

"That's what I do. I spend more time writing and analyzing reports these days than anything else. Thanks for the compliment. Did I leave anything out that you can think of that won't point back to you?"

"Nope it's perfect, I just hope it don't stir up anything between the bikers and the police around here."

"Don't think it will unless they fit the description. I just wish I could put more in it based on what happened to Mark, maybe a description of the bikes. May be able to with the video on youtube. I've got to be careful, those Feds are real suspicious types. They might be coming by to talk to you, anyway."

Mark spoke up, "they can bring it on if they want to, I don't hassle easily unless it's in cuffs."

"So when is this note gonna turn up . . . you know it's got our prints all over it."

"No shit, Sherlock! I ain't stupid you know. It'll be reprinted and the note will be left on somebody's patrol car tomorrow. I pity that guy, he'll be in the hot seat with the FBI for hours. Got just the right guy in mind. Pissed me off when he gave my daughter a ticket a few months ago without even giving me a call first. Could have given her a warning, but nooo—gave her a ticket and scared the crap out of her. New cop . . . I caught some ribbing about that."

"Sounds like you got it all planned out, bro. Now about us; what should we be doing?"

"Business as usual. You have that Daytona trip coming up soon. Do it, act as if nothing is different. Write your stories, go to work, try to put it out of your mind. *Do not* confide in anybody else. Just watch your back and call me if you see either of those two or anything else suspicious. I'll keep you guys in the loop with what's going on from my end. Oh yeah, one more thing. Keep a low profile and stay out of trouble this time, please!"

"All right then, what do we name those two? Don't we need some kind of code names?" Mark asked in a way that suggested he had watched way too many movies. It was obvious he was joking.

Wolf joined, trying to break the tension of the moment and said, "maybe Big and Bigger or, even better, Big and Blondie?"

"Yeah, anybody listening would just think we're talking about biker babes."

"You guys should hire on at the comedy club with that act—just don't lose your day jobs." Lute said, then sat down and took a long pull on his beer.

No one spoke for a while, all three lost in their thoughts of what the future would bring and the impact on their lives. Many minutes went by before anybody spoke.

Wolf broke the silence first. "I'm going outside for a smoke." He stood and walked outside before anyone answered.

Lute and Mark looked at each other. "Better check it out and make sure he's OK. I'm going to go on line and see if there are new developments."

Mark grabbed two beers and went outside.

"What's up buddy?" He handed a beer to Wolf, then took the leftover joint out, lit it, and passed it to his friend.

"No thanks, I gotta keep a clear head and there ain't nada to celebrate. I gotta bad feeling it's gonna get real bad soon and I'm not feeling good at all about dragging you guys into this shit. I sure don't feel good about going to Daytona with this stuff getting ready to hit the fan."

"Dude you gotta go to keep everything looking as normal as possible. Besides, Lute's got everything all planned out. Don't worry so damn much, it's all gonna work out and they'll catch those assholes. What you need is a long ride. You need a wingman?"

"Naw, you know me, I ride alone. But, you're right, a road trip sounds real good right about now to clear my head and do some thinking."

"When ya leaving?"

Wolf thought for a minute before answering. "Probably Wednesday or Thursday, depends on when the funeral is. I'll be leaving after that. So when are you putting that pool in? It'll be getting hot before you know it."

"I figure another good month of getting customer's bikes ready for the riding season and I'll have enough cash to do it right. It's a surprise. When the family goes to the beach after school gets out, it'll be done when they get back. Contractor's already lined up to do the work and the old lady's birthday is the day they get back. Put it on that calendar of yours, gonna be a big blowout party that night."

Both looked up as Lute came out the door. "Funeral for Stag is gonna be Wednesday. Should be twenty or more bikes there. Oh yeah, Mark you're an internet movie star now, your video has more than ten thousand views. Can I get your autograph?"

"Screw you, dude. Did they get my best side?" he said primping and grinning.

"Your ugly ass ain't got no best side. Come on in, I've got it on the big screen. Y'all have got to see this, it's funny as hell and I enhanced it so you can see that big dude ride by in the background."

They filed in and took a seat. Lute stopped the video and zoomed in on the biker riding by. The picture was grainy and blurred, but it was easy to see that the bike was a CVO Street Glide with a very big man riding it. No other details were clear enough to add to the anonymous note.

"That the guy you saw, bro?" Lute asked.

"Can't tell for sure, but the bike and probably the rider are the ones I saw outside the Hawg that night. Not a lot of those CVO Street Glides in that color out there."

"Well, it gives us somewhere to start, anyway. Anybody got anything else? If not, let's all go get in some family time before all this crap comes out tomorrow."

With that, they went outside, Wolf and Lute mounting their bikes. Mark's cute young daughter ran over and gave them hugs, then stepped back and was picked up and held closely in Mark's arms. She waved as they rode off down the gravel driveway. At the end of the driveway, they stopped. Lute held out his hand to his friend.

"You packing dude?" he asked.

"Always," Wolf replied, patting his tank bag.

"Keep it close at all times and get some practice in. Don't worry, we'll get those two real soon. Stay in touch and watch your back." He reached out and they bumped fists.

"Likewise," he said as he twisted the throttle and let the clutch out. Lute revved his throttle and rode off in the other direction.

CHAPTER 16

Blondie, aka Cheetah, aka Ronnie, aka, numerous other names, had been on the computer for more than an hour when 45 came roaring up the gravel drive, sliding to a stop at the front door and throwing loose gravel against the side of the trailer. She had gotten the address of the owners of the two Vulcans that were at Resort 25 and had already entered the info into the GPS on the table. An easy task, she had looked at other websites, including Facebook, VROC, and others, and then, on a whim, googled "Resort 25" and found a link to a very recent posting on youtube. She was watching this as 45 came strutting through the door. As she watched, she laughed as the scene revealed the acts of the bumbling cop, then froze as she recognized the biker she had so recently seen at the service riding the red and black Vulcan. She paused the video when the window broke out, seeing her now present companion ride by on the road outside the restaurant in the background. Saving the still shot, she resumed the video to the end. She slowly stood up, and turned to face 45.

"What are you watching, Blondie?" he asked.

"You, you dumbshit, stupid motherfucker." She slapped him hard upside the head, taking him totally by surprise. He froze, his hand on the gun in his belt.

"What the fuck was that for, bitch?" he asked in a threatening manner.

"Take a look at this," she said, bringing up the saved shot from the video. She enhanced and zoomed in on the biker on the road. The picture was grainy and unclear, but to one familiar with bikes, it was easy to tell it was the CVO Street Glide, ridden by a big man.

"You want to tell me about this? It's gotten more hits than you can imagine in just a few hours."

"Well, for one thing, I'm pretty damned sure I found our witness. That guy knows how to handle his bike real good, even in the dirt. That's the guy that was riding the red and black Vulcan with the batwing."

"Well, while you were being stupid, I got his and the other's addresses from their plates. That other Vulcan rider rides pretty good, too. I followed him all the way to Harperville before coming back here. He handles curves like a pro. I don't think we should take any chances, we'll do them both to be sure."

"You got a plan?" he asked, relaxing and taking a swig from his beer, then pulling out and lighting up a joint.

"I've got to do more research, but until then, you need to stay around here and not be seen on that bike of yours—let's take no more chances. If your guy's the one, he'll be on full alert now. My guy's got no clue I was following him. He'll be the first to die. He rides that road a lot, judging by the way he rode it. Might just be easier to kill him there if we do it right."

"Alright, you set it up. *I'm* gonna kick back and work on my bike to change its appearance. You don't look too good dressed as a man. Do something about it and we can have some fun later."

"And you can do yourself. You keep that stupid shit up, you'll be having fun with a bunch of guys behind bars."

"Never happen, Blondie, I figure I'll end it all in a hail of lead, my blood and guts spread all over. I'll make sure there will be more that go down with me, too."

"If you don't mind, I'd prefer to put that off for a few years, so don't be in a hurry to be a desperado. Let's just finish this job and then get the hell out of this redneck county. After that, you're welcome to fly solo if you want to do the outlaw bit."

She resolved to kill him herself when all the loose ends were tied up. She had no doubt he would do the same without hesitation. For now, she needed him. 45 went outside and took his bike to the garage, while she returned to her research on the computer. She was doing background checks on the two bike owners. As she suspected, the biker she had followed lived just past Childersburg, an area from where Hwy 25 would be a scenic route to his workplace in Leeds.

The other plate belonged to one Tommy Moore, and further search turned up that he was a judge in a nearby county. *What would a judge be doing in a place like that at night and riding a bike?* Puzzled, she continued to dig deeper and found out he had a pilot's license, wrote for a local paper, and was currently up for re-election. She pondered on the last item for a minute. Why would a judge up for re-election pass up an opportunity to get publicity by catching criminals? Maybe he himself, had been up to something that would not look so good if it was discovered. The biker in the video certainly was not this man. Just who was the biker in the video if not the owner of the bike? She wrote down the phone number and decided to give the Judge a call.

The phone was answered on the second ring. "Hello, Judge Moore."

"Judge Moore, this is Alice Johnson from the Birmingham News. Have you seen the video currently on youtube that was filmed locally and is very popular right now, with several thousand views in less than a day?"

"No, Ms. Johnson, I don't spend my time surfing the net like so many do these days, I have more serious business to attend to. What is in the video and how does it involve me?"

"Judge, your bike, a red and black Vulcan was being ridden by the biker in the video. The bike is not in the video, but a witness places it at the scene."

"Ms. Johnson, I'll have you know that the bike you referred to is in the shop and has been since last Wednesday. Was it involved in an accident or a crime?"

"Sir, we know you weren't riding it, but we are trying to track down who was."

"I don't know. The bike should be at the Twisted Iron motorcycle shop where I left it. Was a crime committed involving the bike?" He was beginning to sound alarmed and was demanding in the way he repeated the question.

"Not at all, sir. Just a minor incident that was entertaining to watch. How long have you owned the bike?"

"Just a few months. As a matter of fact, my friend is doing some performance modifications and may have been test riding it. You said the video is on youtube? How would I search for that?"

"Go to the site and search by putting in the words, "biker" and "cop", that should bring it up. Could you provide us with the name and number of the friend that is working on it so we can get in contact with him?" she asked.

"I'll tell you what, Ms. Johnson, give me your number and I'll have him call you. I'd like to see this video before I give out any more information. What's your number?"

"Sure, I understand sir. Please tell your friend we just want to get a few details about what happened before the video." She gave him a fictitious number. "By the way, where is Twisted Iron?"

"Whiteville, on 31. I'll let him know. It's up to him if he wants to call."

He hung up, went to his study and pulled up youtube.com. He was both astounded and amused as the events unfolded on the screen. He dialed Mark's number and waited until he answered. He relayed the information to his friend, who assured him the bike was fine and that he had indeed, been on a test ride. Mark apologized for the call from the reporter, saying he would call her immediately to clarify the facts. He was surprised that the bike had been reported and that a reporter was asking questions.

Mark dialed the number and was very concerned to find the number was to a restaurant. He googled the reporter's name and did not find her listed on staff at the Birmingham News. He decided to call Lute and advise him about this recent development.

Lute was indeed troubled to hear about the mysterious caller.

"Based on what the woman said in the call, I believe that may have been the female killer that called the Judge. With the answers that he gave her, she probably removed both of you from her list of possible witnesses. How sure are you of the facts?"

"He's a judge, Lute. He only deals in facts, and in fact, is one of the most conservative bikers I know. He was very detailed when he relayed the conversation to me, and I took notes. His main concern right now is how this might look in the news—you know he's up for re-election."

"No I didn't. You know, if someone had written down the bike's plate and given it out to the news or the police, the judge would have had a lot more calls by now. No, I think the only one that would take notice of the plate would be the ones searching for you. Inadvertently, the judge cleared you in their minds as to being the witness they're looking for. I'm also sure they would never think the judge was the witness mainly because he is a judge. What really bothers me the most is that these two are very resourceful and will not stop until they find and eliminate anyone they think could be the witness. I keep coming back to a question that has been on my mind. Why was the mayor killed in the first place?"

"Certainly a mystery—I didn't like the noise ordinance, but overall, he was pretty good at getting things done in the community, even if his old lady was pulling his strings."

There was silence while Lute was thinking. "Whatever the motive was for the hit, it doesn't change the fact that those two are looking for the witness and will find a way to eliminate anybody they think it could be. A very dangerous situation for anybody riding a bike like Wolf's."

"You said it."

"Things will change quickly when the note is found. Be ready, it's going to be a busy day for yours truly. Don't be surprised if you get visited by the FBI, too."

"I guess you could use some sleep. Talk to you soon."

"Yep, you got that right. I'll talk to you later."

At the trailer in Shelby, Blondie was not completely convinced the Judge wasn't the one they sought. The bike was taken in for upgrades—why? She knew he was a pilot and deduced he would have excellent riding skills as a biker. She decided to investigate further with some surveillance. She resolved to do the work herself, having little confidence in the discretion of her partner. After checking the weather for the next day, she decided to take a break. Grabbing a couple of beers, she went out to the shed to check on the alterations 45 was making to his bike. Surprised by the drop in temperature and the total darkness outside, she hurried to the shed where she knew the space heater would have the interior warm and comfortable.

His bike was in pieces—the fairing, tank, and hard bags in an area that was surrounded by opaque plastic sheets hung from ceiling to floor. The smell of paint permeated the air, an indication of the painstaking work of her partner. He was a skilled painter, as evidenced by the paintwork on his collection of bikes at the farm where they lived. What was most surprising was the fast pace at which he worked. The parts now had reddish-orange tribal flames, enhanced by glimmers of chrome that covered the ghost flames of the factory paint. It seemed like such a waste to ruin a great factory custom paint job, an opinion she shared with her partner.

"That's the real beauty of this job, Blondie. It's all a peel and stick latex wrap that can be removed quickly if needed. Cool, huh?"

"I gotta admit, if this career doesn't work out for you, you might have a new one disguising stolen bikes or maybe painting cop cars in prison. Nice work." She handed him a beer. "I've got an early morning tomorrow, so I'm going to crash soon. I need you to come up with the plan for the biker that works in Leeds. I left his bio and details on the desk inside. Be creative, we'll do it together. The weather looks good for a few days, he'll probably be riding. The funeral for the dead guy is Wednesday. They're burying him at the veteran's cemetery in Montevallo. I mapped it out for you."

"Thanks for all the help," he said with extreme sarcasm in his voice. "Don't know how I ever survived without you."

"Alright, I got it, just trying to be helpful. You set it up. Just don't get busted or have your picture on the web—again. Later." She walked out the door, letting it slam behind her. She could hear him laughing as she walked towards the trailer. It really pissed her off, but she let it go for now.

At seven the next morning, Blondie, disguised as Ronnie, was parked in a plain rental van across the road and a hundred yards from where the judge's driveway turned off county road 21. According to her research, the Judge was an empty nester living with his wife. His children were grown with their own separate lives. The judge did alright for himself, living modestly in a one story, ranch-style home on five acres. When the garage door opened, a newer Camry backed out. The open door revealed a grey, cruiser-style bike parked inside. A Chevrolet pickup was parked outside the garage in order to leave room for the judge's bikes in the garage. He had his priorities right, she thought. She watched through binoculars as the Camry sat idling in front of the garage. In a few minutes, the judge came outside through the garage and stopped at the Camry's side and bent down to kiss his wife. As Blondie watched, the garage door closed and the Camry drove down the driveway and entered the highway, turning in the opposite direction from where she sat watching. The judge got in his truck and drove down the driveway, not giving a second look up the road to where she was parked. She gave him a long lead, certain she knew where he was headed. To her surprise, he turned away from his expected route to work and headed north on US 280. She narrowed the gap and followed.

Almost an hour later, the Judge's truck stopped outside a motorcycle repair shop in Whiteville. The sign outside read *Twisted Iron* painted on a black background. Blondie slowed but kept on going, pulling a U-turn a few blocks past, and then parked across the four-lane road from the shop, got out her binoculars, and watched as the Judge and the biker from the video engaged in conversation. They walked over to a red and black Vulcan parked outside, where it was obvious that they were going over the bike's features. To her, it seemed that the Judge was not happy with what was being discussed. She continued to wait, intrigued by this turn of events. The judge got back in his truck and headed south towards the courthouse. She continued to follow until he pulled into the courthouse parking lot and went inside.

As she had neared the town, Blondie saw several signs staked in the ground with the Judge's face and "re-elect Judge Moore" in bold letters upon them. She began to devise a plan to interrogate and then murder the judge, making it look like a home invasion.

At noon, she was parked outside the diner a few blocks down from the courthouse when, just as expected, the judge came walking up to where she, dressed as a man, was sitting astride her Vaquero.

"Nice bike! I've been thinking about trading mine in for one. You like the way it handles?" he said as he stopped next to her. He was quick to stick out his hand like most politicians do.

"Appreciate it and yes I do. Say, aren't you that judge," she said pointing to the picture in the diner's window. "I never would have figured you as a rider. What kind of scooter do you ride?"

"I ride a Vulcan, too. A Nomad. Been thinking about upgrading to a Vaquero. I'm having mine souped up a bit, but I really like the idea of a six-speed. You had lunch yet?"

"Nope, just pulled up. This place any good?"

"Best home cooking in town and also the *only* place in town to eat. Come on in, my treat if you don't mind me bending your ear about your bike. My name is Tommy Moore."

"Mine is Ronnie Smith, Judge; glad to know you. I don't mind talking bikes at all, thanks for the invite. Always a pleasure talking with a fellow biker." Blondie dismounted, then walked with him into the small restaurant and then taking a seat at a table by the window.

After talking about the Vaquero for a while, Blondie turned the conversation to family. The judge was not hesitant to talk about his family, obviously proud of his kids who didn't visit often enough, he said. Blondie asked if he had any dinner plans and learned that the judge was planning to surprise his wife with a quiet evening at home. Blondie was a master manipulator and agreed to meet the judge at his home after work to let him ride the Vaquero which she said was up for sale. She told the judge she would consider a trade for a lesser cruiser and cash. The judge readily agreed and told her about an almost new Harley Sportster 1200 he had with low miles. He was almost apologetic in his explanation for not riding it, saying it was due to his love of the Vulcan's more comfortable ride. He added that it was a shame not to ride such a great bike, then asked if it might be of interest as a trade. Blondie feigned interest, saying she liked the Harley's sporty ride. The judge gave her his address. Because his wife got home earlier than he due to her job as a teacher, he said she could get there early and check out the bike. He'd let his wife know to expect him.

As they were leaving the restaurant, the sheriff walked up and whispered in the judge's ear. The judge nodded, and the sheriff walked back across the street. Blondie decided to put the plan for a home invasion style killing on hold for now, not wanting to be the subject of a manhunt later. She decided to call the judge later and arrange a fatal meeting at a better time. Blondie and the judge said their goodbyes like old biker buddies. The judge walked back across the street as Blondie started her bike. As she sat there allowing the oil to circulate and thoroughly lubricate the engine, four sheriff vehicles, 3 of which were patrol cars and the other a cargo van, pulled out of the lot and headed northwest towards Clanton. Blondie wished the judge was still there so she could ask what was going on.

Back in Leeds, 45 sat in a bar on Main Street, looking out the window to where a black Nomad with a fairing sat in the parking lot across the street. He had called the biker's workplace and learned from a helpful, and very chatty employee about her boss' habits, which included his departure time around four pm. 45 already knew the road the Nomad's owner typically took home after work. He had quickly devised a plan to terminate the man, leaving his body broken and bleeding beside a little county road a few miles south of Resort 25. With the assistance of his partner and a little luck, the plan would work well. He knew it would be deemed an accident due to the planned interaction of a medium-sized doe with the bike. He had trapped the deer near the trailer, and it was now tranquilized and sleeping peacefully in the van.

As he watched, his intended victim came out of the office building across the street. Glancing at the time on his cellphone, 45 made a call and told his partner the plan was a go. As expected, she was already at the rendezvous along the lightly traveled back country road he knew the biker used as a short cut home. She would hook up with him along the lonely road where she had parked her bike. It was just off the pavement in an overgrown clearing behind an old abandoned house along the route he had scouted earlier in the day. The van would be used to carry out the plan. 45 came out and got in the van, started it, then drove slowly off, watching as his intended victim was fastening his helmet. He drove as fast as he dared, not wanting to chance being pulled over by the cops. Several miles past Resort 25, he went right where the road forked. Seeing his partner standing beside the road, he stopped to let her get in.

"See anybody?" he asked.

"Everything's clear, only 2 cars have been by in the last 30 minutes. You sure about the plan?"

"You just grab that doe, remove the zip ties, and get ready to plant it in his windshield. He should be just a few minutes behind us. In two point five miles, we'll go around the curve where I'll put on the blinker and slow down. He should go to pass us at that time. Pull the cord when I sound the horn. The doors will open and the bike will be right behind the van—don't miss. Here he comes now."

He accelerated rapidly while she cut the ties on the sedated deer. As anticipated, the bike narrowed the gap, then slowed and took a position four car lengths behind. 45 sped up, went around the sharp curve, then slowed quickly by downshifting the van and turning on the right turn signal. As the black Vulcan started to speed up and pass, he blew the horn and moved left while speeding up. At that instant, the bike was just a few feet directly behind the van, its' rider cursing and braking hard. The twin doors of the van sprang open immediately, and Blondie, inside with the deer in her arms, extended and tossed the deer onto the front fender of the Vulcan. The lone biker jammed both brakes on out of instinct, causing both wheels to lock up and skid. The front of the bike wobbled rapidly, then the rear of the bike swung around and caught up with the front as the deer and bike separated. The biker had the handle bars in a death grip while the rest of his body began to come up and over the bike. Both bike and rider left the road, sliding down the slope along the roadside.

The bike came to a halt with the sound of crumpling metal and breaking tree limbs. The rider came right behind the bike crashing into the side of the small tree the bike had hit and sheering off several limbs. Both came to a rest a few yards inside the tree line, twenty yards off the road. A few yards further, the van came to a stop and the driver, dressed in camo, jumped out and ran back towards the crash site. Blondie jumped out and ran to the open driver's door. She got in and drove off. 45 descended the slope to where the biker lay, moaning and writhing in pain. He took the crash victim's helmeted head in both hands and, while looking into his eyes, twisted violently upward and to the right. The victim's body went as limp as fresh road kill. 45 continued to look at the man's eyes as his lids closed. He detected a slight movement of the man's chest, so he hoisted him by his armpits, his head lolling backwards, neck obviously broken, then walked back to the tree with the broken limbs. With the ease of a parent carrying a child, he hoisted the body and thrust it violently onto the remains of a protruding, sheared off limb on the tree that had stopped the bike and its rider's plunge into the woods. He was satisfied with the results as the sharp edge of the limb protruded from the biker's abdomen. As he stood there admiring his work, the body slid off the branch, hitting the ground and rolling downhill a few yards, coming to a rest next to the wrecked and shattered Vulcan. He walked to the front of the Vulcan and looking closely, he could make out a few hairs from the deer in the headlight housing. He smashed the lens, then removed a few shards of glass.

Taking his camera out, he snapped a few pictures of the scene, wishing the body had stayed in place on the tree. He smiled at the thought of a first responder's reaction to the sight. At that moment, the van came to a halt on the slope above, and 45 scrambled up the hill, being careful to leave no tracks. The deer was starting to move where it lay next to the road. He walked over and stepped on its' heaving chest, then thrust his size 14 boot downward and was rewarded by the feel of snapping ribs. He bent over and inserted some headlight glass in the deer's chest area where his boot had been. He dropped the remaining pieces onto the road's asphalt surface, then ran over to the van and got in. Blondie accelerated rapidly away.

"Congratulations, that was under three minutes from start to finish. I'm impressed."

"All in a day's work. I don't think he's our man, he didn't know how to handle a skid, but it was good practice anyway. I always hate to mess up a nice bike, but at least it's not a Harley. They can mass produce those rice burners. What's up with the judge? I thought you would have a plan for his demise by now."

"I did, but the sheriff saw my face, so now we're going to have to make it look like an accident instead of a robbery. Don't worry; I'll set it up so he'll come to us. We'll do him in the morning on his way to work."

She pulled off the road near the old abandoned house and got out, walking quickly down the overgrown driveway to where her bike was hidden. She called the judge and apologized profusely for not being able to meet that evening. She requested that instead, he ride the bike to work the next day, saying she could check out the bike on the judge's lunch break. The judge, excited at the prospect of owning a Vaquero, readily agreed to ride the Sportster and meet the next day. She requested that he bring his title with him.

Judge Moore spent the evening cleaning and polishing his 2008 Harley-Davidson Sportster 1200, then installed the new windshield he had purchased for it but never gotten around to installing. As many wives do, his could not understand his enthusiasm for the trade, saying he already had one Vulcan, and asking why he needed a second one. He had given up on her understanding the differences in bikes and why one wasn't enough, but secretly hoped that one day she would understand, and even want to learn to ride herself. After detailing the Sportster, he went on the internet and did research on the Vaquero, reading reviews and studying specs. An hour later, he was disappointed and more than a little upset when she turned her back on him in bed, rejecting his need for affection and not quelling his excitement at the prospect of owning a bad-to-the-bone Vaquero. He fell asleep thinking of riding the Vaquero on the twisty road leading to Mt. Cheaha.

CHAPTER 17

O fficer John Walker began his shift like most days with role call then a briefing on activities in the community. He received several routine assignments for the day. As expected, he would do traffic duty at the middle school and then act as the resource officer for the first half of his day, covering for the regular officer that was not available that morning. As had become the new normal, an FBI agent was in attendance, but had nothing new to add to the morning's briefing.

Officer John Walker had been on the force for almost a year, and was accepted and liked by his fellow officers. He had joined the force after being discharged from the Army where he had been an MP for four years. Growing up in the nearby small community of Vincent, he already had local connections and was hired on due to the economic expansion going on in the small southern town. He had ruffled the feathers of a few on the force, but overall was known as a dedicated and fair police officer that played by the rules and could be depended on to keep a cool head in an emergency. He was of Cherokee Indian and black descent, and as could be expected, was jokingly referred to as "Johnny Walker Red", or sometimes just "Red". He smiled when he thought it could have just been "Black", but knew that it would have been too politically incorrect.

Directing traffic was his least favorite activity, but he was appreciative of the smiles and waves from local parents dropping off their kids. It was not unusual to find an occasional thank-you card tucked under his wiper with a gift card for a local restaurant tucked inside. Sometimes, there was even a name and phone number included. He never responded to these obvious flirtations, knowing that no good would come from doing so. He figured they were from lonely housewives that were turned on by the uniform and had way too much imagination, or perhaps just needed an exciting break from their monotonous daily lives while the kids and husbands were away.

At mid-day, Officer Walker went to his patrol car and found an envelope tucked under the wiper. He stuck it on his clipboard, then got in his patrol car. He was hungry and looking forward to enjoying the home-style cooking at the City Diner while meeting his buddy there. Many on the force ate there lately, mostly due to the distance from the station—close, but far enough away. As he sat at the table waiting for his buddy to arrive, an unmarked unit pulled up and the lead detective known as Lute got out, accompanied by the FBI agent that was at the morning's briefing. They came inside, Lute stopping by his table to say hello, and asking if he was eating alone. When he said he was meeting another officer on break, Lute offered to join them and took a seat.

Officer Walker was pleased at this, knowing Lute was respected by all and had a lot of influence when it came to promotions and policy. He was relieved at his friendly demeanor, remembering a ticket he had given Lute's daughter a few months past. Maybe he could get the inside scoop on what was going on with the investigation into the mayor's disappearance, and be on the inside for a change. The FBI agent's name was Watson, and he seemed pleasant. The talk turned to family and previous experience. Officer Walker mainly listened, offering little about himself except when asked. He was pleasantly surprised when he was asked about his background and pleased at the reaction when he told of his Army experience.

"So John, I don't see a ring, you got a lady friend out there?"

"No sir, not yet sir, but I'm working on it."

"I can tell you are—that card to someone special?" Lute asked, pointing at the card on his clipboard.

"No sir, the card was on the windshield of my patrol car when I came out of the middle school. I figure it's another thank-you card. We find them from time to time like that. Folks around here sure are nice and show their appreciation all the time. This sure is a friendly little family town and it's a pleasure to serve here."

"Enough politicking—you going to open it or you saving it for later? You know, I think we could all use a little appreciation right about now."

"Sure sir, be glad to." He then tore open the sealed flap. Instead of a card, he withdrew a single sheet of paper. He opened it, and then drew an inward breath, the color beginning to drain from his face.

The FBI agent reacted first. "Let me see that!" he said in a bit too loud commanding tone of voice, causing several in the small diner to turn and look in their direction. Lute was expressionless as he observed, secretly pleased with the way the note's discovery had gone down, but feeling a little sorry for Officer Walker and what he figured would soon be coming his way. The agent grabbed the note and started to read. Lute looked over at the note, then sent officer Walker to get his evidence kit from the car.

The agent was still studying the piece of paper when Officer Walker returned inside, another patrol officer behind him. Lute withdrew gloves from the kit then turned to the agent and said, "you might want to use these. Mind if I take a look?"

"Go ahead, but don't touch it until it's bagged," the agent responded as he too, put on gloves and bagged the envelope. Lute placed the letter in the baggie and began to read. He took his time, but knowing what the letter said by heart, he was more interested with the events unfolding around him. The agent had stepped away and was having an animated conversation on his phone with what was probably the agent in charge. The two officers had taken a protective stance, seemingly to ward off possible intruders. All activity in the diner had come to a halt as the small lunch crowd watched with fascination. Lute looked up from reading, and then stood.

"Don't let anyone near this table. I've got to call in." He stepped outside and called the chief. As he hung up, he could hear the sirens of approaching units growing in volume as they got closer. He lit a smoke then tried hard to suppress the need to laugh at the events now occurring around him. Two unmarked FBI units, followed by a plain dark blue van came screeching into the lot. A minute later, units from the city police department started pulling in. As he stood watching, an agent put crime scene tape around Officer Walker's patrol unit and directed another officer to stand guard.

Minutes later, the FBI agents came out of the diner, and his friend, Agent Watson, invited him to ride back with them. He declined by saying he was driving, but would be there as soon as possible. Not used to being told no by local cops, Watson seemed a bit perturbed when he went to another FBI agent's car and got in. He resolved to hurry to keep from upsetting him further, as Watson was a potentially good source of inside information on the FBI's investigation.

He advised Officer Walker to hightail it back to the station with the next available unit. He got in his own car and drove to the middle school. He went inside and asked to look at the security camera display. He knew from a time he had investigated a break-in at the school, there were no cameras that would catch activity around the police resource officer's parking spot. He made a digital copy anyway to take back to headquarters. He then called Watson and asked him to dispatch some agents to interview all drivers when school got out. He called three of his own detectives to question the teachers. He knew it was a futile use of man hours, but it would be expected. He decided to remain at the scene and wait for Watson and his team to join him. He went to the principal's office, a place he knew well from visits on behalf of his own son, along with a few others on official business. He and Principal Jones had a great working relationship, and they flirted with each other whenever meeting. Both knew it was but a facade. They enjoyed it anyway as both had great, if a little warped, senses of humor.

Just as he finished informing his friend about the pending teacher interviews and warning about the FBI's intense interview style, as if on cue, agent Watson came into the office without knocking, two other agents in tow.

"You got a roster, Lieutenant? We only have two hours to talk to all the teachers and staff."

"Got it covered dude. Have your guys start on the first hallway, my guys will get the rest. At three, I need two of your agents to help question the drivers picking up kids. Here's a list of questions." Lute stood in his official stance, using his best authoritative tone of voice.

"I'll take a look at the questions and see if we need to add anything. Three pm is when school lets out?"

"3:10 actually, but the drivers start lining up around three. I figured we needed a head start."

"Great, and really, thanks for your support—I'm making note of your efficiency. See you back here at 2:45 sharp." He turned and walked out of the office on his way to watch the security video.

Principal Jones came over and gave him a hug. "That's for good luck; I think you're going to need it. See you later, Lute." She blew him a kiss as he left.

The interviews went smoothly, with all but a few readily answering questions. The others, when told of the importance of finding the letter writer, agreed to cooperate. However, no information of use was obtained. Everyone hoped the driver interviews would turn up something, except for Lute, who was silently amused because he knew nobody had seen him drive by at eleven am and place the envelope under the wiper.

Lute therefore, was not at all surprised when nothing of use was learned from the drivers who were alarmed by the police presence. They agreed the interviews would be repeated in the morning, as at least 35 of the drivers were not the same as the ones that dropped the kids off that morning. Agent Watson agreed to get his team to conduct the interviews with the support of two city officers to handle traffic. Lute was pleased that he would not be wasting city time on what he knew was a dead end.

Consequently, he was very displeased when he learned that an agent had detained a citizen that was found to have a joint in his possession and was being interrogated as if he had left the note. The agent had detected extreme nervousness by "Ole Smokey" as he was known in the community. This Vietnam vet that stayed to himself had a purple heart for the napalm burns he suffered over half of the lower part of his body in the war. Indeed, the only time people saw him was at veteran events and when taking his grandson to school. Lute knew he smoked marijuana to handle the never-ending pain from his wounds. Everyone tended to let him be out of respect for his sacrifices for his country.

Lute inwardly felt bad for the unintended result of the note's discovery. Nothing he could do now but try to do damage control by calming down the aging veteran. He called the Southern Veteran's Motorcycle Club's president and explained the situation. A call to arms was issued and about thirty minutes after four, more than fifty bikers from the club came rolling into the municipal parking lot, revving their loud pipes, and creating a rumbling vibration throughout the building. He smiled when he looked outside his second floor window, noting that every biker had backed against the curb, pipes pointed directly at the building. In unison, the bikers all revved their engines, causing several windows to crack. The window in the office that the FBI was using as their command post, shattered and fell inward. Opening his own window and looking outside, he noted several assault weapons jutting from the shattered window and pointed at the bikers below. He acted quickly, running down the hallway while yelling for all to stand down. He burst into the office and ran to the window. Hanging out the empty window frame as far as he dared, he gave the cut engines sign. The signal was repeated by the bikers outside, and within seconds, there was an eerie silence.

"I think they're trying to tell you that you got the wrong man in the sweat box. I don't want to tell y'all what to do, but I'd finish up with him real quick, and get him out of here soon," Lute said with enthusiasm. He added, "in case you didn't notice, there are some real nosy reporters with cameras out there, all just looking for a juicy story about the Feds hassling a decorated war hero. Something to think about."

The agent in charge agreed, and said, "we were about to let him out. You want to press charges on the drugs?"

"Not today after what y'all put him through." He turned and looked at the chief, standing in the doorway listening. "What do you say chief?"

"By all means, let him go. And have the officer taking him home stop and get supper for the whole family. Please extend my apologies to all. Where's his grandson?" the chief asked, giving the agent in charge a scathing look that only surfaced when the chief was extremely pissed off, as was obviously the case now.

Lute spoke first. "He's down in the simulation room shooting bad guys—having one heck of a good time, I hear. Chief, I'll take them home if you don't mind. I'm a friend of the family. Their kids know mine real well."

"Thanks for volunteering Lieutenant, I really liked the way you handled the noise problem. I'm sending the FBI the bill for the glass." He turned and looked at the FBI agent once more. The agent remained silent.

"Y'all need to tell me what you got. I've got to face the mayor pro tem who just happens to be the missing, and now most likely, dead mayor's widow. She'll demand answers. Lute, you get out of here and get Ole Smokey home. I got this."

"Good luck sir, I'm glad I'm not in your shoes—be seeing you." Lute walked quickly out of the room with a smug smile, having a good idea of the anger that was about to be unleashed upon the agents. He almost felt sorry for them.

The trip away from the station with Ole Smokey and his grandson was uneventful, the dark windows of the cruiser hiding the passengers from the reporters. Lute was pleased to hear the boy excitedly tell his grandpa about the fun he had shooting bad guys. Lute knew that the memory of the questioning the old vet had undergone would quickly fade, and probably by the time they got home. Such was the memory of old pot smokers—CRS was a common ailment with them and one he was thankful for now. *They'll love KFC chicken for dinner, courtesy of the city.*

After delivering them to their family home, he went to his own house, changed, and hopped on his bike, a Harley-Davidson Road King with way too many accessories including pipes, seat, and chrome everywhere. He had the Screaming Eagle conversion done, so his bike pumped out gobs of torque. He knew a spirited ride would ease the tension and guilt at the way the day had turned out.

An hour later, he turned into Mark's driveway. As he rode up, the garage door opened to reveal two fully dressed Vulcan Nomads, both complete with batwing fairings. One was Wolf's, and the other he had seen the Judge and more recently, Mark riding. He dismounted and went inside to brief his friends and catch the news.

"Dude, you gotta watch this clip on the news. You're some kind of TV star now," Mark said with a grin, extending his hand.

Mark replayed the 30 second clip showing Lute hanging out the window and quieting the motorcycles. You could hear and see him a few seconds earlier bursting into the FBI office and yelling. The clip ended when the agents lowered their assault weapons, and the noise from the bikes was silenced.

Wolf piped up, "Kind of reminds me of Moses or maybe Bruce Willis in one of his Die Hard movies, minus all the blood. Oh, did I mention they're both a lot purtier than you? But really man, great job—I'm glad you're on my side!" He grabbed Lute's hand and gave a solid chest pump to his friend.

"Y'all going to kiss, hurry up. I want to hear the details of what happened at city hall today. What did they do to piss off so many bikers like that?" Mark said, pointing at the recliner while handing him a beer.

"Thanks, man. I really need a beer and maybe something a little stronger after the day I've had. Overall, it was a pretty fun and productive day. Y'all are just seeing the culmination of the day's events. Lute took a long swallow of beer, then was handed a shot glass of tequila. Glasses were lifted in a toast.

"Here's to a well-executed plan! Tell us all about it, we're sitting on the edge of our seats here," Wolf said, gesturing with the bottle of Jose. "Another one, dude?"

"No thanks, I'm good for now. It all started around eleven this morning at the middle school . . ." He continued giving a detailed explanation of lunch and the note's discovery, and then went on to astonish his friends when he told about the interviews. He finished by telling about Ole Smoky and the surrounding activities that led up to the news clip.

"So that's how the vet's club appeared on the scene. I thought you might have had something to do with it. Why get them involved?" Mark asked.

"Well, I was feeling pretty bad about the hassle those FBI jerks were giving an innocent, decorated war vet. I had no idea it would turn out like that, but in the end, it seems like it turned out pretty good and Ole Smoky and his kin got a free supper on the city's dime."

"Turn the sound up, looks like they've released info from the note to the reporters." As soon as he spoke, his cell phone rang with his Dragnet ring tone for official calls from the brass at city hall.

As they watched, descriptions of the two killers were given to the public. They were described as "persons of interest" and the public was advised to avoid approaching them and to call in on the special tip line. The nickname for the woman was given, and a substantial reward was offered.

Mark and Wolf exchanged knowing looks. They pitied anyone matching the description. Lute closed his cell phone and frowned.

"Crap! I have to go check out the church. The chief wants me to call the shots and supervise the search. It's going to be a long night."

"We're feeling your pain Lute. Anything we can do?"

"Just stay clear of that area—no telling who may get stopped and questioned. If it's like the school fiasco today and you're riding a bike in this county, you can almost depend on getting stopped. You guys got any new ideas?"

"Nope. Wait a minute, what if we put out the word for all the clubs to ride—they can't stop everybody on a bike; there aren't enough cops out there to do that."

"Yeah, but those they do may get pissed off and do something stupid. Did you forget what happened today with Ole Smokey at city hall? This town's an overheated pressure cooker ready to explode. Advise everybody you know to just stay calm. This will blow over soon." Lute stood up to leave.

"Dude, I'm real sorry for the extra BS you're going through on my account. You are taking way too many risks, and I really appreciate it."

"You would do the same, bro, besides, I would have played it the same way if I had been in your boots. Don't sweat it. Get packed and take your trip to Daytona. I'll keep you up to date with what's happening around here."

They all shook hands. Minutes later, the sound of Lute's bike was heard as he started it and let it warm up, followed in a few minutes by the rumble of his exhaust that faded as he rode away.

Lute was glad it was only a few miles to the church. The temperature had dropped drastically when the sun went down. He was brought to a complete stop a half mile from the murder scene by the line of cars ahead. Not being able to identify the reason for the delay, he figured the FBI might have a hand in the traffic backup. He decided to ride the shoulder around the stopped cars, smiling at the signs of displeasure from the drivers in the cars he passed. Several even honked their horns. As he topped the hill, he saw the reason for the long line of traffic. No less than five patrol units lined the road, blue lights flashing and casting the eerie blue-tinted light on the surrounding area and blinding the drivers going by. There were units from the two neighboring towns, a highway patrol unit, and a sheriff's car on the road. He was stopped a little too enthusiastically by a young deputy whose hand was on the gun in his holster. Lute slowly pulled his jacket up to reveal his badge. He was allowed to pass and turn into the entrance to the church. As he ascended the hill and rounded the curve around the church, he was astounded at the scene before him. It looked like a law enforcement carnival—several tents, crime scene trucks, and dozens of cars from many different agencies were there. Spotlights were in place and the sound of radios and generators made it difficult to hear the exhaust on the bike he was riding. He parked next to the tent with the most activity, noting the abundance of agents with jackets with the big letters, FBI emblazoned on the back. Agent Watson walked over and extended his hand.

"What a zoo you guys got here . . . what gives with all this? A little overkill, don't you think? Also, can you get them to tone down the lights on the road down there . . . pretty blinding to the drivers." Lute asked.

He was rewarded by Watson making a radio request to the officers manning the checkpoint on the road below.

"Maybe it does seem like an overzealous response, but after this afternoon's fiasco, the boss thought this spot would be better to set up a temporary HQ in order to control the press. That video made us look real bad, and as a result, there's a lot of heat from Washington."

"Yeah, but all this as a result of an anonymous note? Do we even know it to be real?"

"That's the best part. We pulled a 45 caliber slug out of the side of the church wall. Found a shell casing in the field that's pretty fresh, but no prints. Bad news is the cadaver dogs haven't found anything. There is what looks to be a fresh grave, but it's empty," he said, the disappointment evident on his face.

"What kind of gun was it from—any idea?"

"Our expert says it's from a Model 1911 Colt, used to be standard issue for Army. Everything fits the note, but no body. You know any bikers that carry that kind of gun?"

"Too bulky and heavy for most that carry. Bikers don't exactly show their pistols to many unless they're of the two legged variety. Seriously, most I know carry Glocks," Lute said with authority. "What's next on the agenda?"

"We're calling in all the support we can to search any possible body dump sites in a 50 mile radius. Governor's called the National Guard in to help, starting in the morning. We're going to use this as a command post."

"Great, the town could use a boost to the local economy. Wonder if it might have been planned that way. What do you think, maybe the Mayor's wife took out the hit. *That* would really make for a good story," he said laughingly, slapping the agent on the back. He looked at the straight, non-humored expression on agent Watson's face. "Just kidding, my friend—don't they let you guys smile every now and then?"

"Only when we're off duty. We're not as rule bound as the secret service," he said, a glimmer of a smile crossing the corner of his mouth. "When this is over, we're hitting a biker bar and I'm buying. Got an extra bike?"

"Damn, you ride Watty? I knew there was something about you I liked. Damn right I got you a ride if you don't mind planting your butt on a metric."

"Anything with two wheels is fine within certain limitations—I'm not going to ride a crotch rocket." He extended his hand and they shook in the traditional biker way. A bond that had not been present before was created in that moment.

"Sounds like there's not much left to do tonight. You got any bunks in that trailer of yours? I could sure use some shuteye."

"You got it bro. You eaten yet? We got some pretty good barbeque in there and we really need to talk in private."

Lute's eyebrows arched up as he replied. "Sounds good to me."

Minutes later, they were sitting in the agent's car, finishing up the tasty remnants of their plates of food from a local restaurant. Lute spoke first.

"So what's up, Watty?" he asked in a way indicative of the new connection they shared.

"I'm going to need your help checking out the local bikers for the gun. You are right, we do seem to be heavily involved in this, but there's good reason. Can I trust you to keep some background info to yourself? It may shed a little light on the murder. We need an inside man on the force we can trust."

"You can, and that goes both ways. I'm not going to violate the trust of my biker or work buddies to achieve short-term results—I live here," Lute said, unblinkingly staring him in the eyes.

"Not going to ask you to do anything unethical, illegal, or immoral."

"Immoral might be ok, especially if it involves good looking biker babes." Lute paused and grinned to ease the tension. "No, seriously, we can work together, but we must readily share information if we're going to catch those killers. They're pros, so I'm sure they didn't leave many leads to follow. Actually, I'm very surprised we found the casing; pretty sloppy for a pro—they must have been in a hurry to leave. Sounds like this witness is our hole card. Only problem is we have to find him before they do. Now let me ask you a question. What gives with all the agents in town before the hit? Why was there a hit on the mayor, anyway? And lastly, why me?"

"That's three questions, but who's counting? Here goes, but you might want to buckle up."

Lute feigned buckling his seat belt, but instead of actually doing so, he hit the record button on his cell phone.

Agent Watson checked the mirrors to be sure no one was near his car before continuing. Lute could tell this was not a planned or sanctioned conversation. The agent took a deep breath.

"First off, we were conducting the last phase of an ongoing investigation into bribery involving the mayor. We had him nailed, and that night we had it set up for him to lead us to the money man in the case. Without him, we don't have enough to go any further towards making a case that will stick. We can connect the dots, but we don't have a way of proving it. The mayor's wife is involved, along with some distant relatives in the construction business. There may also be a couple of council members and a lawyer involved. Also, we might have a judge if we get lucky. That answer your questions?"

"All but one—why trust me?"

"We ran a background on you and many others, and you have the connections and a long history of success. You're the right guy, I'm sure of that. Today proved it. You in?" The agent held his hand out.

"Yeah, I'm in, I don't have any tolerance for that bribery shit. Anybody on the force involved?"

"We don't think so, but we can't be sure. The mayor and the chief were pretty tight, but we think he's clean; he just trusted his buddy too much."

"Alright then, what's next? Your guys still handling the interviews at the school in the morning?"

"That plan hasn't changed. Oh yes, we've asked your chief to assign you to our team as our liaison. You should like this, your job is to be a biker for a while and try to gather some intel. You got a problem with that?"

"That part sounds good; living the dream and getting paid for it. It's a deal, Watty." He stuck his hand out again to seal the deal.

"One more thing—don't call me Watty unless you need to meet, and never around anybody else. It will be our code to meet privately."

"Got it. When do I start being an undercover biker. I guess you do know that most of the locals are aware I'm a cop."

"Right now. We got it set up that the chief, with your approval of course, will announce that you put in for a leave of absence because you were unhappy with today's events and refused to have a part in it. We need you to start putting feelers out tonight. I'm sure the rumors are starting already, and we feel you can serve us better by being undercover. I'll bet you'll be pretty popular with the biker community trying to get the inside scoop. Play up that renegade biker image." Agent Watson had reverted back to the authoritative tone of voice agents are known for.

"This could be fun, I always wanted to be a renegade biker. Makes you real popular with the babes. I'll bet they peg you as a G man the moment you walk in a bar, even when you're riding and leathered up."

"You reckon the white shirt and skinny black tie under the leather jacket might be giving me away?" the agent asked, grinning again.

"You are so full of it, it'll be fun doing some riding and then throwing back a few when this is done. If you have nothing more, like some FBI secret code or maybe an undercover biker babe for me to hang with, I'm going to get started before you change your mind." He opened the door and swung his legs out.

"You gotta get your own babe. Oh yeah, there is one more little thing—"

"I knew it, here comes the—" He said shaking his head.

Agent Watson cut him off before he could finish. "Shiny side up, bro, be careful out there."

Lute walked over to his bike and mounted. While he was putting on his lid and gloves, a coworker from his department walked over.

"You're in charge, I can't handle this shit anymore! See you." He put his bike in gear and rode off, not waiting for the reply from his police buddy, who for the first time he could remember, seemed to be at a loss for words.

Departing the scene, he headed towards the Hawg Corral, happy for the cold bite of the night air on his face, clearing his mind of fatigue while allowing him to plan his next moves. Lost in thought, his bike seemed to be on auto pilot, surprising him when he neared his favorite bar. Before going inside, he made a call to the chief to confirm the plan, then called Wolf and asked him to join him at the bar. Walking in, he saw a dozen or more regulars seated at the bar, with more playing pool as was normal for pool league night. He got a beer from the bartender; a cute, blond, but streetwise young babe named Comma. Pleasing to the eye, she seemed to have a bit of knowledge about almost any subject, and announced this fact to the patrons with a sign on the bar that stated, "the doctor is in".

As he expected, the topic of conversation was the day's events. Most had seen the news clip, and Lute was overwhelmed with the attention. Many had opinions about the situation. This started Lute thinking of ways to take advantage of this pipeline of information and theories. He knew this could be a good thing. He let it slip that he had told his boss where to "stick the job," and that he was taking a break for an indefinite amount of time.

The pool league games were ending when he heard Wolf's Vulcan pull up outside. A beer was waiting for him when he came up to greet his friends at the bar. Before he got sucked into a long conversation, Lute pulled him aside and walked him out the back door to the patio where they could talk in private. Lute had already had a look around and was certain the location was clear of unseen listeners.

"What's up dude, you made it sound purty darn urgent on the phone," Wolf asked, concern evident on his face.

"I just landed my dream job as a renegade biker and I'm getting paid for it—how about them apples?"

"Sounds too good to be true man; must be a catch there somewhere. More details, please. I might just want to get in touch with your employer and see if there are any other job openings."

"I'm sure you don't want to talk with my employers, but I'm certain they'd like to talk with you, and may be going to do so in the future if we're not real careful. Let me tell you all about it. You'll get a real kick out it."

Lute went on to fill him in on the evening's events. When he finished, he took a long pull on his beer and set down the empty bottle.

"So the way I see it, that makes you some kind of triple agent now, right? This will definitely work in our favor and give you a chance to have a little fun while working. Feel like a little brainstorming activity now?"

"I thought you'd never ask . . . fire that sucker up!" Wolf did as asked, pulling out a joint, lighting it, and then passing it to his friend. After two round trips, Lute held up his hand palm out, indicating he'd had enough. Wolf agreed, snuffed the roach out, and put it away.

"So, when does this stuff hit the news?"

"In the morning. Why?"

"Stag's funeral is in the morning at eleven. You going?" Wolf asked.

"I'll be there. We can meet at Mark's shop before riding over."

"You got it. I'll be there at seven before his employees get there. You hanging here for a while?"

"Nope, I need some rack time after the day I've had. Tell you what, you leave first and I'll hang back and see if you are followed. Take the back way tonight. Be safe bro, see you in the am." They headed inside and said their goodbyes. Wolf headed outside to his bike first, while Lute lagged behind and grabbed a magazine. After giving Wolf a suitable head start, Lute took a route he knew would intercept his buddy a few miles away, allowing him to check for a tail without being seen. No one was following him as he went by, and both arrived at their homes safely without spotting any signs of being followed.

Chapter 18

T he bottom of the high thin clouds on the eastern horizon were just beginning to turn a rosy hue of pink when the white van pulled into the parking lot. The old abandoned country store was on Highway 231, not too far from Rockford. A lone biker, dressed in black leather was waiting in the parking lot as the van pulled up alongside. The van shielded the biker from the view of passing motorists, of which there were few due to the early hour.

The tinted window of the van slid quietly down. "Any questions before we split up and get in position?" Blondie, dressed as Ronnie, asked quietly.

"The three lane starts in 3.8 miles. I'll be ready, just hit the button," came the quiet, gruff reply from inside the van. "You really think a judge could be the witness? Seems unlikely to me."

"It doesn't matter, we take no chances. Besides, it'll work well with the rest of the plan. We'll talk and have some fun afterward if all goes as planned. The plan will cover our asses later—I didn't like that guy Wolf, but instead of whacking him, I figure we can use him as a patsy for the killing. All we got to do is plant a glove of his where we dumped the mayor."

"Enough for now, we focus on the task at hand, and then we'll talk." he checked the time. "This could be fun—too bad I won't be able to see his eyes,"

Blondie started her bike and rode off. 45 turned on the radio and heard:

"Local law enforcement officials are asking for your help with information regarding the missing mayor of Whiteville. Anyone with information is urged to come forward or call the anonymous tip line immediately. A $100,000 reward is being offered for information leading to the apprehension of the person or persons involved in the mayor's disappearance. Foul play is suspected. In a connected development, the disturbance at city hall yesterday was followed today by an announcement from the Chief of Police that the lead investigator has taken a leave of absence. No more details were given. A news conference is scheduled for noon today where there will be more information provided. We will provide live coverage and request you stay tuned to this station for updates." The announcer's voice was replaced by a commercial.

45 knew in his gut that the judge was not the witness. He reasoned that if it was the judge and he didn't want to come forward for whatever reason, he certainly wouldn't be taking any risks by inviting unknown bikers to his house. He decided to go with the plan anyway, and reassured himself that his partner knew what she was doing. He was not happy that this was the first he had heard of Blondie's plan until now. He would find out more later, and resolved to focus on the work at hand, not allowing himself to become distracted with speculation. He would be sure to watch the news conference and get more details about Blondie's plan later.

Forty minutes passed. He got the signal when the judge left the house, headed in his direction on a black HD Sportster. 45 knew it would be about ten minutes before they reached where he was parked, but started the van and moved into position anyway. While waiting he saw two vehicles go by in the direction he was headed, but several trucks and cars were headed the other way toward Birmingham and most likely, their driver's jobs. He heard his cell phone ring, and pulled onto the highway, heading south. As he approached the area where the highway began a three-lane stretch, two of the lanes headed south, he checked his mirror and was rewarded with the sight of two bikers a few car lengths back. He noted that his speed was 50 mph, just as planned.

He entered the stretch and stayed in the right lane. The first bike was the flamed Vaquero, ridden by Blondie. Behind her, he could see a second bike a few car lengths further back. As planned, Blondie sped up and began to pass in the left lane. As agreed, he began to speed up, holding his speed at just over 55. He could see a large truck in the distance coming towards them. Blondie sped up and took position a few feet ahead of him in the other lane. As he watched the mirrors, the second bike was just about even with the rear of his van. As the truck neared, Blondie sped up, and the second bike did likewise. As the large truck passed Blondie, the second biker was even with his rear axle. 45 put on his left blinker, and changed lanes swiftly. The move caught the second biker by surprise and, out of habit, he swerved left to avoid contact with the van, not seeing the large truck hidden from his view by the van as it went around the sweeping right curve.

It was too late to react, and the Sportster rider had nowhere to go when he saw the truck twenty yards in front of him, closing the distance between them at a combined speed of more than 110 mph. Neither the truck driver nor the biker had time to swerve before colliding. As 45 watched his mirror, he saw smoke come from the truck's rear tires, debris and smoke from the front of the truck, and unrecognizable bike parts bouncing under the truck and out to the side in all directions. He did recognize one part—a biker boot that flew out from under a tire and was spit down the road in his direction. He wondered to himself if a foot was inside. A smile crossed his face as he uttered the familiar words, "mission accomplished."

They continued on at exactly the speed limit towards Rockford, with a quarter of a mile of distance between them. They were a mile from the center of the little town when a fire truck and two sheriff cars passed by in the opposite direction, sirens screeching and lights flashing. Neither Blondie or 45 slowed or stopped until they reached the four way stop at the crossroads. Turning right, they continued west towards the interstate. They stopped and grabbed breakfast at a restaurant near the entrance to I-65. A good meal afterward was a customary way of celebrating a clean kill. They did not speak of the morning's activities or of Blondie's plan, but instead, discussed the differences in metric and American made bikes. Any observers would swear that the two guys in the greasy spoon were only interested in motorcycles.

Just before noon, Blondie pulled into the secluded driveway leading to the trailer in Shelby. She parked her bike in the shed, then went inside to change into more feminine attire, biker style, complete with a revealing bodice and leather chaps, minus the jeans. She poured two generous portions of George Dickel, then set two beers on the bar. Next, she turned on a local TV channel and was rewarded with the breaking news of the motorcycle accident. A reporter was on the scene, and the truck could be seen in the background. Traffic had been rerouted to county roads while the accident was under investigation. The reporter had been busy. He said that according to a local who had been the first to stop at the scene, the trucker said the bike had run head on into him while passing a small cargo van in his lane. He had no time to avoid or even slow before colliding with the motorcycle. The biker's name was being withheld until the family was notified. Blondie hoped they found a wallet, because she knew the biker's body was mush. He had been wearing a full-faced helmet, so she knew at least that part would be largely intact, even if separated from the rest of his smashed anatomy. As the reporter finished, she heard the crunch of gravel as the van pulled up in front. She glanced out the window to be sure it was 45.

He pulled open the door, and ducking slightly as he entered, walked over and set a case of beer on the counter. He turned and grabbed the beer and the shot, holding the shot up to Blondie, who had walked over and grabbed hers.

"Here's to a job well done, even if it was for free," he said. They clinked glasses and threw back the contents in a single gulp, chased by a swallow of beer. Blondie poured two more fingers in each glass, handing one to 45.

She held hers up and said "here's to the plan and its' successful implementation." Blondie then grabbed his hand and yanked him towards the couch. No more was said as they went through their ritual of sexual activity after a successful kill, fueled partly by adrenaline, but enhanced with alcohol and other drugs.

The afternoon shadows reached the windows, causing a deeper gloom to fill the room where they lay. 45 awakened instantly at the mention of the Judge's name by a reporter on TV. News of disaster or any other stories of misery had an energizing effect on him, and both he and Blondie enjoyed making morbid jokes while uttering snide comments about the victims. She laughed when he told her about the boot flying out from under the truck. Too bad he had no video of the efficient, instant kill. He put this way of extermination in his top three of efficient ways to complete a contract. With Blondie's assistance, he had completed several hits by pushing an unsuspecting victim's vehicle into the path of an oncoming vehicle. She was a real asset as a partner with fringe benefits thrown in. Indeed, she competed with him on ruthlessness and cruelty, and had an uncanny way of reading the future outcome of an action. The mayor's murder was the first time they had left a witness. He held her partially to blame, but in his mind, he blamed himself for having too much faith in her ability to foresee all the angles of future outcomes. *Never again will I totally trust her judgment*, he vowed silently to himself. He sat up and prodded his companion.

"Wake up bitch, the day's almost gone. Check out the news."

"Screw you, big head, what are you talking about?"

"Make us some coffee and tell me about this plan of yours."

Blondie flipped him the bird, but got up and started a pot of coffee anyway.

He went to the john and took a shower. When he came out, Blondie was dressed and had a cup of black coffee waiting on the table beside the recliner.

"Alright, listen up. It's really simple. We hang the murder of the mayor on that Wolf guy." She went on to explain in more detail about planting evidence to implicate him. She knew that once the ball was rolling, the various law enforcement departments would jump in to look for any evidence that could help them build a case. They would use all the resources the Justice Department had at their disposal to try and convict the suspected criminal. Wolf would be the ideal scapegoat with another well-executed plan.

The only complication was what she had read in the latest edition of the biker magazine he wrote for. He would be at Daytona Beach Bike Week that started this weekend, and would be leaving in the next day or two. It was vital they plant the evidence before the body was discovered for the plan to work. She knew that with all the resources that had been brought in to look for disposal sites, that it would not be long before the body was found. She knew he would be attending the funeral of Stag being held Wednesday morning. There would be little opportunity to steal a glove there safely, as he would discover it immediately. There would be witnesses to the fact it disappeared. No good at all. Daytona was the place, and Wolf normally would be traveling alone. There would be an abundance of bikers around at his destination, providing ample opportunities to lift a glove.

They worked out the logistics of the trip, both traveling separately, with plans to be at locations he would be certain to visit. 45 felt better after hearing the plan and was reassured by taking part in the logistical planning. He would leave during the funeral and station himself along a favorite road Wolf was sure to take. Fortunately for them, Wolf liked to travel out of the way routes that most others didn't. However, that did seem to change once he gave out the route in his stories. 45, being an expert at recon and camouflage, was sure he could spot and tail him if he took the same route as last year. Blondie planned for the other possibility, following and locating him at Daytona Beach during one of the most popular bike rallies in the world with around 500,000 extra visitors to the area, most of them bikers. No problem, she thought. With a little planning you can find anyone if you stake out the right places.

Plan in place, they each began to work on their own part. Kickstands up was an hour before Stag's funeral, leaving plenty of time to get in position to watch for Wolf on River Road, a route he favored for the water and fishing along the way. They also knew he was an avid member of ABATE and the AMA, and as such, detested Georgia's motorcycle checkpoints and avoided them whenever possible. Blondie, dressed as her alter-ego, Ronnie, would provide surveillance from the funeral. Different flames had been applied to her Vaquero. She knew there would be bikers that had never met in person, thanks to the internet and sites like VROC, BON, BK, KOC, along with countless others that tied these biker brothers together. Too bad that they had recently encountered such a succession of biker brotherhood losses. So sad—

When all preparation was completed, Blondie sealed the deal with a shorter version of the day's earlier lustful activities. She'd have to be sharp when following Wolf, as he was suspicious already, and she had last lost him before when he was riding in a group, him peeling off unseen down a side road. *She would not let that happen again.*

The morning came earlier than she wanted it to. 45 was up and watching TV when she came out of the bedroom. She invited him out on an early morning run in the clear, brisk air. He accepted. She had to push herself hard to stay up with his long strides. No matter, this was one of the ways she kept her body toned and ready.

Fifteen minutes before the agreed upon time found 45 sitting astride his running motorcycle, letting the oil circulate and warm. Blondie, dressed as a man, came out and backed her bike out of the shed, starting the bike as she rolled it out. While he waited, he went through his ritual of checking tires, fluids, and eye-balling his entire bike. They were both dressed in black leather, 45's noticeably more worn than hers. At exactly the agreed upon time, they put their kickstands up. They knocked gloved fists and 45 screeched off, spitting gravel to warm his tires before hitting the cool asphalt. Blondie gave him a two minute head start, then turned north onto the highway at the end of the driveway.

Blondie was across the road from the church where the service for Stag was being held when it ended. She pulled out and attached herself to the rear of the procession headed to the Veteran's cemetery where he would be buried with full military honors. She spotted Wolf along with another Vulcan with a fairing in the group of more than thirty riders. She got his plate number and added him to her list for a later close encounter of the terminal kind. She noted that Wolf was not loaded for the trip, and surmised he would be going home to load up after the funeral. She pulled up behind the last bike parked near the graveside, taking up post near the rear of the group. She was familiar with the proceedings, having attended several others in the past as she reveled in the misery of the surviving families, most times a result of her grisly actions.

After the ceremony was over, several in the group split at the entrance. She stayed with the group headed back towards town. At the first light, she realized she had picked the wrong group. She knew it was too late to catch up with the other riders, so she took up surveillance at the hidden vantage point she had found just off the main road in his neighborhood. An hour passed and dusk was approaching. She made a call and advised 45 of the situation. He was not happy, and described her effectiveness in the most demeaning fashion he could. She said she'd be there within two hours.

CHAPTER 19

After Stag's funeral, Wolf headed to Mark's house where his gear was packed and waiting. He hated leaving this late in the day, but with almost four hours of daylight left, he knew he'd be bucket-less before dark. He loved the thought of a week riding bareheaded in Florida, and hoped the weather cooperated.

Rain was not in the forecast for the next two days, but the weekend forecast was calling for intermittent showers. After going thru Eufala, his route followed the river along the Alabama side of the GA-AL state line. He was finally able to remove the skid lid at the intersection of SR 2 and CR 64 in Florida before dark. Setting the GPS to take the shortest route to the southeastern corner of Lake Talquin, he avoided Tallahassee and enjoyed the ride with little traffic and scenic backroads the entire trip. From there, he would take SR 20 to CR 267, then US 98 to Perry, FL.

This year, instead of going straight to Daytona Beach, he planned a side trip to see his buddy, Big Jim in Dade City. They planned to do some bass fishing, followed by a trip to Big Cat Rescue in Tampa for some extra story material. Big Jim lived up to his name at six foot seven, and in the past had played college football then enjoyed moderate success as a competitive bass fisherman. He now operated a pest control company with the most advanced termite detection equipment on the market. A biker himself, Big Jim now spent most of his time with the day-to-day operation of his company. Wolf knew the only way he'd step away from his business was if he came down and motivated him to take a break for a few days. He was not alarmed when he noticed a pair of riders a half mile behind him as he turned off River Road near Sneads, Florida.

Ouzts Too is a great biker oasis with good food next to a waterway on Hwy 98 in Newport, FL, and Wolf typically stopped there to eat and hydrate. As usual, Wolf stopped at the familiar watering hole for supper and a beer. He had just ordered food at the bar when he saw two bikes pull into the crushed shell parking lot out front. He recognized the CVO Street Glide and its rider as the biker he had spoken with briefly at the Hawg Corral. His riding partner looked familiar, but he couldn't place him. There were several other bikers in the bar, many of which he had seen during previous trips, and as a result, was not worried about immediate danger. He was sitting at the corner of the bar when the huge biker walked in. He scanned the bar, then locked eyes with Wolf and headed in his direction. As Wolf watched him approach, he saw the biker's companion riding a Vaquero with a flame paint job, ride off. Wolf didn't wait for him to speak before greeting him with the ritual handshake.

"What's happening, you headed to Daytona, too?" He tried to keep the banter as normal as possible to keep from raising suspicion.

45 ordered a beer and turned back to look him in the eye. "Got some business to attend to in Orlando, but I'll be in Daytona by the weekend. You?"

"Yep, gonna check out the new bikes—that's an awesome paint job on your scooter out there."

"Thanks, I like it. That's your Vulcan out there, right?"

"Yes it is, we've been together for a lot of miles," Wolf replied. He thought 45 was acting way too buddy-buddy, especially considering his disdain for Jap bikes, a feeling he had been quick to reveal the last time they met.

They continued talking until Wolf's food was placed on the bar in front of him.

"Where are you staying in Daytona? I heard you're an expert on where to stay and such."

"I'm not so sure about the expert part, but this year I'm staying with a friend in New Smryna Beach."

"Must be a real hot babe. Well, I have to hit the road if I'm going to make Orlando tonight. Be seeing you." He threw down a five and got up to leave, but turned and said, "You got a card? Maybe we can get together for a beer while you're there."

Wolf hesitated for a few seconds, then reached in his wallet and pulled out a card. "Yeah, give me a call if you want to." He watched as the biker drained his beer in one long draw.

They shook, then 45 headed out the door. He heard a loud belch just before the door came swinging closed. Wolf watched as he started his bike and put it in gear. His rear tire kicked up crushed shell from the parking lot as he went rumbling onto the blacktop.

Wolf was pleased he left, but wondered what accident the two had in store for him further down the road to Daytona. He went out and got his GPS, then looked for a way to bypass US Highway 98 for a few miles. Not many options presented themselves, so he decided to hook up with anyone going that direction. A pair of bikers was also headed to Daytona, and agreed to travel with him. One even mentioned that the road ahead to Perry was loaded with deer. A bit later, they left and headed east on Hwy 98. As predicted, Wolf saw the glow of no less than 38 pairs of eyes, the deer grazing on the side of the dark, two-lane stretch of road to Perry. He also noted a motorcycle's headlights a ways behind them. The bike behind missed the light in Perry, and had to stop.

A few blocks later, Wolf turned right onto a side street and, after a few quick turns through old sparsely-lighted neighborhoods, turned onto US Hwy 19 and headed south towards Dade City. Seeing no other vehicle lights ahead or behind him on the long, lonely stretch of 4-lane highway, he decided to ride straight through to Big Jim's. It was a clear and cold night, especially for Florida, with no lights along the deserted stretch of road other than the half-moon overhead. Wolf normally enjoyed traveling at night, especially when staying true to the phrase, two lanes by day and four lanes by night during times when deer were active. This evening, he had an uneasy feeling that he had narrowly escaped a fatal accident more than once.

Blondie and 45 were sitting out of sight of the highway near one of the few crossroads on Hwy 98. The spot had been carefully picked out due to the streetlight that lit the highway there. As the three riders went by, Blondie gave the signal, and 45 pulled out to tail the group, leaving lots of distance in between. Blondie followed suit a minute later. As they approached Perry, 45 narrowed the gap between himself and the riders ahead. He slowed as he neared the stoplight on Hwy 19, not wanting to alert Wolf to the tail. As he looked ahead, the light turned green. The group proceeded thru the intersection. He twisted his throttle open to make the light before it turned red. It turned yellow when he was but 50 yards away, but spotting the police car parked at the corner, he downshifted quickly and came to a complete stop. He quickly turned right then took the first left, giving his bike full throttle after he was out of sight of the cop. Many blocks later, he made a left and pulled up to a stop on US 27. Looking to his right, he saw two motorcycle taillights. To his left, Blondie's bike was approaching. He turned out in front of her and they both continued until they were behind the two bikes. It was easy to see that Wolf was not one of them. 45 motioned Blondie to pull over. Looking at the GPS, it was apparent that US 27 was the likely and most direct route from Perry to Daytona. They continued on, then pulled off the road and waited for Wolf to go through the crossroad in Mayo on his way to Daytona Beach.

An hour passed without seeing him go by. They returned to Perry and cruised by every motel in town shown on their GPS. Next, they checked outside the local bars of which they found only three, two of which were not hospitable to Anglo-Saxon bikers. The other one was slow, it being a Wednesday night, and as such, had only six women and two men inside. All eyes were on 45 as he ducked his six foot seven head under the door frame. Blondie came through next, her dark hair windblown and wild. She looked around the room at the staring women, locking eyes and establishing that this man was taken. 45 didn't care about the bad vibes in the room. He went up to the bar, stood next to the best looking woman in the room, and ordered two Coronas and "whatever she's having", pursing his lips in her direction. She blushed and smiled with obvious pleasure at the attention he had bestowed upon her. In the most gentlemanly way possible, he asked if the seat next to her was taken. She put her hand on his arm, and invited him to sit. Blondie left for the restroom.

"Gal, you are the hottest babe in this joint. Would you like to have some real fun tonight?"

She looked at him with her forest green eyes, paused as if considering the offer, and then said, "What did you have in mind?"

"Pizza party complete with the beer, whiskey, weed, and the best looking woman around. It don't get much better than that. There's even a pool there," he said, gently rubbing her knee with his huge hand.

"Sounds like fun. What's *she* gonna think? When are you talking about?"

"Now. The woman won't have a problem with it. We're just riding partners."

"Ok, let me pay my tab."

"I got ya covered sweet thing. Let's ride." he threw a fifty on the bar.

"What about her?"

"She can get her own stud." He grabbed her by the hand and led her outside. He stood her up against the wall and gave her a deep kiss, cracking open a drug capsule on his tongue and placing it deep inside her mouth. She returned the kiss with the fervor that comes from a lifetime of being with overfed and under educated, beer drinking, Nascar-watching rednecks. It didn't take long for the drug to have a calming, cooperative effect on her.

She climbed behind him on his Street Glide and rode off to a secluded motel on the edge of town. He showed her a picture of Wolf and learned she had seen him before, but not recently. Not one to pass on opportunities, 45 spent the next hour showing her things that redneck women typically never experience and probably wouldn't want to. She passed out afterward. He left the room and went a few doors down to where Blondie's bike was parked outside.

Blondie had taken advantage of what was perceived by the other women at the bar as a snub by a low down, cheating man, and as such, created a bond with them due to their own experiences with men. She ordered a round for all, and was readily accepted into the group. After spending too much breath berating men in general, she showed a photo of Wolf astride his bike and asked if any had seen him tonight. No one had, but the bartender remembered him stopping by the previous year. She asked if he had a local babe or buddy, but no one knew.

Getting little information of use, she left shortly afterward, heading for the motel at the edge of town for the night. Arriving at the motel, she saw 45's bike a few doors down from her room, and noted the animal sounds coming from within. She was grateful for the sacrifices the bimbo was making that would allow her time to unwind and do research online.

She had just finished inputting into her GPS all the places Wolf had mentioned in previous Daytona stories when she heard a familiar knock on the door. She opened it to find 45 in his shorts, sweaty and smelly from his activities. Telling him to go take a shower, she went back to work dividing up the places each would go, searching for the elusive Nomad. She booked a room online at a motel he had mentioned in last year's story. 45 would be spending time at the racetrack venue, knowing Wolf was expected there for the test rides. She would cruise the other local venues looking for him. She knew the clock was ticking for them to steal and plant evidence at the dump site that would implicate him in the murder. It was just a matter of time before the authorities found the Mercedes at the bottom of the abandoned, water-filled rock quarry. Luck had not been on their side when it came to anything regarding the illusive Vulcan rider. She had a hard time understanding how he had slipped away yet again.

After his shower, she went over the plan with 45, who thankfully had no objections. They both sacked out in anticipation of an early morning departure, followed by a full day of riding. They left separately and met at the motel in Daytona at dusk after a fruitless day of searching. To their frustration, Friday brought more of the same.

Meanwhile, outside Dade City, Wolf was having a great time catching fish and hanging out with Big Jim. The big bass were biting, and the day was filled with joking and partying as was their custom. Thursday night, Wolf let his oldest friend in on the details of the dilemma he was in. After hearing about the run in with 45 on his way down from Alabama, Big Jim committed to be his wing man for the rest of his time in Florida. He said he was looking forward to meeting the big S.O.B, adding that it had been years since he last went to bike week. Wolf resisted, due mainly to his fear for his bro's safety. It was futile to argue when his giant buddy made up his mind, and he was looking forward to more partying with his old friend. They made plans to leave after fishing on Friday.

By mid-morning, they were tired of pulling in large, healthy bass, both itching to get on their bikes and ride. The weather forecast for the day called for intermittent showers, and they could already see dark bottomed clouds forming on the horizon of Lake County. After covering the boat, they were sweaty and more than ready for a leisurely ride to Daytona. They planned to take a winding, scenic route on rural back roads through Lake county, avoiding traffic in and around Orlando. They took 98 to 50 to 19 thru Mt. Dora, taking side roads in an effort to avoid the scattered showers. The sky was beautiful as it normally was this time of year, with towering, puffy white clouds with dark bottoms floating in a robin's egg blue sky. They saw several rainbows along the way, created by the sun shining through the roving rain showers.

Outside of Mt. Dora, their luck suddenly changed. The fuel pump on Wolf's bike stopped working. Good karma was with them, and a passing biker with a truck and empty trailer gave Wolf and his bike a lift to the local Kawasaki dealer, a few miles away. The diagnosis was confirmed, and with a few calls, the service manager arranged to have a fuel pump flown in to be installed the next morning. They spent the evening at a buddy's house in nearby Lake Mary.

Leaving around noon the next day with the new fuel pump installed in the Vulcan, they rode aggressively to make it to Daytona. Arriving there midafternoon, the rain finally caught up with them. They checked into the motel across from the speedway, then went to main street to catch the band, *Razorback*, at the Bank and Blues club. After a couple of hours, the downpour let up, so they continued on as planned to the Broken Spoke on A1A to meet up with another friend of Wolf's. The attractive blond artist was extremely proficient at quickly drawing caricatures that enhanced the features of her subjects while stripping away the years. The rain had thinned the crowd, but the band, *Lucas Hoge*, played on with enthusiasm to spare. Most of the bikers and venders were there under the big canopy, avoiding the rain that had come back with a vengeance.

No one noticed the black Vaquero pull up next to Wolf's bike, parked behind a vendor's tent on the perimeter. The lone rider was fast and efficient at her task. Dismounting quickly, she knelt down between the two bikes and jimmied the lock on Wolf's hard bag. She picked up the helmet on top of his tank bag, and a pair of leather gloves fell out onto the ground, landing in the puddle next to his bike. She picked them up, placed one in a baggie, then took the other one and jammed it under the tool bag inside the hard bag. Satisfied that no one had seen her, she slid back on her bike and rode off slowly to avoid attention. Across the muddy parking area near the entrance, a CVO Street Glide with a black leather clad rider slowly turned out onto A1A and headed north, stopping at the huge Harley Davidson dealer just off Interstate 95. There was only a small crowd outside under the large tent due to the intermittent rain, so no one noticed him pull up and stop beside the Vaquero. The rider handed him the baggie with the glove inside. They bumped gloved fists, and the Street Glide took off, turning and heading north on 95.

He rode straight through, stopping only for gas while taking the fastest route his GPS showed. Around three am, he entered Shelby county from the south, turning off interstate 65 at the exit for the small county airport. He continued on after a few turns toward Pea Ridge, passing through little groups of houses and churches on his way to the rock quarry near the river. He was reassured by the passing of only one vehicle along the way, and parked his bike in a clearing a few yards off the muddy gravel road, throwing camouflage over it to insure it remained unseen.

He donned night goggles and started walking the mile to the quarry. The trail was devoid of any light, the half moon and stars hidden by the low hanging clouds overhead. Reaching the downward sloping track going around the crevice in the trail, he looked for a place where a glove could easily be dropped. Finding a suitable spot where a hiker would have to climb up the slope, he removed the glove from the baggie and tucked it under the roots of an overhanging tree, partially covering it with leaves. He turned and went back the way he had come.

Back at his bike, he stowed the cover and goggles, then headed back to the trailer in Shelby, passing only a few more vehicles along the way. Blondie's bike was already in the shed as he pulled the Street Glide inside. She was standing at the trailer door when he closed the doors to the shed. She raised her eyebrows to form a questioning look as he neared the front porch.

"Mission accomplished; everything cool at your end?" he asked.

She handed him a beer and a big fatty, holding out a lit lighter. She smiled and grabbed his crotch.

"Good, let's party before crashing." She grabbed his hand and pulled him inside. An hour later, both were naked and passed out on the bed, sleeping soundly.

Wolf was pissed off when he got to his bike after the band quit at the Broken Spoke Saloon. His helmet was on the ground, half filled with rainwater, and his tank bag where the helmet had been, was soaked. Even worse, the gloves he had worn for years were gone. He was loudly cussing up a storm when Big Jim walked out of the porta potti nearby.

"What's up dude—something wrong with your bike?"

"Nothing's wrong with Beast, but some asshole stole my gloves. Oh yeah, did I mention my helmet is full of water?"

"What a shitty thing for anyone to do! Must be a real low life to do that kind of shit. Probably some local trailer trash cracker that lives hereabouts. No real biker would think of screwing with a man's bike. Must have a death wish."

"I'd like to fulfill that wish. You see anything?"

"Nope, we can ask around a bit, but if someone saw anything they'd probably have already come over and kicked the thief's ass. Don't hurt to ask around, though." They went their separate ways, asking vendors in the area if they had seen anything. Unsuccessful, they returned to their bikes and headed back to the motel.

The week passed way too quickly. They attended races, saw old friends, and rode the newest bikes the manufacturers had at the racetrack. Wolf was loaned a new black Street Glide to test ride for a few days for a review he would write for the magazine. Sunday morning they were packing up their gear and getting ready for the ride home when a breaking news story on TV caught their attention.

"The vehicle belonging to the missing mayor of the city of Whiteville was found in a rock quarry not far from the city in the nearby community of Pea Ridge. It is not known at this time whether the mayor's body is inside. The submerged Mercedes was located by a search and rescue team from the National Guard late yesterday—" As they watched the story, Wolf's phone rang. A quick glance showed the caller was Lute.

"What's up Lute?"

"You watching the news? They found the mayor's body yesterday in his Mercedes at the bottom of that rock quarry near the old crossing on the Cahaba river. The hunt for the killers is going nuclear here, with every lead being examined and reexamined, and there is again an army of forensic experts canvassing the area around the quarry. Bikers are being stopped and hassled indiscriminately, and anyone known to have said anything unkind about the mayor in the past is being sought out and questioned. You are near the top of the list." He paused, took a deep and audible breath, and then said, "so how was Daytona Bike Week? You're heading back today, right?"

"It was a righteous week, Big Jim was with me the whole time. We rode a lot of new bikes, saw a lot of old buddies, and I got a great story with some super pictures."

"You see any more of those two bikers?"

"I didn't see either again after running into the big guy at the bar on the way down. I did have a bit of bad luck when Beast broke down, but we got it fixed and back on the road the next morning. The worst thing was that some asshole stole my gloves the first night we were in Daytona. Other than that, an outstanding trip."

There was silence from the other end.

"Lute, you still there . . . Lute?"

"I'm still here, just thinking. Wolf, tell me every detail about when your gloves went missing." Wolf did as asked, telling about the rain, the band, the tents, and the muddy parking lot. He was asked specific questions that, after a week, were hard to give specific details about. Lute as usual, knew what questions to ask to draw forgotten facts out.

"Wolf, when you are a couple of hours out, have a beer or get something to eat and give me a call. I want to meet up and escort you in. Don't forget, this is extremely important."

"Why so dramatic, dude? You know something you're not telling me, don't you?"

"You're pretty damn astute, maybe too damned much this time for your own good. Just do what I say, will you?"

"You got it, officer. I'll call you later."

"Okay, you be careful and watch your back. Let me say hey to Big Jim before you hang up."

"Ok, thanks for everything. Here he is." He handed the phone to his buddy.

Big Jim said little, but listened for a few minutes before hanging up. They quickly finished packing, both sensing the need to hurry. They were sitting on their bikes letting the engines warm when Big Jim punched Wolf in the arm and then took his hand and shook it in the matter that close biker brothers do.

He looked Wolf in the eye and said, "Dude, I'm your wingman until we meet up with Lute. No arguments, I'm under orders from the establishment, and I sure don't want to piss the man off." He squeezed Wolf's arm until he agreed.

"Man, I can't seem to get no dang alone time since this shit started. I don't need no babysitter—however, it will be good to have you along, it's been a great trip. Let's ride!"

Gas tanks were kept filled at night to prevent any accumulation of humidity moisture from condensing inside the tanks during the cool spring nights. They stopped for gas near Albany.

"Man, I hate this way, but it sure beats interstate. I feel like I lost out on an hour of bareheaded riding." Wolf frequently bitched about having to put a lid back on when leaving Florida. They resumed their ride after giving Lute a call to tell of their location. He indicated they would meet sooner than two hours out and urged them to keep an eye out for tails and not get stopped for speeding.

Lute had taken the same route to Daytona before, and estimated where they would intercept. As he sat at the station where he had filled his tank, he heard the familiar sound of Beast's new pipes in the distance. As he looked down the barren stretch of road, three deer ran across the road between him and the approaching bikes. The two bikes slowed, downshifting almost in unison, and then pulled up to the pumps at the station. He walked over and warmly greeted his friends. He pulled out his cell phone and handed it to Wolf. Wolf stared at the picture intently.

"Damn, you're good Lute. You found my gloves already," he said, clapping him on the back. "They did find them both, right?"

"No, this was found many hours ago at the crime site where they recovered the mayor's car. Not a good thing, bro." The serious look on his face easily conveyed his concern.

"There ain't no way that they found my gloves there, unless someone put them there." It was obvious to his friends that he was stressing about this new development.

"I know that, dude. Jim, I need you to film every detail of what I'm about to do. I've got a hunch. Wolf, you stay out of camera range." Lute handed Jim the camera. He went to Wolf's right saddle bag and took everything out and laid it on the ground. He then repeated the procedure on the left side, stopping suddenly after removing the tool pouch.

"Jim, you need to get a close up of this," he said, pointing inside. Wolf, use this camera to take some still shots."

Wolf was obviously surprised, and this was accidentally caught by the camera in Jim's hand. Lute took out an evidence baggie and using his pin, picked up the soggy, muddy glove and placed it inside. He scooped up the mud that was under the glove and placed it inside another baggie.

"You can probably guess what all this means, right?" Lute said with worry in his eyes.

"Yep, I'm in some deep doo doo. You got some chrome bracelets for me?"

"You know, I've spent most of my riding time on a beautiful day thinking this eventuality thru, while trying to figure out what to do if it did. This glove is potentially the proof you got set up for the murder. My guess is that the glove the FBI found has the same type of mud in it. As soon as I make a call, there will be a team out taking soil samples at the parking lot where the gloves were stolen. The next part is not so easy and there's no guarantee of success. The FBI's going to want to hang this on somebody, and you'll be a very good target for their investigation. We have to get you out of town and safe. Make the killers think their plan worked. The only way to do that is make you the subject of a manhunt, or put you in jail—your choice."

"When you put it that way, there's only one choice. Never did like being in the shower with a bunch of guys. Tell me what to do."

Lute's plan was for Wolf to leave the day after next, giving him a chance to arrange a leave of absence from his job with the cover story that he was distraught over the breakup with his wife, Sue. Not happy with the plan, but understanding the need, he hesitantly agreed.

He spent the rest of the ride home thinking up a reason that would cover him leaving for an indefinite period of time. It wouldn't be the first time he had felt the call for a long, extended ride, and had to come up with a plausible reason. In fact, it was the main reason Sue had taken up riding her own bike. Lately, he suspected that for her, the thrill of the ride had been waning. He decided to take advantage of that with the help of a female friend that loved to ride her own bike and often invited him to ride along. He remembered that Sue had once asked if there was more to their friendship than just the bikes. Wolf had reassured her, but was also aware that should he ever lose Sue, the other woman would gladly step in to take her place. He figured with a few well-worded emails, he could get a chain of events started that would cover him leaving and staying gone for a long time. He hated to do this to Sue, but knew it would help keep her safe if the killers thought he had ditched his wife for another woman.

His boss would not be happy, but the breakup was a good cover for work. He hated to think about the hassles that would be experienced by his friends, coworkers, and family when the investigators came calling. He knew that Lute would do whatever he could to reduce the impact of the inevitable invasion into their lives, and the resulting embarrassment it would bring to his family. The news media would go into a feeding frenzy. A stupid thought popped into his mind. He needed to cut the grass and trim the bushes in the morning before going to work. Funny—

Monday went as expected for Wolf. His boss was extremely distressed when told about his need to take a leave of absence, beginning the next day. He knew his peers weren't happy either, but even worse, he sensed they were suspicious of his questionable reason for leaving. He did not say anything about another woman. The shit would hit the fan soon enough, and he knew better than to confuse matters. He knew he would be suspended or fired when the authorities came looking for him at the workplace. He did the best he could, delegating and reassigning tasks to his sales team for the time he would be gone, if indeed he was able to come back at all.

The talk in the store revolved around the new developments in the mayor's murder. He inwardly winced every time the subject came up. The media had gotten wind that bikers were likely involved, and he was asked more than once what he thought about the connection. He really hated lying, but had no alternative.

As bad as his day at work was, what Wolf dreaded most was going home to face his wife. He knew Sue's radar was up due to the recent late nights, overnighters, and changes in his behavior. He suspected she had been reading his emails, and if so, would soon see replies to the message he had sent to his female friend. She would be extremely hurt, and their kids would be upset at the distress he caused their mother. The thought of talking with his son and daughter was too hard to even imagine. He took the long way home to think.

Finally arriving at home, he waited until supper to tell Sue of his intention to leave the next day. At first, she seemed surprised when told of his plans, but to his relief, did not ask many details other than where he was going and why it was so sudden. He knew that she could smell a lie and therefore had carefully rehearsed the story in his head. He sensed she knew something, but wasn't speaking what was on her mind. As was her habit, she had washed and folded his favorite riding clothes and put them neatly in a stack in the closet, causing him to feel even more intense shame for what she would go through all too soon.

CHAPTER 20

A faint reddish glow was beginning to lighten the sky as he backed his loaded down Vulcan Nomad out of the garage. The neighborhood was quiet except for the shrill whistles of early morning birds. Wolf had cleaned and checked Beast over last night, then packed his camping gear in the same methodical way he had done so many times in the past. This time was different—he had no idea how long he'd be gone, or even if he could come back at all. His kids believed this was just another road trip to the Appalachian mountains, a favorite spring and summer destination. Wolf knew differently, and had spent the evening paying close attention to every detail of the evening's activities.

Supper had been Sue's meatloaf with the usual fixings. He had requested she make an extra sandwich for the next day's trip, and watched as she assembled it with care. He regretted that his son was off at school and he would not see him before leaving, but he was extremely thankful his son would not see firsthand what would soon happen. His daughter was at home for supper, so he drew her out in conversation about her plans for the summer. After a nightcap with Sue, followed by a muscle relaxer to help him sleep, he had seduced his wife, slowly and with a loving touch, paying attention to the details she enjoyed when they were intimate. As they lay there recuperating from the passion, she looked him in the eye and asked with concern when he'd be back, sensing the change in his normal preride behavior. He'd done his best to put her fears at ease, but knew she suspected that this trip was different. They had fallen asleep later, Wolf sleeping lightly and rising before the alarm rang. He quietly showered, then dressed quickly, trying not to wake her as was his normal routine.

He mounted his bike and hit the starter, putting on his gloves and helmet as it idled, the Vance and Hines pipes putting out a low pitched, reassuring sound while spouting foggy exhaust into the early morning chilly air. The door opened and Sue came over and gave him a long, silent hug. He reached in his jacket pocket and pulled out an envelope containing a note explaining his situation and the passwords she'd need to manage his accounts while he was away. He had planned to drop it in the mail, but knew by her appearance that this was the time to give it to her.

"Don't worry, everything's going to work out; we will be ok. Whatever you do, wait until tonight to open this. It's important that you trust me."

She looked him in the eyes for a long minute and then in a flat tone said, "You're riding with that bitch Kelly, aren't you." She didn't wait for him to reply before continuing. "I hope you understand what all you are throwing away. You will hurt some people that really love and believe in you." She turned and walked back inside, slamming the door shut behind her.

Wolf drew in a long, deep breath, thankful that Sue had not made a big and tearful scene. He did not know if he could have handled the heart ache. He stepped on the shifter, let out the clutch, and slowly started down the driveway. In his mirror he could see Sue watching from the window upstairs as he pulled out of the driveway.

He would not miss the middle-class neighborhood with its white collar, uppity homeowner's association rules, and the conservative, self-serving attitudes of the residents. He *would* miss the good roads, restaurants, and bars where he had made so many connections over the years. He put the thought away as he rode through town, headed toward the Twisted Iron where his buddy and the best wrench he knew were waiting.

As he pulled up in front, the door to the motorcycle work area slid open, and Mark beckoned him inside. The door slid down quickly behind him. His buddy Big Jim was standing next to the lift and motioned him to pull up on it. After Jim secured Beast, Lute, in his police jacket and riot helmet, stepped around the corner, gun in one hand, and cuffs in the other. All color drained from Wolf's face, to which his friends reacted by doubling over with laughter, while Mark came up and slapped him on the back.

"We're just screwing with you, Wolf—I just wish we had gotten a picture of your face for that danged magazine. You turned as white as one of those Yankees after spending the winter inside with no sun."

Still shaken, he climbed off his bike and stumbled but was caught before he did a face plant by the big arms of his tree-like friend, Big Jim.

"What the hell are you doing up here, and how is this funny to you assholes?" he stammered. His relief had turned to anger, his face turning crimson.

Lute spoke in a solemn tone of voice. "We wanted to get your attention by doing something you'd remember in the weeks ahead. You must be constantly on guard more than any time in the past and extremely careful who you trust. If this thing goes as bad as it could, every cop in the nation will be gunning for you and putting the squeeze on everyone you know. Anybody that helps you could be charged as an accessory. Luckily, with a few changes, you'll easily blend in with other bikers."

Wolf looked hard at Big Jim, then grinned and gave him an enthusiastic greeting followed by a hard punch in the back.

"It's good to see you dude, but why are you here? You sure are a long way from Florida."

"Mark called me, and I was looking for an excuse to put some miles on my new ride, anyway," he said, pointing at a black Kawasaki Vulcan 2000 Classic LT in the nearest bay. "I figured you could give me some tips on how to be a road dog."

"Nice looking bike, but you heard what Lute said. You don't want to be anywhere around if they find me."

Big Jim looked Wolf dead in the eye and said slowly in his best southern Alabamian drawl, "ain't no way in hell you're going on this adventure without a wingman whether you like it or not." He paused for effect while his demand sank in. "I figured I'd need a fast bike to keep up with you, so you're stuck with me. Besides, everybody knows you travel alone, so you'll be less obvious with a buddy riding along."

"I don't want to break up this tear jerking family reunion, but we got work to do and not much time to do it," Mark said, pointing at a tank, fender, and the hard saddle bags sitting on the workbench. "Hope you like red, Wolf."

Big Jim said, "let me have your jacket, bro."

He handed it over and watched as Jim disappeared into the room in the back.

An hour later, Beast had been fully serviced, with many changes made to its' appearance. The Nomad was now red and black with matching red flame decals on the batwing fairing.

"There's an envelope inside the left bag's pocket with some traveling money in it," Mark said. "Let me know if you need anything and it'll be there for you. You've got a lot of friends if you need 'em."

"I can't—"

Mark cut him off, "you're good for it. We have a plan to catch those two that set you up. Just be cool and enjoy the ride this summer. I'll keep an eye on Sue for you. She know anything?"

"I left her a note with an explanation. She'll be strong."

"Good, I'll call her tonight. Don't worry about anything but staying safe and free." He put out his hand and they shook.

Lute was next. "Listen closely, my friend. I need your wallet, belt, phone, and anything else on you or in the bike with your name on it." He waited as Wolf did as he was told.

He continued. "Here's a new wallet with a driver's license, insurance card, credit cards, and some typical stuff most guys have on them. Your name is now William Little. Your biker handle is "Pack". Always use that name when you call or text Mark or me or anyone else. Our numbers are programmed into your phone and on cards inside the wallet. There are a few business cards of people you can trust in an emergency. Use them only if you have to. Next, you've got to change your appearance. You are going to shave that purty mustache before you leave. When you get where you're going that I don't want to know where, stay there as long as you can and grow a beard and long hair. Here's the new phone. Use it until you get the word to lose it. Get a disposable, call twice and hang up each time, ten minutes apart. Got it?"

"Sounds pretty cloak and dagger—should I even bother to ask about the name?"

"Nope, but if you get pulled, it's clean. You're retired now. Wolf, this is very important. When they start looking for you, it will be with more resources than you could ever imagine. Hunker down and just try to blend in. Many a fugitive has been caught by just a seemingly minor slip up, hence your new name. Do not call anyone you know; their incoming calls will be tracked, you can count on that."

"Lute, I don't know how I can ever—"

He was cut off again before finishing when Lute said, "you did many years ago. Just get rid of that mustache and smear this on where it was. Hurry it up, you have to be gone before anybody shows up outside." He went and sheared his bushy mustache off, then returned to where his bike and friends were waiting.

As if on cue, Big Jim stepped from the back room and threw his leather jacket at him. Weathered motorcycle club insignia was now sewn on the back, and his wolf patch on the front had been replaced by a name patch with the handle, 'Pack' on it. He put his well-worn leather jacket on, then looked at his oldest friend.

"Didn't know you could sew, old buddy; not bad at all."

"Just one of my many talents I never told ya about. We'll have plenty of time for me to enlighten you later. Let's ride," he said with an exaggerated, but fake grin.

Wolf paused at the entrance. He slowly let out the clutch, gave Beast a gentle turn of the throttle, and pulled out into the light traffic on Hwy 31 followed closely by Big Jim on his bike. The start of this journey was similar to the way many past road trips had started. This time however, he passed by his turn and headed into town towards the hospital where his mom had passed gently in her sleep, three years ago. He turned his bike into the gap in the median on the road below it, and looked up the hill to see the rest home where she spent her final years, her memory slowly failing due to Alzheimer's. The staff had lovingly cared for her during her stay there, and to the staff, she was a favorite due to her gentle, friendly, and caring demeanor. Many would stop by her room in the late night hours to talk about their families, several even seeking her advice on handling personal problems. She never judged them, instead listening and consoling them with understanding and compassion. The staff knew they could speak openly about even their most private issues, knowing that when they left the room, she would promptly forget their conversations due to her total loss of short term memory, a symptom of the disease. They loved her and always treated her with dignity and respect. Many even came to visit her in the hospital after the last heart stoppage, and prayed with the family as she drew her final breath.

As he sat on his idling bike lost in thought, his wingman pulled alongside. Wolf wondered when and if, he would ever again as a free man see this town where his kids had grown to adulthood. Memories of football, basketball, and baseball games came flooding into his mind. His daughter's concerts and awards in high school, along with the sports awards his son had won were all sources of pride in the lessons he had tried to teach them growing up. His deepest fears washed over him as he thought of the strong possibility of jail, and the shame it would bring upon his kids and Sue. He wiped a tear away and resolved that he would rather have a head on collision with a Mack truck then put them through what seemed to him a possible, and even likely ending to this story.

Not wanting to dwell upon these dark thoughts and the distraction they would bring, he turned on the radio and pulled out into traffic, followed closely by Big Jim. He headed for the turn two lights ahead that would lead him to temporary safety in the mountains of Tennessee and North Carolina. He was thankful for all the biker brothers he had there, but was fearful of the possible consequences they might face by harboring him, a fugitive.

As he shifted into second gear and twisted the throttle, the music of a Bon Jovi song, *Wanted—Dead or Alive* came on the radio.

CHAPTER 21

The two bikers took Highway 11 out of town, and then got on Hwy 43, not stopping until they got to Rome, Georgia where they filled up on gas. The temperature rose steadily, predicted to pass 80 degrees by noon. A few miles north of Rome on Hwy 53, they stopped at Panhead City for hydration therapy and to see old buddies. Wolf knew he would need his network of friends for the plan to work. This would be but one of many stops to renew past connections. As usual, they were invited to attend one of the frequent parties planned for that night, and could crash in the bunkhouse afterward. Wolf knew they could spend the day there, forgetting about their troubles and getting lost in this antique museum, filled with toys for kids and adults. The place was filled with Harley-Davidson panheads and knuckleheads, many that had been all over the U.S. and been restored and maintained in pristine and rideable condition. Unfortunately, he knew they had to move on. They said their goodbyes and headed north on 53 toward Ellijay, then on to Blue Ridge. From there, they took 515 to Blairsville where they turned onto US 129, passing through Murphy and heading north to Robbinsville.

Wolf had been in contact with one of the best navigator/bargain finders he knew, Gator, who had on a previous ride, hooked them up with a two-bedroom cabin right off the Cherohola Skyway, a great scenic road that connected Robbinsville, NC with Tellico Plains, TN. You could sit on the porch or in any room and watch the bikes go by just thirty yards away. It had all the amenities of home including Wi-Fi. Two comfortable beds and a refrigerator full of beer and food awaited them when they arrived just after dusk. They unloaded their bikes and then changed into shorts. They then grabbed cold beers and went out to the porch to relax after the long day's ride. Wolf checked his cell phone for messages, and seeing only one with the message, "all clear", relaxed and sat down.

His buddy passed him a lit joint. "Here's to the long vacation, bro, may the ride last to the very end." Wolf accepted and took a long, deep draw, holding it inside his lungs as long as he could. He nodded his head in agreement, then held up his beer in a toast to the shared sentiment. Two passes of the potent weed, and both were satisfied with the relaxing effect. They talked for an hour about biker philosophy, signs, and omens. When the conversation lagged, they both came to the conclusion that they would not be smoking once the hunt was on.

The following week was spent riding local blacktop, mapping out different back roads less traveled for ways to leave the area without being on the main highways. Their exploring led them to some fine hidden away streams, lakeside swimming holes, and great fishing. Wolf was grateful for the rods left at the cabin for their use, as his normal way of traveling with a rod stuck on the back of the bike was a dead giveaway. He was more than aware of the stares of passersby that he reasoned were due to the rod on the back of his bike. In the past, it had often opened the door for many a great experience that had started with the fishing connection. No more traveling with a rod on the back of his bike after the hunt began.

For more than two weeks the two bikers rode the area, traveling further each day in different directions from the cabin. They renewed old friendships and checked out places to hide all over the Appalachian Mountains. On the fourteenth day, Wolf told his friend of an idea he had. Big Jim was against it from the start, but finally agreed to arrange a visit by his wife, Sue. He himself had hit it off with Lisa, the cabin's landlady, a mature, attractive lady with a great sense of humor. He thought a few days riding to quiet, out of the way places down lightly traveled backroads would be fun for both of them.

Sue arrived in the early morning hours the next day. She slid into bed beside the sleeping Wolf, awakening, and then showing him in his favorite ways how much he was missed. Afterward, they talked until the sound of activity came from the kitchen, followed by the smell of fresh coffee. They heard the shower come on and were waiting, coffee in hand, when Big Jim came strolling out with a towel draped around his waist.

"Good morning, Miz Wolf," he said, a big grin on his face. They hugged for a longer than normal time.

"Thanks for keeping him safe," she whispered in his ear. He gave her a squeeze in reply.

"So what's on the agenda for today, dude? You look like you're getting ready for a date." Wolf said.

"Matter of fact I am. Me and Lisa are gonna take us a ride. I hope you and that hot lady of yours don't mind."

"Not at all, I thought y'all were getting pretty friendly lately." He smiled at Sue. "I think we can keep ourselves occupied all day."

"Yep, I thought so. You guys have fun, I know we will. You wanna do supper together?"

Sue spoke first. "I'm cooking, so come hungry."

He left to dress. A short while later they said their goodbyes, then listened as he started his bike and let it warm. Minutes later they watched as he and Lisa drove off, smiles plastered on both of their faces.

The next few days passed quickly as new, lasting memories were made. Wolf was a little suspicious when his buddy came back in time for supper after spending a second day with the Lisa. This came to a head when on the third day, he saw Lisa drive up without him. An hour later, he was waiting as Big Jim rode up, covered in dirt and sweat from head to toe.

"What have you been up to today?"

"Follow me," was his reply. He waited while Beast warmed up.

They rode for a few miles until Jim put on his blinker, then swung his bike wide in the road, turning up a steep, narrow road hidden from view by the trees along the main road. No one could see the driveway unless looking for it. There was no street sign, as this was a private road. After a bend, the road flattened out in an area in front of a 1920's era stone two story house with a small cottage behind it. The cottage had a garage under it that opened onto the road. Big Jim stopped outside and got off his bike. He walked over and pushed numbers on a keypad and the door opened. He motioned for Wolf to back his bike in. The air inside was cool, feeling great after the mid-eighty temps outside. He got off and walked outside. They ascended the rough cut stone steps leading to the two dwellings above, entering a common patio area between them.

His buddy gave him a tour, returning to the big kitchen in the main house at the end. "Here's the best feature of this little getaway."

He opened the door to what looked like a small pantry. He pressed his boot on a hidden release in the bottom. The wall and shelves swung inward to reveal a narrow staircase below. The room at the bottom contained a bed, a small efficiency kitchen, and a bathroom. Jim walked over to the full length mirror and pulled on the edge. The mirror swung open to reveal a small, narrow passageway. Flipping on a flashlight, Jim squeezed through the entrance and walked slowly through the damp, forty feet of tunnel. Wolf heard the sound of squeaking hinges and could see the faint light from the now open doorway at the end. The light suddenly brightened as Jim opened the garage door where Beast was parked.

"What do you think—cool place, huh?"

"Dude, this place is awesome! How did you find it?"

"Lisa owns and rents them out. Our cabin is just one of many she has. The big one used to be a realtor's office and before that, they used it to hide moonshine back during the prohibition. I figure if you ever have to hide out in this area, it might come in handy. Lisa is one cool lady that will look out for you. Sue and her really hit it off, each trying to out cook the other—I sure liked that part," he said, rubbing his belly.

"Sue's leaving tonight after supper. We're afraid to push our luck. We saw the signs today," Wolf said in a low, sad tone of voice. "We're good for the long haul now."

"Thank goodness for vibrators—they got ones that work as well as Harley's for the womenfolk," he said with a big laugh, to which Wolf responded with a punch in the arm. "Just kidding, bro. Let's go see what's cooking."

They returned to the cabin to find supper ready and waiting. After a few hours of talking and messing around, Sue loaded the car under the cover of darkness, planning to arrive home before dawn. No one had come by their house, and their daughter had not seen anything out of ordinary. As far as anyone knew, Sue had simply not left the house, still upset at Wolf for leaving her. She knew that a storm was brewing and could hit at any time. She would be ready.

Jim and Wolf were up at dawn, having just heard from Sue that she was home safely. Sitting in the small screened in porch drinking coffee and smoking, they watched the chickens come down the hill from the coop behind the house as was their daily routine. The clucking and occasional crowing of the rooster was drowned out by a passing biker on a Harley CVO Street Glide with loud pipes. By habit, both looked up and watched the lone rider go by barely forty yards away, them out of sight from the passing rider. A chill went up Wolf's spine when he thought he recognized the huge frame of the biker known as 45 go by. A moment later, Wolf dropped his coffee and crouched behind a chair when a fully grown deer came crashing through the brush from the other side of the road, jumped the guardrail, then headed across the road, running at full speed up the driveway and into the woods above. He looked at his friend, who had drawn his Glock and was looking at him.

"Time to leave," they said in unison then walked inside to pack.

Twenty minutes later they were outside loading the bikes when the familiar sound of a performance enhanced Harley Davidson engine was heard. Still early and a week day, bikes were infrequent travelers at this time of day. Jim pushed Wolf behind the house and watched the receding back of the biker after it passed the cabin in the curve. They waited a minute and, as if on cue, a second bike, a black Vaquero with flames went around the curve. Jim jumped on his bike, started it, and took off spraying gravel from the rear tire of his 2000cc V-twin cruiser. Wolf reacted quickly as well, and was right behind him. They went a few miles then stopped at the lookout point, cut their engines, and listened. No motorcycle exhaust noise was heard, even from the valley ahead and below. Having no clue where the two riders had gone, they rode back to the house to complete packing, leaving ten minutes later.

They stayed on highway 129 until they got to 74, then headed east. From there, they went north at Lake Junaluska on NC 209, a road known as *The Rattler*. The road was much longer than *the Dragon*—very curvy and more scenic, but not as well banked or nearly as notorious. Riding through the valleys, they smelled the sweet smell of freshly cut hay and relished in the view of mountain farmland surrounded by the dense forest growth on the surrounding slopes. Coming out of the valleys, they were as one with their machines on the curvy roads that wound through the countryside, taking their minds off the drama at hand as they headed to the Bobarosa Saloon and Motorcycle Resort in Del Rio, Tennessee.

Arriving late in the afternoon, they stopped and went inside a camper separated from the others at the edge of the camping area. Big Jim set up an improvised perimeter motion detector with low output lights around their temporary home. He tied the detector into an audible alarm for the trailer's interior. After unloading and stowing their gear, they walked over to the bar, ordered food and the first round of a bunch of beers.

CHAPTER 22

The days passed slowly in Shelby. After a week without new developments in the murder investigation, along with no mention of the glove in the news, Blondie was growing extremely impatient and irritable. She snapped and told 45 to take the long way back to the house in the mountains. It took him three days to get there, stopping at bars where he could find and take advantage of the local women in his lust for total domination over his conquests. They never remembered anything between taking a motorcycle ride and waking up in a local seedy motel the next day, sore in unfamiliar places. 45 took care to leave no marks on the victims of his sexually depraved actions.

Blondie spent the next two weeks soaking up the local news and surfing the internet for more local matches to the bike. She returned to the house in the mountains, but after several days went by without additional developments, she got restless and returned to Shelby. She found and read every copy of the biker rag Wolf's story was in. She studied his habits, trip routes, and places he mentioned, programing them into her GPS. They would show on her screen when she was in an area and riding by. She could find no trace of him, and bikers he knew had no idea where he was, typically saying things like, "he's on one of his trips to God only knows where again," or telling her she could "probably read about it in next month's issue."

She decided it was time to plant the note and take advantage of Wolf being gone. Not knowing what or how the first anonymous note was written, she decided to go for simplicity.

On the note were the simple words: *Wolf is who you are looking for.*

Blondie placed the note into the water bill drop box in Whitesville late that night. She went back to Shelby and packed to leave. The next day was spent watching the news and the internet for any mention of the note. On the six o'clock news, it was reported that an unnamed source in city hall had told a reporter that another anonymous note had been found. There was no information about the note's content. As the sky began to lighten early the following morning, she started her bike and rode north on a route leading back to the mountains of western North Carolina.

At police headquarters, there was frantic activity, examining all available information about Wolf, aka John Trotter. The note was not probable cause for a search warrant, so all other possible reasons were examined in order to obtain a search warrant. FBI analysts looked for motive, and based on previously examined information put together while looking for a suspect, determined that what Wolf had said at the protest of the noise ordinance constituted a threat, and therefore, were able to coerce a judge to issue the warrant. They were waiting for the go ahead and staged in an undeveloped cul-de-sac inside his neighborhood when the go ahead was given to proceed with the search. They were to obtain DNA samples, along with any other items that could be evidence of the crime or that would help determine Wolf's present whereabouts, and specifically, a glove.

The warrant was served at three pm by a team of FBI agents led by Agent Watson. Sue was at home with their daughter when the doorbell rang. After taking her time reading the warrant, she was escorted outside by a cold, impersonal female agent. Standing outside her home, she could hear the sounds of the search as the team of agents went through her home from the attic to the garage. As she stood there holding her daughter's hand, she heard a familiar, reassuring voice saying her name. She turned and saw Lute. He hugged her and whispered that she must continue playing the part of the shocked, but loyal wife who would never think her husband capable of a heinous crime like murder. He asked about the note Wolf had left, and she told him it was in her journal. Lute knew it would be found and hoped there was nothing written that would cast more suspicion upon his buddy. Lute had been asked to stay outside with the family until needed, and was advised to console Sue in order to ensure her cooperation later.

The city police department was there in a support function to handle traffic, nosy neighbors, and especially the media. The streets were lined with police cars and support vehicles. Members of the media were unable to turn down the dead end street and had to walk from as much as six blocks away. Neighbors' cars were allowed to pass thru, but only after proving they lived there, a problem for some that had not changed the address on their driver licenses. The handling of the search and the questioning of the neighbors that were on their way home was later described as a three-ring circus and an imposition to residents going about their daily business. As the curiosity and anger of the neighbors grew, the media became more vocal, even seeming to stir up bad feelings towards the authorities. By five, there were more than thirty vehicles lining the street, and the crowd numbered more than a hundred and consisted of media and law enforcement personnel, with spectators from the neighborhood mixed in. There was standing room only in the cul-de-sac in front of Wolf's home. A spokesman for the department had "no comment at this time" for the media. Undeterred, the reporters sought out Wolf's neighbors to interview and get opinions as to what was happening while seeking background information on the biker and his family for the next newscast.

At the dealership where John Trotter, aka Wolf worked, similar activity was going on. His office was searched and his coworkers extensively questioned as to his whereabouts. The bikers that worked with him were given extra attention. His boss, normally outspoken in his opinions, was tight-lipped when questioned, and upon the advice of the legal department, had nothing to say to the media except that they were giving their full cooperation to the authorities and that John Trotter was on a leave of absence. He advised his employees to cooperate fully with the police, but to avoid the news media's questions and cameras. Those that worked with him daily could tell he was extremely distressed at the unwelcome attention, and was trying hard to hold back from voicing his opinion of the situation or to say anything about who many were certain would soon be their ex-coworker and sales manager. Wolf was well thought of by the team, and consequently, morale was at an all-time low as the ramifications of the events were realized. Few sales were made that day, even though there was a tremendous amount of customer traffic coming through the front door and into the customer parking lot.

Unfortunately for the dealership, their manager, John Trotter, wasn't there to put his typical positive spin on the development and then prod them to make connections with the inflow of potential new and future customers. Instead, the common thought was more about the damage that was being done to the dealership's reputation, and how it would negatively impact future sales.

On the five o'clock news, the top story was that there were new developments in the investigation into the murder of Whiteville's mayor. The authorities were seeking the whereabouts of one John Trotter, aka Wolf for questioning as a "person of interest" in the crime. Details would follow as more information was obtained. A few short snippets from interviews were shown. Most portrayed him as a good man, dedicated to his family and supportive of charities and the biker community. The authorities were not nearly as fortunate, and were shown to be more than a little inept in the handling of the investigation. Several short news clips were aired, including the recent fiasco at the municipal center. The news anchorman promised more to come on the newscast at ten.

By seven pm, the FBI investigators had completed their search, and had obtained most, but not all of the evidence and information they sought. DNA samples were easily obtained, and the note in Wolf's wife's journal was found.

Several motorcycle gloves were found and taken, but the one that matched the glove found at the crime scene was not located. Wolf's family spent the evening putting their home back in order, while attempting to console each other. Bud, their son, had come home to help his family. Sue remained close lipped, telling both of the kids that this would all blow over soon, assuring them that their dad would be found innocent of any wrong doing. Her mind was cluttered with worries about the truth of these reassurances to her son and daughter. It had been mentioned to her by investigators that her husband could be charged with obstruction of justice and hindering an investigation in a murder case, and was a suspect in the murder. She did not mention this to their son and daughter. When she was alone behind the closed bedroom door, she again watched the news, becoming even more fearful of the outcome, and feeling less reassured by the soothing words of their friend, Lute. After a long cry, she fell asleep with the TV turned to the local news channel.

CHAPTER 23

Wolf and Jim spent the week riding, again looking for little-known backroads and hideaways around Del Rio, TN. Wolf's beard was growing nicely, and those he had met in the past did not recognize him now. He practiced talking in a way that mimicked the local mountain dialect. Wolf enjoyed singing along to country and rock-n-roll music, and had purchased several CDs of mountain ballads in order to learn and practice, much to Big Jim's dismay. Their daily routine typically included exercising, riding, and watching the news. They competed to see who could come up with the most creative and outlandish stories, many with ties to their current situation and the potential outcome. They tended to avoid others, a tough thing for both as they enjoyed the camaraderie of fellow bikers and typically, were outgoing and talkative, especially after a few favorite beverages. In the bar, they were often sought out by "flat-landers" looking for tips on roads to ride. Avoiding the numerous good looking biker babes was extremely tough, especially for Big Jim.

They were having a beer, sitting on the deck perched over the fast running, clear waters of the French Broad river, the full moon reflected in the ripples on the water, when Jim received a text. It advised them to watch the local broadcast from the Birmingham TV station, available on the internet. Doing as instructed, they watched the newscast highlighting new developments in the murder investigation of the mayor of Whiteville. They turned the TV on and saw a similar story on the national news. A knot grew in his stomach when the camera panned the crowd in front of his home, followed by a shot of the dealership where he worked. A substantial reward was being offered for information on his whereabouts, followed by an ominous reminder of the consequences of not coming forward.

They sat watching and searching the internet for more information for over an hour when the phone rang. It was Lute. Wolf went outside to talk in private. Minutes later, he came back inside and handed the phone to Jim. What followed was not pretty, with Jim generously using common four letter words typically used by bikers along with some terms not so often heard except in the most heated discussions. A short while later, Jim handed the phone back. Wolf listened for a couple of minutes more, took a few notes, and hung up.

Jim spoke first. "You on-board with this, dude? You and I go way back, and I'm not feeling good at all about bailing on you now when you need me most."

"I appreciate that, bro, but what Lute said makes sense. You do tend to stand out in a crowd, and now that they're looking into all my "known associates", you'll be one of the first they look for. I'm one hundred percent sure they're at your house as we speak. Lute knows his shit, and I agree with him that you need to hightail it back to Florida in the morning. You'll be asked where you've been and if you've seen me. Those guys are experts at picking out lies, so be ready with a story that will check out. Include this place, but leave out Robbinsville, I may need that one later."

"I know you trust Lute and he's a cop, but they gotta be looking at him, too."

Wolf thought about what to say next. "They are, but we have a connection that will ride with me that no one knows about. He'll be riding as my wingman for a while. Don't worry, I'll be in very good hands. Be looking for a message—we may need your help catching those killers down the road."

"You know you—" he looked at Wolf with tears welling in his eyes.

"Not another word, bro. You get packed and ready to leave at dawn. You've got a long ride ahead of you tomorrow." He stood up and extended his hand, looking him in the eye. They both knew this could be the last time they shared a night of freedom on the road.

Big Jim left before dawn the next morning. Wolf packed quickly and left an hour later, now comfortable in his altered looks. His beard was full, he had lost over twenty pounds, and now looked more lean and muscled than he had in many years. He was confident in his disguise, but was uneasy about returning to Alabama for a bike rally at Boogie Bottoms, near Locust Fork. The plan was to meet Lute at a cabin there. The ride today would be relatively short, traveling roads popular with bikers on his way to Tellico Plains. He was meeting up with another lone wolf and old buddy, known only to a few as "Navigator", at a secluded cabin in Caney Creek Village.

Wolf had met Navigator several years earlier at the Bamafest rally near Demopolis, Alabama. They traded shots for beers and spent most of an afternoon and early evening sharing tales from the road. The old road dog was mostly retired, earning his traveling money as a lone watchman at secluded high-security projects for months at a time. He would have many months to ride in between jobs, and like Wolf, preferred to ride alone. He seldom spent more than a day or two at any one location, and knew the backroads in the southeastern states extremely well. He supplemented his income with occasional visits to casinos, always traveling on his bike and riding in areas where the temps were comfortable during that time of year. Little more about him was shared. Wolf had his suspicions about his past, suspecting he was ex-military and an expert in covert operations by the way he planned his trips, among other things. Another thing they had in common was their appearance, including approximate height, weight, age, and even the same hair and eye color. Some thought they were blood brothers when seen together. They ran into each other from time to time, and frequently shared new discoveries and unique places to ride with the other. "Navigator" was shortened to "Gator", the name he was known by with most of his biker acquaintances.

Wolf was within three miles of the cabin when the deluge of cold, spring rain came pouring down, forcing him to pull under an old oak tree along the long, upward sloping drive that led to the small Baptist church at the top of the hill. He had waited a few minutes too long, and consequently was soaked for his determination to beat the rain. He always carried a full faced helmet with a rain suit rolled up inside, so after putting his rain gear and helmet on, he continued on to the waiting dry cabin.

Pulling up outside the cabin in the driving rain, he used the combination he knew by heart to gain entrance to the two bedroom temporary refuge from the elements. The cabin was one of ten fully furnished ones that made up the small, secluded resort, all equipped with a kitchen, full bath, and satellite TV. In the cabins nearest the office, there was even wireless internet available. As he was toweling himself dry after stripping off his soaked clothes, he heard a familiar knock on the rear door.

As he opened the door and greeted his buddy Gator, they heard the sound of tornado sirens from the top of a nearby ridge. The surrounding hills amplified the sound, causing the hair to stand up on his neck. At that moment, a bolt of lightning struck the tall tree at the edge of the field behind the cabin, momentarily blinding and deafening them from the boom of the thunder. Startled, Wolf dropped the towel wrapped around his waist. Not noticing his nakedness, they both looked up in awe at the dark, swirling mass of clouds overhead. A sound similar to a far off train was heard as they watched the clouds change color to hues of dark brown and orange. They watched in amazement as large sheets of metal roofing and other debris were carried high aloft by the winds.

Gator was the first to speak. "I know you're glad to see me, but put some pants on, will ya?"

Wolf, suddenly embarrassed, went in and returned quickly, hastily pulling on jeans and a shirt while watching the storm.

"You reckon we ought to find shelter?" he asked Gator.

"Probably too late for that now. Is there a shelter close by?"

"Never asked or seen one. Guess we could tie ourselves to a pole or go lie down in the stream, but I'm too lazy," Wolf replied.

"How about a beer while we watch—may be hard to find a cold one later."

Wolf looked at his friend in the way one does when hearing an unexpected off-the-wall remark. He laughed and said, "what the hell, why not? You sure know how to make one hell of an entrance."

The siren stopped suddenly, and the noise of the wind picked up. They watched as what looked like a small RV crashed into the woods on the ridge. Minutes later, the winds began to calm and the rain stopped. Little damage was seen in the immediate area, but the smell of fresh pine wood saturated the air.

As they stood there watching, they heard a truck from the cabin at the end start up, and as they watched, two men wearing jackets with the large letters DEA on the back start throwing supplies into the rear. Gator ran over and offered their help. He motioned for Wolf to join them. They jumped into the rear as the driver put the truck in gear and started off.

"I hate to ask, but are you real sure about this?"

"Yeah I am. You ever heard the phrase, "hidden in plain sight"? I met these guys earlier today—they both love to ride. There are a couple of dual purpose bikes on the other side of their cabin. This will be a good test of your disguise and who would ever think to look *here* with all the emergency personnel that will soon be all over the place. Besides, the roads most likely are blocked judging by the debris we saw being tossed around."

"You've got a point there, bro. Sorry I doubted you. In fact, I'd have a hard time just sitting here with my thumb up my butt while people need our help. It is amazing that we still have power."

Less than a mile from the entrance, highway 360 was blocked by a tree that had fallen across the road. Grabbing chainsaws, they helped cut and then winch the cut sections of the downed tree out of the roadway. This was repeated again as they made their way closer to the little town of Tellico Plains. About a mile outside of town, they saw where the tornado had touched down, breaking and uprooting trees, tearing off roofs, and throwing large man-made items around like toys. The tree he had been under when he stopped earlier had been uprooted.

Just before reaching the intersection with the Cherohala Skyway, they saw that the KOA campground had been leveled. Emergency vehicles and personnel had converged there, and were setting up shelters and caring for the injured. As they drove up, a helicopter landed, loaded two occupied stretchers aboard, and then took off as the sun began to set with an amazing display of sunset colors.

The following days were spent helping the locals clear debris, cutting fallen trees, and putting tarps on the roofs of damaged homes. As they worked alongside others, Wolf became comfortable with his new identity and lost his fear of being discovered by public safety officials. He came to think of the two DEA agents as friends, and shared many a beer with them at the end of the day. The town bounced back quickly, and within a few days, all local businesses were open with the exception of the KOA campground, now a small pile of bricks surrounded by a barren field. It still looked like a campground with all the trailers and disaster relief tents pitched around the site.

They rode out on Wednesday, as dawn's early light cast a reddish-yellow glow on the layers of low-lying clouds hovering over the mountains behind them. They headed south to Locust Fork and a favorite rally of theirs, Boogie Bottoms. Situated on the banks of the Locust Fork River, this was the perfect base camp to explore the curvy roads and beautiful landscape in Blount county and the surrounding area. There was swimming and fishing in the river, activities enjoyed by many, but especially this pair of bikers after a long day of riding in the hot sun. The water was refreshingly cool and clear.

Upon arriving, they rode straight to cabin number 2 and unloaded, preparing for a weekend of biker games, great music, and beer drinking. More importantly, a rendezvous was planned with Mark and Lute to share the latest news on the investigation and manhunt for Wolf. They joined up with a group from BON at their camp known as 'Speedy's Bar and Grill'. Wolf had met many in the group at previous rallies there while enjoying the warmth and comraderie while gathered around the "Alabama hot tub", a firepit inside an old, discarded cast-iron bathtub. He believed this would be a true test of his new identity and great practice using his newly acquired mountain dialect.

Both were in their element, seeing old friends and making new ones. It was difficult staying relatively sober amongst this entertaining bunch of bikers or not, as some preferred to be backseat scooter riders. A bright side was that there were plenty of volunteer bikers readily offering their services during the rally as taxicabs from campsites to the stage area. After the bands were done, firepits were stoked as groups gathered around them in the chilly night air to talk and keep the party going. The sight and smell of burning wood made the bikers hungry for food and companionship. As the night grew late, couples would drift off to their tents and RVs. Laughter and moans of pleasure were heard across the land.

Gator hit it off with a petite, mature, attractive blond with a great looking tush. Wolf smiled when they disappeared into a small RV parked a few yards away. He realized how much he missed the company of his wife, Sue. Sitting at the fire, he stared at the full moon overhead and was again reminded of how his predicament got started. With that on his mind, he leaned back in the chair, closed his eyes, and drifted off to sleep. He dreamed of many things, including an angel that laid him to rest in a golden tent. He suddenly woke up, as the sun did indeed make the tent light up like gold in the rays of the rising sun. Looking under the quilt, he noted he was fully clothed and there was a familiar, well-endowed woman gently snoring beside him on the large air mattress. Thankful for his apparent restraint from amorous activities, he drifted back to sleep.

Saturday was entirely different from the previous day. Mark and Lute had ridden in at noon, seemingly accompanied by a group of riders known as the "White Knights". The small group was from Whiteville and was making a hydration stop at Resort 25 when they met up. They too were headed to the rally, so the two of them followed the group on their ride to Boogie Bottoms. Mark participated in the biker games held in the afternoon, coming close to winning several events. Lute mingled with the spectators, scanning the bikers for anyone that seemed suspicious or out of place. He made eye contact with Wolf and Gator more than once. As the band started to play near dusk, Lute gave the all clear signal for the meeting at the cabin.

Cabin 2 had been chosen for its location. It was situated on a slope with low visibility from casual observers, easy access to the river, and next to a seldom used trail leading out of the area. Exactly at nine pm, a familiar knock was heard on the cabin door. Without looking outside, Gator opened the door and stepped out. He put on the night vision goggles Lute handed him as he and Mark went inside. Taking post where he could easily spot anyone approaching, he clicked the radio's transmit button twice and got an immediate response. Unknown to all but Lute, a lone hidden sentry was posted near the entrance to the rally.

After filling Wolf in on the investigation back in Whiteville, the talk turned to devising a plan to catch the killers. Lute dropped a bombshell when he told them that a top FBI agent had been advised of the real situation. He went on to tell about his current assignment and his connection with Watty. He reassured Wolf that the film would clear him of the charges that were sure to be brought against him due to his glove being discovered near where the mayor's body was found. The general consensus was that he had become a bit of a "folk hero" due to the videos seen on TV and the internet, but thankfully not like Eric Rudolf, the Atlanta bomber, who had also been referred to as a "lone wolf". As they shared a laugh at the thought of being outlaw bikers, Lute wondered how his friends would react if they knew there was a hidden sentry watching the entrance to Boogie Bottoms that was a senior agent in the FBI.

Over a couple of beers, Lute began to outline a loose plan for finding the killers. The plan involved Wolf and Gator attending bike rallies that he had written about in the past. Thunder Beach, Shine in Lapine, and Faunsdale were a few mentioned that were within a few hour's ride. Others discussed were Monteagle and Rider's Roost. Leesburg and Sturgis, along with several others were brought up, but discarded as too risky due to the long ride. An idea was suggested that he should continue sending in stories to the magazine, covering the rallies and proclaiming his innocence. The idea was quickly squashed. With the new intel provided by Lute to the FBI, research was being done looking for patterns of unusual motorcycle accidents, especially fatalities that had occurred recently involving Vulcans with batwing fairings. The reason for the research had not been disclosed to others involved in the manhunt, and as such, the news media had no idea of the number of local Vulcan rider deaths. As is typical with the media, stories loosely related to the headlines were created and aired. One story mentioned that motorcycle sales were up, and pointed out that sales of Kawasaki Vulcans was at an all-time high.

By eleven, the plan and resulting itinerary was complete. They would meet at each rally to catch up and tweak the plan as needed. Wolf didn't like that the killers had apparently left the area and gone back to wherever they had come from. Lute really wanted them to meet Watty, but knew no good would come of it for any of them. Mark and Lute left quietly after saying their good-byes before the band stopped playing. They left the rally along with several others, Lute giving a thumbs up as they passed by agent Watson's hidden location.

Unknown to anyone, Blondie was dressed to kill and had her intended victim in sight. She was standing at the edge of the rowdy crowd of bikers gathered around the stage where the band was playing classic rock-n-roll, mixed with country rock. Beer was being consumed in great quantity, firepits were blazing, and the smell of wood smoke, along with the occasional whiff of weed, filled the air. The band was good and loud, the women were dressed in revealing and for many, too revealing biker attire, and the crowd was enjoying themselves immensely. On the big screen, pictures from past rallies were shown as if to encourage newcomers with ways to "let it all hang out".

Blondie was among the best looking women at the rally and as such, had been frequently encouraged to participate in the various lewd activities and competitions typically found at bike rallies. She declined, waiting for the ideal opportunity to hook her prey, a biker from Whiteville known to his friends as "Toad". He was a bit of a loner, but occasionally rode with a group from his hometown known as the White Knights. The group was not an MC per se, but rather a bunch of guys that attended high school together and later bought motorcycles as an excuse to get together to ride and party without their wives. They chose the name for the symbolic meaning it implied.

Toad exhibited much skill during the games with his bike, a 2008 black and silver Vulcan Nomad with a batwing fairing and unique flashing taillights. Blondie recognized the bike as the one she had seen outside a bar near Whiteville. She had come to the rally looking for its owner after reading his post on the internet. After winning the barrel roll, she had made it a point to congratulate him.

Toad was not unattractive, especially for a 43 year old accountant. While most of his coworkers were overweight and happy to watch others participate in sports, he had bonded with his teenage son by frequently participating in activities most boys enjoy. They regularly went for rides on their dirt bikes through the Cahaba Wildlife Management area trails and gravel roads. Weekends were typically spent camping in out-of-the-way places around the state, spending quality time riding trails while camping, fishing, and hunting in order to avoid becoming a couch potato like most of his friends. He thought of the computer as a tool, and was determined his son would not fall into the habit of preferring games and surfing the web to spending time outside, enjoying nature's gifts to man. His ex-wife had never liked the outdoors and could not understand his love for it, leaving him for a more sophisticated businessman. After the divorce, he made a pledge to himself that he would not marry another woman that didn't share his love of the outdoors.

In the past year, his son had become active in outdoor clubs including the scouts, and had recently told his dad of his plan to attend Auburn and become a forest ranger. Toad could not have been happier, and with his son away on a camping trip with the scouts, had agreed to join his high school buddies in a camping trip to the Boogie Bottoms bike rally. In his mind, he secretly hoped he would find a woman to share his life with after his son went off to college. With this in mind, he had agreed to participate in the biker games after much prodding from his friends. To his surprise and encouraged by his buddies' cheers, he had won the barrel roll, and come close to winning the slow race. A big bonus at the end was the congratulations offered by an attractive biker that appeared to be an outdoor lover herself.

After supper, Toad and the others headed over to the stage for the entertainment. He hoped he would run into the woman he had met earlier. His buddies were more interested in watching the band and checking out the women, while partying and guzzling beer. The band, *Buck Wild*, was one they had rocked to at other rallies in Alabama. The lead singer was skilled at working the crowd into a frenzy, especially the women who would dance on stage or utilize the stripper poles nearby. He stood at the edge of the crowd, enjoying the music while hoping the attractive brunette was not attached. His wishes came true when he felt two strong, feminine arms circle his waist, accompanied by the press of a pair of firm, ample breasts against his back. He turned to face the owner.

"Let's go somewhere we can talk," she yelled in his ear. He nodded and followed as she led the way to a table in the shadows at the end of the concession stand shelter.

"I was real impressed with the way you handled your Nomad today. You compete in those events often?"

"Nope, first time I ever tried it," he smiled sheepishly. "Don't mean to brag, but it was actually pretty easy." He looked her in the eyes and said, "My name's Tim, but my buddies call me Toad."

"Mine's Cheetah. You must ride a lot to handle that 850 pound Vulcan like you do." she held out her hand.

"Every chance I get. I love to ride my dirt bike, too. Sounds like you know your bikes. You ride?"

"That's my bike right there," she said, gesturing to her black, flamed Vaquero.

He stood up and looked her bike over closely. "2011 or 12?"

"2012. I like it way better than my old Road King. So how did you get your handle, Toad? Sure don't describe your looks—you married?" She squeezed his bicep, while looking into his dark brown eyes.

"Nope, I've been divorced for almost ten years. How about you? Is there a lucky man out there?"

"No there isn't, but you're avoiding my question," she said, smiling as she propped herself against the seat of her bike.

He grinned. "It's easier to just show you." With that said, he flicked his long, pointed tongue out and touched the tip of his nose.

"Oooh, now that's real sexy, Toad. You know how to use that thing?" she asked in a low, sultry voice, while smiling in the most sensual way he had ever seen.

"Haven't had any complaints, but I've had a few compliments, if you don't mind me bragging," he replied with a lusty grin that came from years without a steady sexual relationship.

"I'll be the judge of that." She grabbed his head and stuck her tongue deep inside his mouth, stroking his tongue with her own. "I'd say you've got lots of potential. Let's take a stroll down by the river—my tents down there." She put her arm around him and led him down the hill toward the river.

Excited at the expectation of getting laid, he went along without hesitation. He could not believe how lucky he was to have found such a sexy woman with a passion for the outdoors and biking. As they entered her campsite, she snapped on a dim light inside the tent and picked up a folding chair.

"Let's go down by the river." She pulled out a joint, lit it, then passed it to him.

"It's been a long time, but . . . what the hell." He took a long draw and held it, then coughed explosively, and passed it back to her. "That's some bad ass weed."

"It'll mellow you out a bit." She ducked inside the tent and came out with two beers, handing him one. Grabbing his hand, she led him down the path to a secluded sandy area next to the river's edge. With a near full moon overhead, they could easily see as she pushed him into the chair and handed him the re-lit joint. Determined not to cough, he held the aromatic smoke in his lungs until he coughed through his nose.

"Here, baby, let me help." She straddled the chair, sitting on his lap and shotgunned the smoke into his mouth and nose. She could easily tell he was aroused. They continued until the joint was gone. She removed her skimpy leather top and placed his hands on her breasts, while fluidly moving on his thighs like dancers do when giving a lap dance at strip clubs.

"You like?"

He laughed and mumbled an acknowledgment.

"I thought so." She stood up and removed her shorts. "Let's see what you can do with that tongue of yours." She pulled him up and took his place in the chair, her long, strong legs wrapping his torso and pulling him down until his face was just above her crotch. He knew what to do, and soon she was moaning and writhing with pleasure.

She pulled his head up when he began to slow down, exhausted from his efforts to please her. "My turn," she said as she pushed him down into the chair. She slowly removed his clothes, pausing and lightly brushing his engorged penis with her fingertips. As he leaned back and closed his eyes, he failed to realize she had used zip ties to connect his ankles to the legs of the chair. When she quickly placed them on his wrist, then fastened them to the legs of the chair, she reassured him, telling him that she would soon show him things he had never dreamed of.

She began to question him, soothing his growing feeling of unease by saying it was part of the pleasure to come. As she lightly stroked him, she told him she was really into role play, and he would be her prisoner while she was the interrogator. She began by asking questions about his sexual preferences, mixing in questions about where he lived and worked, along with roads he regularly traveled on his bike. In his drug-induced state of mind, he eagerly played the game, laughing and embellishing his answers. The laughter did not sit well with Blondie; in fact, she had been called a control freak more than once by ex-lovers having too much fun.

The game became dangerous for Toad when he nervously confirmed he knew where the church was and regularly went by it. At the mention of the mayor, he panicked, drew in a deep breath as if in preparation to yell for help. He was prevented from doing so by the zip tie suddenly pulled tight around his neck, cutting off his scream before he could exhale.

She took her small led flashlight and shone it briefly on her face as she said, "that's right asshole, it was *my* leg you hit after I killed that pervert of a mayor." Blondie suspected he was the witness, but still had a nagging doubt that comes from deep in one's own subconscious mind. She watched in satisfaction as his eyes opened wide in the realization he was helpless to prevent his certain death and why. As he struggled to breathe, she tightened the wide strip of plastic a few more clicks. He rapidly succumbed to the loss of oxygen to his brain. His body convulsed and became still. She shone her light into his eyes and watched in pleasure as his life expectancy ran out.

Blondie began to put her exit plan into motion, quietly breaking down her tent and stuffing it into a nearby trash can. She got her bike and returned to pick up the rest of her gear. As she was about to depart, she had an idea. She returned to where Toad's body was growing cold, cut the zip tie from his right wrist, and then replaced it with another after making sure his index finger could touch the ground. She drew a "W" in the sand with that finger. As if by reflex, she quickly stood, grabbed his head in both hands, and twisted until she heard the snap of his neck as it broke. Satisfied with her efforts, she returned to her bike and started off. She took the steep path up behind the stage, then followed the narrow gravel trail that bypassed the crowd as well as the camped bikers, drawing little attention from those still partying hard. She stopped near the exit to see if anyone was following, then smiled as she heard Bon Jovi's song, *You Give Love a Bad Name* being played by the band. Much later, she stopped in Rome, Georgia, and spent the night at a small rundown motel, paying cash and disguised as a man.

Wolf and Gator were miles away, riding east on 231 as an orange glow began to lighten the sky in the direction they were headed on the overcast Sunday morning. As the sky began to lighten, those camped at Boogie Bottoms began to make rapid preparations to head home. As was typical with most rallies, it seemed like a race to see who could pack and depart the fastest, with all but a few stragglers gone by 11 am. By noon, all tents were rolled, folded, and packed but one—Toad's. His Nomad was still parked in the field near the concession stand where his three riding buddies were gathered, impatiently waiting.

Their conversation revolved around the good looking babe they had seen briefly with Toad, and they were trying to decide whether to leave him there, or check for him at the three remaining RV's of vendors still parked behind their display tents. He did not answer his phone, not surprising due to the lack of service. Toad had said more than once he never could understand why everyone was in such a big hurry to leave, especially after a night of partying and listening to great music. Many still felt the effects of the previous night when they rode out.

Each chose an RV to check out. Having no success finding him, they started searching for him on the outskirts of the camp and then down by the river. The comment was made that he could be fishing, another adding that if so, he would "strangle him" for making them wait.

They rode their bikes, parking in an abandoned campsite overlooking the river, then went by foot along the freshly-cleared path along the bank in both directions. One yelled his name loudly when he saw Toad from the bank above, apparently asleep in a chair on a small sandbar next to the water. After noticing the unnatural tilt of his friend's head, he yelled for his buddies to come quickly, and then ran down the steeply sloping bank, almost falling over the chair holding Toad's stone cold body. After checking for a pulse, he went back up the bank to watch over the body, while one went for help. They had noted the W written in the sand by Toad's right hand, a detail that was discussed while waiting for the authorities. As they stood waiting, it started to rain. The police had been called immediately, and by five, Boogie Bottoms looked like a rally again, but this time for police, fire, and rescue personnel. Wet yellow rain suits were the uniform of the day, and by dark, the reflection of red and blue flashing lights glimmered off the wet tents and canopies.

CHAPTER 24

After identifying the dead biker, the FBI, along with the Whiteville police were immediately notified. Agent Watson was dispatched to the scene. He contacted Lute and arranged to meet him there. The agent in charge was looking for a connection to the mayor's murder, and spared no expense in collecting evidence. After examining the log in sheets from bikers that attended the rally, investigators learned that most attendees did not give their full name or any contact information. In fact, most just used a nickname. There were two with names listed as "Wolf", along with several more that were variations with the word Wolf in them. Successful identification of bikers would be extremely difficult, and they would have to rely on fingerprints to be successful. Unfortunately, a large portion of those were likely to have criminal or military backgrounds, and as such, would not be forthright in providing information on their biker brothers and sisters. Even more certainly, few would agree to be a witness against a biker that was beginning to be thought of as an outlaw hero, similar to Jesse James in the days of the Wild West.

Forensic investigators and experts were brought in from all over the southeast and as far away as Washington and given the task of sorting through, bagging and tagging, then fingerprinting everything. With over a thousand beer-drinking bikers attending the three day event, this was a task of huge proportions. Over a hundred personnel were involved over the next few days in collecting, sorting, and bagging evidence. The family that ran the rally worked harder and made more money feeding these public servants than they did during the rally. Afterward, they did not have to clean up or remove any debris from the bike rally, and were even able to send a bill to the FBI for damage caused to the property by the army of vehicles that had created a field of mud where plush grass had grown before.

The physical murder scene contained few clues. The deluge of rain in the first few hours had not only washed away part of the bank, but had come close to washing the body into the river due to runoff from the newly cut path turned into a fast running stream that emptied onto the sandbar from above. The "W" in the sand by the victim's hand was gone, only existing in the memories of Toad's buddies, one of which thought it was an "M" instead.

By the time the last rays of the sun disappeared from the watery horizon in the west, Wolf and Gator were slurping down frozen drinks at the Florabama. After riding in from the other end of the state, they were ready to kick back and relax after the tension of the weekend. They were at the bar hydrating, water in one hand and Bushwhacker in the other when the news came on. The top state story was the murder at Boogie Bottoms of an upstanding citizen of Whiteville. He was a biker, and authorities were examining the evidence on site for ties to the current investigation into the mayor's murder. The viewers were reminded that John Trotter, aka "Wolf", was being sought for questioning with a picture from the magazine shown in the background, along with a physical description. A reward of $150,000 was now being offered for information leading to the arrest of those responsible.

Wolf looked at Gator, both nodded, then walked calmly outside to the beach. They were careful to get out of hearing range of the medium-sized crowd of leftover weekenders mixed with locals who were off and ready to spend their money on relaxing after a busy spring weekend.

"What the hell! That's another dead because of me. We gotta put a stop to this right now!" Wolf declared, hate mixed with fear obvious on his face.

Gator looked thoughtful for a moment then replied, "maybe we can get Kawasaki to issue a recall on Vulcans with batwings. Say they are a hazard to your health." With a deadpan look on his face, he remained silent as if he was seriously contemplating doing just that.

Wolf just stared at his friend with a blank, unsmiling look. Both said nothing as they stared into the sea, apparently lost in thought. Wolf spoke first.

"Let's get back to the condo and call Lute," he said in a monotone voice laced with dread. He started walking up the beach toward the condos, barely 150 yards away. Gator caught up and walked alongside. Entering the door, Gator started some coffee, grabbed beers, and then joined his friend in the common area, where he found an intense conversation in progress. He could tell Wolf wasn't happy with what he was being advised to do, but knew when his daily companion for more than a week lowered his shoulders that he had resigned himself to do what he was told. He handed the phone to Gator saying, "your turn bro, Lute wants to talk to you."

Gator listened without saying much more than "got it" and "I understand."

There was no argument from him in reply. He hung up and turned to Wolf.

"Guess you know what we gotta do next, right?" he asked his buddy.

"Yeah, I do, but I don't have to like it. Going to be hard acting normal at Thunder Beach. We'll be constantly watching our backs the whole time while we're staying at the Outpost. Staying hidden in plain sight will be a real test that weekend for sure."

"Who knows, it may help take your mind off the other crap. Draw them out. Gotta give it a shot." Gator didn't look or sound very convincing. They decided to go back and listen to the music and flirt with the women, a favorite pastime of Gator's. The night passed too quickly, both turning down several less than virtuous offers by midnight. It was a test of Gator's willpower when he was approached by a slim, thirtyish blond gal whose boobs were the biggest part of her anatomy. Her lush lips and sea green eyes were too much for Gator to resist, until Wolf pointed out the size of her wrists and feet. Gator backed off, quickly joining a group of middle-aged business women, none of which he knew.

Wolf engaged the she-male in conversation by buying "her" a drink.

"Sorry to mess it up, but he'd have been really pissed when he found out, not to mention what would happen if the manager knew you were hustling in here."

"He'd have never found out, honey, as surely you must know, and the manager, now that's something else." she said, sucking the straw of her Bushwhacker with her frequently practiced sensuality.

"I'm not interested in anything but information. You a local?"

"What does it matter? You a cop or something?"

"No, I'm certainly not. I just wanted to know if you're interested in earning some easy money. Nothing illegal involved, just want you and your friends to be on the lookout for a couple."

"How much we talking, honey, I'd even throw in a freebie for *you*."

"Enough to make it worth your while. Just give a number a call if you see one or both of them. You in?"

"I'm in, tell me what they look like and I'll put out the word with my girlfriends. You got a picture?"

"No, just a description and characteristics." He went on to describe the woman and her possible partner. He mentioned that they might ask about bikes and their riders. Her eyebrows rose at that tidbit, but she nodded her understanding after a few questions.

"You know something?" he asked.

"No, but you described a gal I worked with back on Bourbon street before Katrina. That one was real mean and devious, liked to pick up football players from LSU. Hell, she could have played football if she wanted to. That one is real bad news. I'd hate to get on her bad side, even worse if she's got a big bad boyfriend. The price just went way up if that's the one. You still in?"

"You find them, you'll get paid well, and maybe a lot more if it's them. Here's my number. Don't call unless you're reasonably sure."

As he stood and started to walk away, eyes quickly turned away as he looked in their direction. They all looked back at him when the girl said loudly, "Call me, honey, you got my number." Wolf kept walking without looking back, resisting the urge to do something macho. He rejoined his friend who was watching with a big grin pasted on his face.

"Wipe off the smirk, I was just pumping her for information."

"It looked like she wanted to get pumped by you, if ya catch my drift." Gator grinned way too much.

"Let's get out of here before we get too trashed to use good judgment."

"You got it Kimosabe."

They spent Monday hanging out at the condo enjoying life as tourists, mixed with watching the news and surfing the net for new postings and photos on social websites and blogs. Little new information was being released to the reporters, and no mention was made by the authorities of any connection in the two murders. The local stations used snippets of previous news stories as filler to keep the viewers' attention. Car dealer ads dominated the commercials, the other local dealers trying to take advantage of the negative press Wolf's employer was perceived as getting. In fact, a coworker had posted on line that traffic was up at his employer, selling vehicles at a pace that was thirty percent higher than the previous month. It never failed to amaze him how often publicity, good or bad, helped stimulate many businesses.

Tuesday was more of the same, and all indicators pointed to a week of helpless boredom ahead. Wolf and Gator decided to explore the area thoroughly, with evenings capped by Wolf writing a story for the magazine. Gator continued to pick up women at the Florabama just down the beach. After Wolf wrote the second article, he had an idea that he pitched to Lute—he would send the articles and pictures to the magazine like normal, giving a boost to demand, while hopefully pissing off the killers, and just maybe, motivating them to make a stupid move. Lute went along willingly, and agreed that it would get a lot of people's attention, and not just the killers.

The first story ran ten days later and was a hot commodity at the Thunder Beach Bike rally and places that carried the magazine. He had started the story differently, with the simple statement:

> *"I did not have anything to do with any murder, but owners of Vulcans with batwing fairings, beware—you may be in danger."*

After that opening line, the story went on in the style readers had become accustomed to, sharing routes and places to eat and stay.

FOLEY AND DAUPHIN ISLAND

On a mission to explore '*The Alabama*' battleship in Mobile, I set the ole GPS on shortest route, avoiding I-65 and cutting across the curve east it takes between Birmingham and Mobile, shaving miles off the trip and riding great rural two-lane highways to within 20 miles of USA's campus. Except for Selma, there were few towns, lights, and little traffic the entire route. Leaving at 5:30 pm on Friday, the ride was 4 ½ hours, and after sunset, was very dark with few lights along the way. I had a close encounter of the 'deer' kind, but good karma was with me and I escaped with some fur on the helmet lock and a scuff on the hard bag—that deer came out of nowhere! Her face was a foot from my lap, causing serious puckering if you catch my drift. Still a great ride, though slower afterward.

After jumping on I-65 to go over the "Dolly Pardon' bridge, I started thinking about food and a cold one at '*The Shed*', a BBQ and Blues Joint across from USA's campus at Old Shell Rd. and University Blvd. Great blues music, friendly staff, and outstanding food, especially the pulled pork, baby back ribs, and beans went well with the great selection of beer. A great way to kick back in a rustic setting, there is great scenery with indoor and outdoor seating to hang with your buds. Music is from 7-10 Thursday-Saturday.

Saturday I headed for Bayou La Betreu to see what looks like "Forest Gump Land", and then headed over to Dauphin Island to check out the local accommodations; sleeping, partying, and such. Not much there; one motel, a couple of bars, a few eateries, cottages, campgrounds—and dragonflies the size of sparrows that put a hurting on whatever they crash into. The woods behind Ft. Gaines was on fire, and not being the kind of excitement I was looking for, I took the last ferry out to Ft. Morgan on the other side of Mobile Bay with a plan to visit the Florabama—always great bands there! That night it was *Big*

Earl, Kyle Parker, and Adam Holtz, to name a few. The crowd was worked into a frenzy with mucho great scenery. The remod is fantastic! Being a 98 degree day, 3 waters and my favorite, a frozen *'bushwhacker'* got me in the mood for the party. As bikers tend to do, we discussed women, bars, bands, rides, etc. Being on a mission to check out more local entertainment, I left to check out the scene in Foley. Sure was tough to leave as more great looking babes were arriving—it seemed to be the headquarters for bachelorette parties that night; good karma was still keeping me out of trouble.

I never thought of Foley as a biker destination, but me being open minded, we went to *'Whiskey River Bar'* on 59 as you approach Foley This bar caters to bikers with secure parking out back for your scoot. Sundays there's always something cooking there. On October 16, the "Blessing of the Bikes" is scheduled for 1pm, before the biker games of skill-not a bad idea, considering—

We dropped by Scuttlebutts in downtown Foley, a local bar with a great karaoke DJ—John Henry is his handle. He had the crowd rocking into the wee hours of the morning. "Enter as a stranger, leave as a friend" is their motto—they lived up to it! Easy to miss this place, but don't . . . it is 3 blocks north of AL 98 on 59. I came back on a Wed. night and it was hopping again—easy to see why, the comedy and energy was contagious thanks to DJ Jason Vaughn, staff, and patrons—what an outrageously fun bunch!

Riding a lot, I'm always looking for a good bang for my buck. With prices at summertime peaks at the beach, I found Foley to be a great location that was central to the essentials—riding, the beach, great food, biker friendly bars, and shopping for the women folk. Staying at the Best Western in Foley was a great choice; decent price, a pool, hot breakfast, Wi-Fi, and rooms with nice showers, comfy beds, refrigerators, and microwaves. It was very clean with parking right outside your room. For the shoppers, there are outlet malls and a shopping mecca in Fairhope right down the road. This was a great trip. More to come next month; probably check out Forest Gump land, but who knows where me and Beast will end up. Biloxi is right down the road; may be feeling lucky.

Tips: 2 lanes by day, 4 lanes by night, lather up with sunscreen and consume lots of fluids if as hot as it normally is in July. October and November would be a cooler time to take this ride. Oh yeah, don't pet the deer at 60 mph! Most importantly . . . Enjoy the ride!

Wolf

The owners of the places mentioned in the article were annoyed at first with the attention they got from the authorities, but almost immediately their business increased significantly as the readers began visiting where this "outlaw biker" of growing notoriety had stopped or passed through. Many new advertisers bought ads, resulting in the magazine increasing in size and circulation by more than fifty percent to accommodate the new clients. "Wolf sightings" became a frequent source of frustration for the authorities tasked to treat every lead as the real thing. Accordingly, at the town hall meeting in Whiteville, an ordinance to ban horseshoe mustaches was suggested, but quickly declined. Meanwhile, back at the farm, so to speak, Wolf and Gator shared many a laugh about the publicity. A favorite source of entertainment for them at bars was to start a conversation about Wolf and the murder, then watch and listen to the reactions and opinions, smiling at the thought of the results the story that would run in the next month's issue would bring.

They rode to Thunder Beach as planned and enjoyed a great weekend, listening to the music of the many talented bands, coupled with the beauty of women seen not only in the typical contests, but up and down the beach at the various venues. Maintenance to their bikes was done, and supplies needed for an extended road trip were acquired. Wolf tried to spot unique things to mention in the upcoming story of the places they visited, a way of saying "Wolf was here" metaphorically in upcoming stories.

Constantly scanning the crowds of bikers for the killers, they frequently spotted seemingly out of place bikers that appeared to be paying more attention to the bikers than the bikes and gear around them. Occasionally locking eyes with the other crowd watchers, they got nods of acknowledgment and recognition of purpose. At first, this spooked them, but they quickly came to understand the phenomenon was one of mistaken acknowledgment of a common purpose—to catch the biker for the reward money and fame. Understanding this, Wolf became even more confidant in his new identity.

On Saturday, they met up with Lute at the Outpost, many miles away near Bruce, FL. He confirmed their discovery of the observers, advising them that many law enforcement officers that rode in the Alabama and numerous other states were indeed around them, trying to spot them in the crowd. The word on the streets was that the event attendance was up and all motels were full. No reports describing them had come in, but there had been several riders with horseshoe mustaches followed, reported, stopped, and in one case, a rider even admitted he was Wolf, only to be taken in and subsequently identified as a lawyer from Atlanta. His name truly was Wolf—William Wolfe.

During the meeting, Lute said he had mixed feelings about continuing the stories. He warned about giving names or too much info, and added they would have to avoid those places afterward. Anyone named that could have identified them would get the royal treatment as accessories. Lute advised them to get as far away as possible, and suggested the northern North Carolina mountains. Wolf happily agreed, knowing just the right place near Ferguson, NC.

Gator had a great idea, and passed it along to Lute, who in turn, would get the FBI experts to do a search for biker accidents where broken necks were the cause of death. All accidents would be looked at for similarities or a geographical pattern.

"Damn Gator, that's a great idea! Too bad I didn't think of it."

"I can't claim it, we all came up with it together. We're a team or I guess in Lute's lingo, a task force. I kinda like the sound of that. The "Vulcan Killers" task-force. What do you think Lute? We can be the silent partners."

Lute laughed "You guys are so full of it. Y'all are having way too much fun with this." He frowned as he shook his head and then looked at Wolf. "Dude, this is some serious shit you're in. The investigation has been dubbed the *"Lone Wolf Murders"*, and they are looking for serial killers. If the police get nervous or over excited, they may just shoot you. Only a few in the FBI know about the bikers that were killed and the relationship between them. Some fine, upstanding men have died. Could be more soon, you never know, those two are serial killers, and for hire. They're pros, so be careful if you run into them. Call me before doing anything stupid. They would kill you just for having met them more than once. Don't forget, they know you real well, thanks to those stories of yours. I'll get you some help before the next story goes in. Send it to me first, and I'll forward it to the editor."

"I appreciate it Lute, but you need to send it back to me first, otherwise, the editor will suspect something's up. Cool?"

"You got it. Damn, but it's good to see your mug, or what can be seen of it. We gotta be getting out of here soon—a beer for the road?"

The planning done, they went outside to the tables and relaxed. They listened to the band, while eying all the bodacious biker babes parading by them on their way to the bathroom. An hour later found them leaving, Lute heading back to Whiteville, while Wolf and Gator headed north towards the mountains of North Carolina. They rode together to Auburn where they split up, Lute staying on 280 while the other two went due north on 431 towards Roanoke, AL. They stopped for the night outside of Rome at Panhead City, where Wolf wrote his story for the next month's edition of the magazine, forwarding it to Lute as agreed.

THUNDER BEACH, TELLICO PLAINS,

AND BOOGIE BOTTOMS

This month may be the last for a while, so I offer a tip . . . leave way early and stop whenever and wherever you see something interesting. Having a deadline and being in a rush can be dangerous. It also reduces the pleasure and freedom of the ride and stops. You never know when your ride may come to an end, so enjoy it now!

On the last few long overnight rides, I followed my own advice and stopped to discover new places along roads I had ridden before. I took new backroads when I missed my turns. I put the GPS on "shortest route" avoiding highways and interstates, resulting in some great rural backroads along with some super fishing, restaurants, and one heck of a residence. A few are listed below:

Cooter's is on AL Hwy 87, a few miles south of Troy in Spring Hill. Nothing is for sale there, but there is an impressive collection of old nostalgic relics the owner has collected and restored for over 40 years, displayed both outside and inside his 5,000 square foot warehouse/home. The most impressive part was the man-cave and outside deck that would be the envy of even the best bars. He even has a "turbo toilet" outside, the result of a few too many beers, according to him. A six-pack from the guys, or a pair of panties from the babes, might just buy you a tour if you're real friendly.

Another find this trip was the *Sunset Cafe* at Hwy 87 and 52 in Sampson, AL. They had a great all-you-can-eat country buffet with some really tasty fried catfish among other things. Get there at lunchtime for some great home-style cooking.

After the big venues die down at Thunder Beach, you'll find a great hole-in-the-wall karaoke bar 3 doors down from Hooter's called *Sweet Dreams*. Not only do they stay open until 4 am, but the place was full of energy and has a tasty drink invented by the bartender called a "Pink Pussy".

I was blown away by a new bar, the Wicked Wheel in P.C. and their fried chicken, redbeans, & rice, and especially the service and facility—WOW!

Thinking back on the weekend before, I discovered a new place to stay, the Mountain View Cabin Rentals overlooking the Tellico River. It was like walking inside the pages of a Bass Pro Shop catalog. Prices were reasonable. Their facilities ranged from simple cabins to condos to a log palace suitable for a very large group on top of the mountain with a breathtaking view. While there, I ate at the restaurants, *Nut n Fancy* and the *Outpost*. Both were excellent. Tellico Plains is a great place to stay while exploring the curvy backroads in the area. It is at the start of the Cherohala Skyway. Maryville, TN and Robbinsville, NC are the other ends of a popular riding triangle that includes "The Dragon".

Back in Alabama, another great place is found just down the scenic road from Locust Fork, AL. What a great location to have a bike rally! Situated on the banks of the Warrior River, this is a super setting for a base camp to explore the curvy roads and beautiful landscape. And did I mention fishing? My GPS led me on a ride during the Boogie Bottoms Rally by the River that took me on some great roads in Blount county. Stopping on the old Hwy 31 bridge, I spotted numerous fish of all types swimming in the clear water below. There are a great many roads with sweeping views to ride nearby. It was an enjoyable ride exploring the area east of Hwy 31 and north of 160. Those riverside campsites at Boogie Bottoms are outstanding and available anytime—makes for a nice secluded base. There are a couple of cabins there that can be rented, but it is best to call ahead to do so. Go on Friday or Saturday nights, and you can catch the latest movies on the big outside screen at their drive-in movie theater.

I hope to stay free to ride the backroads, but that is really up to the authorities and the success they have in their investigation. I say again, it is not me you are looking for. I wish them luck in finding the real killers, and will continue to help by sending in any information on the killers that I find. To Blondie, along with your butt-ugly ape partner; your rides are numbered, the truth always comes to roost in the end. To all others, enjoy the ride!

Wolf

Gator liked the story, but wasn't happy about the mention of Tellico Plains or Boogie Bottoms. He knew they wouldn't be safe staying at either place once the story was out, and was concerned that the FBI would access the story the second Wolf hit "send" on his laptop. After sighting who they thought were the killers, he wasn't planning on going anywhere near the area, anyway. Wolf's thinking was that by pointing the FBI in that direction, they might get lucky and stumble upon the two killers.

After staying two nights, they left before dawn on Tuesday, headed for their favorite place, Rider's Roost. As was Wolf's custom, they arrived early with plans to rest, party with the operators, and ride before the big weekend party started on Friday. They both were skeptical of Wolf's ability to maintain his new identity, and discussed the impact of alcohol and weed on the success of pulling it off. They had both been seen together at the Roost, so they agreed to arrive separately this time, Wolf staying overnight several miles away at a motel just off the Blue Ridge Parkway, while Gator checked everything out. Taking a back road, they would be less than a 30 minute ride apart.

Tuesday night was a blessing for Wolf. It was the first day in weeks he had spent alone. He used it well, writing and then hanging out at the bar next door, drinking beer while he ate and watching the races. He hated that he could not write there, knowing it would be a dead giveaway to his real identity. He left before he got engaged in conversation with the after-work crowd. It made him extremely uncomfortable that a TV was turned to the national news channel which ran his picture at least once an hour to go along with the breaking news from Whiteville. Wednesday, he rode to a nearby lake and went for a swim. Afterward, he fished in a creek then, after not being able to fool any fish with his artificial worm, he explored the roads in the surrounding area. At dark, he was back at the room and surfing the internet.

At the Roost, Gator was having a serious reunion with his old biker brothers. He and "uncle" Jake had partied together for more than fifteen years at various weekend events held yearly at the Roost. Gator filled his old friend in on Wolf's dilemma. A brainstorming session seemed to be in order for all in attendance. Ideas were brought up, written down, then frequently thrown out. They were able to devise a loose plan for the next original Roost party, two weeks away. Wolf and his wingman would stay in the two bedroom apartment, allowing them to remain secluded when necessary and provide a hiding place in plain sight of all at the Roost party. A surveillance camera would be installed to monitor new arrivals. They would even be able to see the live feed by remote. The plan was to lure the pair of killers in to complete their unfinished business with Wolf. After enjoying an excellent home cooked meal accompanied by way too much alcohol, they sacked out. It would be an early morning for Gator. He planned to meet up with Wolf for breakfast at the restaurant next door to the motel.

CHAPTER 25

Whenever Wolf thought of biker heaven, he envisioned it to be like Rider's Roost in Ferguson, NC. Near Blowing Rock and the Blue Ridge Parkway, there was clear, running water for swimming and fishing, a waterfall, and cabins and tent sites next to the water. A seemingly endless supply of curvy, scenic roads was nearby. Throw in the biker humor, rock-n-roll music, and bikers passionate about riding, and it was easy for Wolf's friends to understand his feelings for this small piece of heaven in the mountains of North Carolina.

Founded by biker author and comic Uncle Roy, BC, along with their brothers, this biker resort allowed no cages and was the ideal "roost" for bikers riding in the area. There are several laid-back, summer weekend parties which typically have open mike comedy and karaoke on Friday, a great band playing on Saturday, and food for breakfast and dinner, all at very reasonable price. Bikers could stay in the serene setting to enjoy the peace and quiet during the weekdays when there was not a crowd.

Wolf was dreaming of Rider's Roost. In the dream, the party was going strong with everyone partying and enjoying the band and camaraderie of fellow bikers. When the Harley ring tone on his phone went off, he hit the snooze button without awakening. When a hungry Gator began to knock on the door, he fit that into his dream also, and slept on. When he heard his name being quietly called, he sprang up wide awake. He could remember only the last part of the dream in which the killers were yelling his name while pointing their weapons at him and the crowd of bikers.

The knock became more insistent and the voice got louder. "Wake up in there—daylights burning."

Realizing what was happening, he opened the door and was handed a fresh cup of coffee by his buddy. After a few sarcastic remarks not suitable for the tender-eared, he took a shower and walked over to join him for breakfast. Gator told him all was clear for the Roost weekend, and without being specific, told him they had a plan and the details would be shared with him when they got to their destination.

The back way to the Roost consisted of steep, winding old asphalt, with a long stretch of dirt road along a mountain creek, followed by more blacktop in better condition. The road was not technically difficult and left them wanting more, so they went right, making a big loop before heading to the Roost. Upon arrival, they immediately went inside the "condo", where Uncle Jake was waiting. It was to their advantage that they both generally looked and dressed similarly. They would capitalize on that later as part of the plan.

Supper was of generous proportions, consisting of chicken pastry and copious amounts of beer. They talked of old friends and past parties, mixed in with lots of BS. All knew the seriousness, and no known on-duty cop had ever stayed at the Roost during an original party weekend. There were sure to be on and off duty cops staying on the weekends now. Unmarked cop cars had been spotted frequently, and a camera had been noted on the side of a pole alongside the road in from the main highway. The camera had been disabled by a well-placed road-killed raccoon. Its' carcass was still hanging from the broken camera, a type of biker early warning for those that passed.

The weekend went by quickly, with a small group ride led by Wolf and another one by Gator. Wolf's identity was never questioned. Several prying questions were heard by several from time to time, and the suspected cops were "marked" as such by the regulars. No trouble was in store for them over the weekend, but there was a marked reserve in the partying of the locals. One well-endowed newbie tried to get a "mark" stoned, and almost succeeded until she found his badge in his underwear. She loudly advertised this fact, calling him many choice names. The officer packed up quickly and left.

Monday caught them having breakfast with Uncle Jake at the little store down the road. Gator had learned from Lute that Wolf's fingerprints were found on a beer can at Boogie Bottoms. The police were in a frenzy to locate and bring him in, and the FBI had a statistical lead based on motorcycle crash data, but had not given him any details. A blitz by the authorities was planned for an unknown area.

Wolf and Gator decided to head to Robbinsville and do a little scouting for the killers themselves. Both were still puzzled by the rapid disappearance of the two bikers on the Cherohala Skyway. They were determined to return to the cabin and do a little surveillance of their own. They took the Blue Ridge Parkway to Asheville, then got on US 64, following lightly traveled country roads whenever possible. They finally arrived at the cabin just after dark. A refrigerator stocked with beer and frozen pizza awaited them, along with fresh eggs and homemade jam for breakfast. Before they could finish their first beer, they heard a knock on the door. It was Lisa, the landlady with fresh fried catfish and homegrown cooked veggies. She insisted on leaving, knowing they were fatigued from their trip. She was right, especially if you added the weekend party into the mix. They promised to have a cookout the following evening. Gator asked if fresh grilled chicken would be on the menu and pointed at the chicken coup. An elbow to the ribs was his reply from Lisa.

After a good night's sleep followed by breakfast, they took off on their quest to find Blondie and 45, who they were sure were the killers. They knew they had to have stopped within a few miles of the cabin, so they stopped at the nearby store to inquire. They still had no pictures, just descriptions that consisted of size and general body type. No one remembered the couple together, but several large men had stopped in recently. Many Street Glides had been seen, but no one could put the bike with the big man for sure.

Blondie was mounted on an ATV checking the hidden back entrance when she heard the sound of two Vulcans coming around the curve near the steep rear entrance to the farm where they lived. The entrance was completely hidden from view from one direction, and was just a gap in the underbrush before the guard rail around a curve from the other. The entrance was marked only by a reflector that was easily removed. County records did not show this entrance to the property.

As she stood hidden from view by the landscape, she saw a red and black Nomad and a Vulcan 2000 LT come around the curve, both riders dressed similarly with helmets that covered their eyes with dark visors. She noted that the Nomad had Alabama plates. She instantly decided to head after them, and tore down the road to the barn where the bikes were parked. Jumping on her Harley Davidson V-Rod, she tore up the driveway and came roaring onto the highway, headed in the same direction as the Vulcans. She knew they had a big head start, but knowing the road well, she took each curve at the maximum speed possible without flying off the road.

She came within sight of them as they were getting off their bikes outside a small house just off the curve in the road not far from the end of the Cherohala Skyway. She made a U-turn in the road after the next curve and got her camera ready. She came slowly around the curve and got several shots as they entered the house through a small, screened-in side porch. She immediately went back to the cabin, this time riding just above the speed limit. She saw this as an opportunity to remove another threat and got the plate number to do more research. There was something familiar about the walk of one of the riders. She would have to give that more thought.

At the cabin, Wolf was prepping food for the cookout, while Gator reviewed the photos captured by the motion-activated webcam set up in the window closest to the road. He watched the photos starting with the most recent first, and by doing so, caught Blondie, dressed as a man, go by twice from different directions in a matter of minutes. The picture showing this biker taking photos was extremely disturbing. As he went to get Wolf, his cell phone rang. Seeing it was Lute, he answered immediately. He joined Wolf on the porch, both listening as Lute advised them of the authorities' plan. Robbinsville was to be the staging area for a massive manhunt and investigation into the deaths of numerous bikers that had died over the last five years. Many had died from broken necks and not internal injuries. Just two weeks ago, an experienced Vulcan rider from Alabama with a fairing had died going off a drop less than ten miles from their cabin.

Sharing information, they learned that agents were converging on Robbinsville. The local sheriff and police departments were already setting up checkpoints on all highways leading to the area. Special units were being set up at both ends of the Cherohala Skyway, the Dragon, and Moonshiner 28. The news media had begun to refer to Wolf as a "lone wolf murderer", creating additional pressure on the task force to hunt him down. Gator gave Lute information to access the webcam after telling of the biker with the camera. Hanging up, they concluded it was time for Wolf to move to the hidden rooms at the other house owned by Lisa. He left in her vehicle, followed by Gator on Wolf's bike.

Unknown to them, 45 and Blondie were in route to the cabin as the sky began to darken. Going by the store a mile away, they saw several cars belonging to various law enforcement agencies parked there. There was only one bike outside the cabin as they went by, so they kept going. Taking the left turn that went by the lake and cut over to Hwy 29, "the Dragon", they saw even more law enforcement units. It was beginning to look like a cop convention was in town. They were fortunate to make it back to the farm without being stopped and hassled by the law by using the main entrance from the county road that cut through from the other side of the lake. They made plans to leave the area, but decided to let things cool down for a few days before leaving via the lesser known county roads.

The next week passed slowly for Wolf. Being cooped up underground while Beast sat idle in the garage gave him too much time to reflect on missed opportunities and alternate paths he could have chosen. He knew it was too late to undo the choices he had made. He was however, still extremely remorseful when he thought of the consequences his network of friends would likely face if he was apprehended, charged, and tried for the murder. He did not like the odds of finding the real killers and proving they committed the murders, even though Lute had tried to reassure him saying he had evidence that should prove his innocence. He knew there would be other charges the FBI could come up with, as they had been embarrassed by the lack of progress and resulting bad press. Eric Rudolf came to mind, and he could not imagine life as a hermit living off the land. Lone wolf or not, he enjoyed the freedom to ride and already missed interacting with other bikers. The only good thing at this point was that Beast was cleaner and had received more TLC than at any point since new. With way over a hundred thousand miles, he knew how important regular maintenance was.

The authorities were indeed blitzing the area with checkpoints, visits to local homes, and extensive questioning of bikers in the area. Merchants quickly grew tired of the perceived threat to the local economy at the height of the summer riding season, and feared bikers would avoid the area for years to come. The press had invaded the area, taking most of the available accommodations typically filled by vacationing bikers. Reports of sightings along with interviews of vocal, enraged bikers were often in the news. To make matters even worse for the authorities, there was an increase in sales of cruiser bikes, and many promptly added fairings to bikes not already equipped with them. A small company in Marysville had a backlog of orders for fairings, and was struggling to catch up. Many bikers made their way to the area to join in the confusion and excitement. At this point in time, Robbinsville was a boom town, and the checkpoints were overrun with impatient, surly bikers.

Wolf and Gator were up and ready to ride out early Sunday morning. The forecast called for temps in the low eighties and little chance of rain. Countless other bikers were already on the roads by 8 am. One group of twelve consisting of many types of cruisers—Harleys, Victorys, and various metric bikes went slowly by, headed downtown. Wolf and Gator pulled out onto the road behind them. The group stopped at Lyn's Place for breakfast, so they too stopped where they met and then shared the camaraderie of the group. The main topics of conversation were the manhunt and the police checkpoints everywhere they went, causing many delays. The group was headed over to Cherokee to get away from the hassles. Wolf understood how they felt, perhaps even more so. He too was tired of being on the run, and often thought his freedom to ride would come to a halt without warning in the very near future. Every day the situation seemed more hopeless. He was past being tired of hiding, forced to leave the place he was enjoying at a moment's notice. He longed for the freedom of the road, but was beginning to feel it was out of reach. As he mounted Beast and got ready to ride once again to an as yet undetermined location, he snapped on the radio. The beginning strains of the song, *Against the Wind* by Bob Segar came pouring out of his speakers.

CHAPTER 26

When the new edition of the biker magazine came out, copies were quickly snatched up and a reprint had to be ordered. It helped demand that the front page had a picture of Wolf with his back turned, sitting on his bike looking over a massive canyon leading into the crevasse below. The editor had done a great job finding a file photo that seemed to symbolize his prospects for the future. When Blondie's copy came, delivered to her local post office box, she was shocked to see the front cover. Turning to Wolf's story, she was incensed. She knew that to 45, Wolf had issued a death wish upon himself. Her anger quickly changed to fear at the thought of 45's hasty reaction and the potential for mistakes. She would be sure to have an exit strategy for the upcoming showdown.

45 reacted as expected, reading even more into the story than Blondie. He took it as a personal insult and challenge. The showdown would be at Rider's Roost.

Once together, they began to devise a plan to draw Wolf out where they could terminate the threat from who they were now convinced was the elusive witness. After watching some news footage, Blondie realized that one of the two bikers at the cabin was Wolf. Only one biker remained there, and she was positive it was not him. With the abundance of law enforcement personnel in the area, they would have to put the plan into action at the Roost, if indeed he did show up for the weekend party. Killing him would be tough enough there, but it would be next to impossible if he was taken into custody.

The plan was for 45 to camp nearby, hidden from sight and within hiking distance of the Roost. Blondie would set up her tent inside the rally and as close to the entrance as possible in order to check out arrivals at the Roost party. After confirming Wolf was there, 45 would kill him in his sleep. As a backup plan, they would ambush him on the back road that led up to the parkway. Blondie would be disguised as Ronnie, and as a man, would draw less attention than as a woman.

182

The most immediate challenge would be to leave their current location without being caught in the police dragnet. They didn't know how much the police knew, and therefore, were extra cautious to avoid the authorities whenever possible.

They laid low until the following Wednesday when they set out just before sunrise, traveling narrow mountain roads until well away from Robbinsville. They rode separately with almost a mile between them. Staying overnight at a seedy, cheap motel in nearby Lenoir, they were able to ride by the Roost and recon the surrounding roads and landscape. Late in the afternoon on Thursday, 45 located, then set up a hidden camp more than a mile away off the side road that went by the entrance to the Roost. Blondie, disguised as Ronnie, rode in and set up her tent. There were a dozen other tents already in place, so she set hers facing the stream, just down the hill from the entrance and the condo. The two bikes that had ridden by the farm back in Robbinsville were among a line of bikes at the edge of the parking area near the two story house at the entrance. There were more than a dozen parked there when she rode in, three of them Vulcans with fairings. She knew that Wolf was there somewhere, and advised 45.

Gator was sure he recognized the lone biker that rode in and set up just down the slope from the condo at Rider's Roost late Thursday afternoon. It looked to be the same Harley Davidson V-Rod and rider that had ridden by taking pictures at the cabin. They trained the camera on the biker and captured him on the webcam. Miles away, in an unmarked surveillance unit disguised as a toy hauler, two agents studied the images that were sent, using the latest in face recognition technology. There were no hits on the V-Rod rider. They advised Gator, and asked for fingerprints. Jake was dispatched to secure them by greeting and offering him a swig of apple pie from his mason jar.

The jar was passed to Lute at the general store just down the road from the Roost. Watty was inside the toy hauler, along with another biker who handled forensics and monitored the equipment. Lute was not comfortable with FBI agents, even biker ones, but in this situation he knew that backup was essential to prove his friend's innocence. To FBI agent Watson's employer, Lute was his operative, and Watson his handler. He knew far more than his superiors, and Lute didn't give any more intel than was needed. No one knew that Wolf was in the condo, and he was determined to keep it that way until necessary to call for backup.

Agent Watson knew his operative well enough to understand the biker code that was in effect. He himself guarded the wooded approach to the cabin that night. Around four am, he thought he heard something nearby, but figured it was wildlife. What he did not know was that he was within six feet of being killed by the huge ex-army ranger. The motion detector turned the spotlights on a minute later, and he watched as a possum stood facing the light, frozen. He heard a rustle to his left and spotted a rabbit as it hopped erratically towards the cover of the underbrush. He would never know how close he came to dying that night, saved only by a possum and a rabbit. Unknown to all, "plan B" had just been activated by 45.

On Friday, the Roost came alive with activity, accompanied by the sound of rock-n-roll music from the pavilion. The Roost operators were busy greeting new arrivals and collecting money, while giving out wrist bands and selling gear at the store. More than two hundred bikers were expected to get "Juiced at the Roost" over the weekend, but there were many more than expected. Roost veterans were advised to steer clear of "newbies", as many were suspected to be undercover cops. This seemed like a challenge over turf to many bikers who resented the invasion of their party sanctuary. The old timers shied away from cameras used by first-timers. Care was taken to bring joints out one at a time, and all knew not to show their stashes at all. Bikers that abstained from smoking weed were "marked" and generally avoided. The whiff of weed could be detected at times, but no one openly displayed the vice. Variations of "Are you with any law enforcement agency or affiliated in any way with one?" was heard frequently. No one but known regulars had wristbands with crabs printed on them, making recognition easier. Just after dark, Mark and Big Jim came rolling in, parking their bikes in line with the others outside the condo. They circulated and greeted old friends, then disappeared one at a time into the condo. Lute and Mark sat outside at the picnic table, eating while keeping close watch outside.

Eastern style BBQ was served by the food vendor, and bikers got their heaping-full plates for six bucks apiece. By eight pm, the party was in full swing with karaoke and dancing, enhanced by the keg of beer nearby. At nine, open mike comedy began, and hilarious jokes and politically incorrect stories were heard. At 9:30, Uncle Jake took center stage in the pavilion and, not using the mike, the crowd quieted and drew closer, listening intently and roaring with laughter as he told outrageous jokes in the redneck, southern road dog style only he could. He picked up his guitar and finished with his infamous "Whale Shit" song. The regulars sang along to his song of a biker done wrong by his woman, joined by the first-timers in the chorus. Joints made the rounds in the room, enhancing the humor being laid out by the aging biker comedian. After he finished, other bikers were encouraged to come up and continue the joke telling, but after two brave souls bombed, the call was made to go back to karaoke, a move appreciated by all.

When he was done, Uncle made his rounds, then headed to the condo to join Wolf, Big Jim, Gator, and Lute for a briefing on Saturday's riding plan. This would be an especially exciting ride if things went as expected. There was a general consensus that the two killers were nearby and planning to take out Wolf. Based on the discovery that the newbie, Ronnie had women's garments amongst his gear, they were sure one of them was just down the hill, less than fifty yards away. Several female regulars in the crowd advised the others of the abundance of bikers with guns hidden on them. The need to stay clear of unseasoned and unaware bikers was cranked up a few notches. The word was put out about the rides for Saturday. Uncle would lead a group to Blowing Rock. Wolf, Gator, Big Jim, and Mark would head to Grandfather Mountain. First timers and select Roost regulars were invited to join the ride with Uncle, while Ronnie, suspected to be the killer Blondie, would be allowed to hear talk of both rides. All went as planned and there were many that committed to ride out with Uncle at nine am. Kickstands up for Wolf and his group would be an hour later.

The morning brought a thick fog to the area, and there were scattered thunderstorms in the forecast for the day. This did not deter any but a few of the riders that had partied late into the night. Seasoned bikers knew that a 30% chance of rain meant there was small chance of rain in the exact place they were riding at any given time. The fog normally would burn off as soon as the sun topped the ridge above. Uncle Jake followed his morning ritual, and all was in place. Lute and Watty would ride out with him and his group. Several regulars were along for the ride and what they thought would be a rolling party with several breaks for hydration therapy and attitude adjustments along the way. The group of fifteen bikes pulled out promptly at eight, thundering up the drive to the paved road above. The valley echoed with the throaty roar of exhausts, a familiar Harley Davidson alarm clock for the camped bikers.

A few miles out, Uncle Jake's Harley lost power, his fuel starved engine sputtering to a stop outside the country store. Lute and Watty stayed with him, telling the others to go on. They said would catch up later if they could get his bike running. As soon as the group was out of sight, Uncle turned on the hidden gas cock and started his bike. They high-tailed it back to the fork in the road and then burned the blacktop up to a fire station near where Wolf and his buddies would turn off and head up Hwy 421 and onto the parkway.

At 8:45 am, Wolf and his closest group of friends were prepping their bikes for the ride, checking oil, fluids, tires, and lights. The familiar routine settled their nerves before what they thought could be an ambush awaiting them, somewhere between Rider's Roost and the Blue Ridge Parkway. All were carrying, and as bikers do, were comforted by their bros that "had their backs".

When ten am rolled around, they were waiting for Ronnie to show. After a few loud, derogatory exchanged words about the missing biker's character, they declared "kickstands up" and headed up the hill, making the sharp U-turn onto the paved road above. Wolf led, followed by Big Jim and Gator with Mark riding tail-gunner. As they all reached the top and turned left, Blondie came out of her tent dressed as Ronnie, jumped on her bike and followed, staying behind, but out of sight of the group. The unusual activity was noticed by several undercover cops in the pavilion, motivating them to run to their bikes and follow suit a few minutes behind her.

Big Jim had the tunes cranked up on his bike's sound system, and did not hear the sharp explosions of shaped C-4 charges against tree trunks on the steep hill above. Wolf did, jamming on the brakes as he saw two huge pine trees begin to fall from above and ahead of him. Big Jim saw his brake lights a second too late, and locked up both wheels and came to an abrupt halt, stopped by a massive branch from the tree. Wolf stopped a foot short of the trunk and immediately drew his Glock and scrambled to his friend's assistance, now trapped between his bike and the limb. He stopped and stood as he heard his name yelled from the other side of the tree. He suddenly realized that a tree had fallen behind them, cutting them off from Lute and Mark. He could not tell if they too had crashed.

As he turned back in the direction of the voice, he heard his name again, this time much nearer and softer. He looked in the direction of the voice and saw 45, dressed in camo, his face smeared with grease in a shooter's stance holding a Colt model 1911 pointed directly at him. An assault rifle hung from a sling at his side.

"You shouldn't have opened your mouth, we were doing you a favor killing the mayor. Let your maker know that an ape beats a wolf every time."

An instant before his finger squeezed the trigger, a huge buck came crashing down the slope from the woods above, apparently startled by the sound of approaching bikes in the distance. 45 caught the movement just as he pulled the trigger, causing him to miss his target. The round caught Wolf in the same shoulder as before, but got more meat this time, spinning him around and up against the limb holding his closest friend. His Glock was gone, leaving him unarmed except for his knife, useless in a gun fight. He stayed where he was, determined to stay between the killer and Big Jim. Realizing his error, 45 swung his rifle up and prepared to unleash a full load into Wolf and Big Jim, followed by another clip at the others trapped by the other tree 75 yards past them.

As he trained his sights on the two downed bikers, a shot rang out that hit him squarely in the chest. Because of his Kevlar vest, the shot succeeded only in knocking him down and spoiling his aim. Out of instinct, he rolled and returned fire, spraying the other fallen tree and the area above and below the trunk with the entire clip. He slammed another clip in and sprang up to finish the two bikers closest to him. As Wolf and Big Jim watched, the top of his head flew forward with a spray of blood and gray matter, followed closely by a barrage of rounds hitting him, causing his body to jump as if pulled by a puppeteer before he finally slid to the ground. A pool of blood began to spread on the pavement under the tree.

Wolf heard the crack of broken limbs followed by the sound of weapons being kicked across pavement from the other side of the tree. Lute's face popped up first, a big grin on his face.

"Y'all alright over there?" He saw Wolf hugging his friend. "I always suspected you two were way too friendly—Hey Wolf, you're bleeding."

"I'll live; check on the others. Did you get Blondie?"

"The other group is in pursuit and have her in sight—she's making a run for it. Don't worry, they'll get her."

Gator and Mark came running up, both bleeding from lacerations on their faces and arms from wood splinters and pavement chips. Greetings and fist pumps were in great supply as they waited for the posse to catch up and cut them out. There were two serious injuries; Big Jim had a bent front fork, and Mark's Vulcan had taken two bullets—one that passed through his radiator and on through the gas tank, and the other that cracked the front transmission cover before lodging in the cooling fins of his front cylinder head. They figured with a bit of gauze, some duct tape, as well as some good drugs, that Wolf would be fine.

Blondie stopped, then made a quick U-turn when she heard the sound of multiple weapons from the road ahead. She twisted the throttle wide open and aggressively rode through the bikers that were in pursuit. One crashed while another did a quick turn and followed her. Two more duck-walked the turn around on the narrow county road, then stopped to assist the biker down. The rest continued on ahead. The sound of approaching sirens was heard clearly in the distance.

She took the turn onto the main highway without slowing, the police car at the store joining the pursuit. The bike in pursuit rapidly fell behind, unwilling to jeopardize his life by using both lanes at top speeds in the blind curves. The patrol unit got even further behind, unable to keep up with the bikes.

As Blondie rounded the second curve in a well banked S-curve, she saw a bike ahead. The lone biker was on a black bike and was wearing a silver helmet with a black t-shirt, similar to the way she was dressed. At the next right curve, she cut inside him in the turn and, with a well-aimed kick, sent him up and across the banked curve, over the barbed wire fence, and airborne into the field below. Not knowing what her pursuers would do, she continued on, turning off onto a narrow county road on the left. She took another quick turn down an overgrown drive with a chain on the ground near the entrance. Stopping her bike in a small clearing under the trees and hidden from sight from the road, she quickly dismounted and ran to put the chain into position by the entrance.

She rapidly morphed into Cheetah, complete with a bright yellow tank top from the Daytona Beach rally. She ripped her life-like mask off. Leaving ten minutes later, she heard sirens in the distance, a chopper overhead, and the rumble of many bikes. She continued on to Hwy 18, then headed south on the quickest route to Robbinsville. She passed numerous units from various law agencies, most with lights flashing and headed in the opposite direction. Blondie was sure they would find the farm in the very near future, but knew she needed to pick up supplies, cash, and take care of a few things before they did. Her identity was safe, as she had never been fingerprinted. She made it to the farm without incident, and left within an hour in the truck, pulling a 26 foot black enclosed trailer equipped with living quarters and two bikes secured inside. One was a new black Goldwing and the other was the Vaquero, its flame decals stripped and burned in the barrel outside the house. She torched the farmhouse and the barn using a time-delayed incendiary device, ensuring her prints would not be found.

As she left the farm for the last time, she made a vow to settle the score with Wolf and his buddies. She already had an idea of how and where to start. A mobile base of operation appealed to her much more than the boredom of a dirt farm.

EPILOG

Good Karma begets treasures. Bad Karma begets tragedy.

Wolf's right arm was put in a cast that he had the doctor set in the full-throttle position that was comfortable while riding. He had insisted the doctor making the cast go with him to his bike parked outside after it had been ridden to the hospital by Big Jim. By six, all evidence had been tagged and bagged and was being examined by the FBI forensics team. Lute's video of the matching glove found in Wolf's hardbag, along with the results of the soil comparisons, was presented as proof that the evidence implicating Wolf had been planted. When Big Jim was questioned, he told the interrogator about the last words spoken by 45, now stone-cold dead, his body containing more than a dozen bullets. This was seen as final proof of Wolf's innocence in the mayor's murder. Mark and Gator were questioned and released. They were unarmed but free, and not entirely unhappy to put some miles between themselves and the jail. They hesitantly returned to the Roost after Lute insisted they leave immediately.

The FBI had set up a mobile command post next to the store, processing evidence and doing interviews inside the toy hauler. Helicopters flew in bringing key personnel from different law agencies, all trying to stake a claim on the investigation. The FBI trumped all others due to crossing state lines, and dispatched orders to the local sheriff and highway patrol to detour traffic and detain anyone leaving. New arrivals were let into the Roost, but no one could leave the area until at the earliest, Sunday morning.

The authorities cleared out from the campground, but guards were posted at the entrance to allow them access to the nearby store . . . beer was the remedy to sooth the restless bikers. Often, the tab was taken care of—Lute had come back to give a hand with biker PR. Two kegs were delivered by a Goldwing pulling a trailer, and the party was on. Later, Lute was joined by Watty, the FBI agent, who had requisitioned bikes from the police departments in Boone and Wilkesboro. If needed, he or one of the several off-duty officers in the vicinity would provide escort for anyone cleared with an extremely good reason to leave. The mood of the bikers was much improved, and the entire encampment was ready for the Saturday night party at the Roost. The only downer was that Wolf had been detained for questioning. The common thought repeated in conversations was that he would likely face obstruction and other charges and be in custody for a while, even if he was innocent of murder.

The party began at dark as usual with the band playing rock-n-roll music and the bikers whooping it up in typical Rider's Roost style. A smoky haze was in the air and hung over the encampment like clouds as they creep over the mountain ridges. Rumors circulated, but there was no news of what was happening to the missing bikers, Big Jim and Wolf. The media converged on the police station in Wilkesboro and the local hospital. Nothing official had been released, but a news conference was scheduled for eleven, just in time for the evening news. Short snippets of information were heard about the capture of the alleged "Lone Wolf Murderer".

Around 10:30 pm, four bikes pulled to a stop at the entrance, shrouded in the smoky, gray fog. When the music stopped, all eyes were upon the mysterious night riders as they slowly made their way down the steeply sloped entrance. As they went around the U-turn halfway down the steep drive, they came out from under the thick cloud. As the four entered the asphalt clearing, the crowd of mostly inebriated bikers parted to let them through. A cheer went up when the partiers realized it was Wolf and Big Jim, escorted by Lute and Watty on police bikes. Backs were slapped, biker greetings were exchanged, and the party got into high gear, lasting into the wee hours of the night.

Meanwhile, Blondie was several hundred miles away, crossing the Mississippi River bridge from Memphis, headed west to parts unknown. She had succeeded in eluding the authorities who had no clue to her real identity other than some film of her disguised as Ronnie. Her fingerprints had not pulled up a match in the national database.

Various law enforcement agencies converged on the farm of one Clyde Coleman, a local hermit not seen for years. They were alerted when an intense fire was detected that had completely consumed the house and barn. They could not approach for several hours after the fire was discovered due to explosions and countless ammunition rounds cooking off. Forest fire-control aircraft were sent in to douse the flames before firemen or law enforcement personnel were allowed within a quarter of a mile of the raging flames.

The real identity of 45 was determined from his fingerprints. The FBI was hard at work tying him to other murders going back more than ten years. The statistical analysis had determined a pattern of crashes of seasoned riders in the Robbinsville area, many with broken necks as the cause of death. A huge spike had been noted in single bike accidents over the past five years. Prior to that, there were many previously unsolved murder cases where the victim was shot in the face with a 45 caliber bullet.

Big Jim sold his company and retired, spending his time fishing and traveling on his motorcycle. He joined Wolf for a cross-country tour, feeling right at home driving the truck pulling a toy-hauler.

Agent Watson, aka Watty, was moved to Washington and reassigned as a liaison to operations that had biker connections. He later scheduled a month off to take a long ride across country with several other law officers he knew or had met recently.

Lute was offered a promotion to captain in the Whiteville police department. He told his buddies he declined because he preferred his biker handle. In addition, he was not particularly fond of the new mayor, the murdered mayor's widow. Instead, he discretely joined up with Homeland Security, leading a group of bikers that patrolled the southwestern U.S. border areas. He kept a loose schedule, and no one ever really knew if he was working or not. The Whiteville police and the FBI kept him on a retainer as a consultant, available whenever needed.

Mark decided to take a much needed vacation, joining his wife and daughter at the beach. He returned home to find a new swimming pool. Mark's business increased to where he had to hire three new wrenches to handle the increase in auto, but mainly extra motorcycle repair business. Mark continued to run the steel man obstacle courses on the weekends. At work, he focused on customizing and building bikes. There were frequent biker pool parties, the man cave very popular with his buddies. His home brew became a favorite of many.

The Federal Marshals took Wolf's wife and daughter and moved them to a small house on a lake, giving them a new identity. The agents knew an as yet unidentified killer was still roaming around free. Wolf's son joined the U.S. Army, enlisting as a combat engineer, specializing in demolition, a job he had been training for most of his teenage years but with much lower grade explosives. Wolf acquired a 28 foot toy-hauler for cheap, prewired with radio, satellite, and internet. He headed west, typically accompanied by any biker buddy he could talk into driving. The Sturgis Rally was fantastic that year, and, like a reunion, all those that played a part in Wolf's run and later rescue were there. To say a major party was kept going all week would be an understatement. Even Watty was enjoying the biker party life. He could spin a tale like no other, and told political jokes one after another. Who to make better jokes about them than those that served the public by enforcing laws that restricted freedoms.

Gator agreed to drive the truck at times when Jim had the urge to ride. At other times, he would ride as Wolf's wingman. More frequently, he would strike out on his own, planning his routes and finding great bargains on unique places to stay and party. His GPS had so many saved points of interest, he could not go 30 miles without a landmark of some type popping up on his screen. His finds were shared with Wolf to visit and use in his magazine stories.

As for Wolf, he got a new Vulcan Nomad, and retired Beast with over 150,000 miles on it. Still riding his trusty iron steed whenever possible, he kept it well-maintained and sheltered. He did ride with others from time to time, but still preferred to travel the blacktop as a lone wolf. When he rolled into Sturgess that year, his new bike was on its' second rear tire. He would show up most nights at the toy-hauler after taking back country routes, often doubling the distance the others covered. He was well aware that a ruthless killer was still out there, and as such, paid careful attention to his surroundings. Ultimately, this became second nature to him, and he didn't give it much thought unless alerted by his subconscious. He was determined that Blondie or not, he would live the rest of his traveling days and moonlit nights mainly to . . . . enjoy the ride!

GLOSSARY

The editor thought a glossary of terms would be useful for non-riding citizens that might not understand the thrill of experiencing nature at 60 mph on a motorcycle, or the bond shared by those that do.

- Bambi—Deer
- Barney—Slang for uniformed police officer
- Battlewagon—Police SWAT vehicle, usually armored.
- Batwing—A fairing on a bike; has short windshield and resembles the outline of a bat with wings extended.
- Cage—Any vehicle with more than 3 wheels. Can also mean an enclosed, secured area such as jail.
- Cager—A person that only drives cages
- CRS—Acronym for "can't remember shit"
- Cruiser—Typically, a comfortable V-twin motorcycle designed for riding long distances
- Dual purpose bike—Street legal bike designed to go off-road
- Fatty—Joint, marijuana cigarette
- Flat-landers—People that live in flat, low-lying areas
- Full-bagger—Bike with windshield or fairing and built in hard bags for carrying gear
- Glock—A brand of handgun
- Goat bladder—Catalytic converter on a Vulcan motorcycle
- High-side fall—A fall where the rider is thrown off the bike towards the outside of the curve—the most dangerous type of fall—bike often lands on top of rider
- Hydration therapy—Consuming liquids, typically beer
- Iron horse—Motorcycle
- Lid, skid lid, bucket—Motorcycle helmet

- Lone Wolf—A biker that prefers to ride alone; is not a member of a motorcycle club or riding group.
- MC—Motorcycle club
- One-percenters—Members of hard-core motorcycle clubs, perceived by many as dangerous gang members
- Rice-burner—Japanese built bike
- Scoot, scooter—Slang terms for a motorcycle
- Thespian—Actor
- Trailer kings—Those that trailer their bikes to rallies, many often stopping miles away to unload and ride into their destination.
- Twisties—A series of curves on two lane blacktop road
- V-twin engine—2 cylinder motorcycle engine where the cylinders are in a 'V' configuration
- Weekend warrior—Biker that rides occasionally